PRAISE

The Book

T0244822

"A furious, jagged and radiant reckoning with the dangers of the man-
ifesto, the mortifications of aging, the mercies and limitations of the
comic posture, the job of the novelist and the indiscriminate desecra-
tion it demands."   —*The New York Times Book Review*

"One reads *The Book of Ayn* with genuine relief that someone has pulled
off a novel of jokes at the expense of the most solemnly protected ab-
surdities of our time."   —*The Wall Street Journal*

"One of the funniest and unruliest novels in ages. It shakes you by the
shoulders until you laugh, vomit or both . . . The author torques her
contrarianism, past trolling, past knee-jerk philosophizing and past
satire, alchemizing a critique of literary culture in all its ideological
waywardness."   —*Los Angeles Times*

"[A] delirious road trip through the age of selfishness . . . Contrarian
and chaotic in the smartest way."   —*Chicago Tribune*

"The last place we expected to find Ayn Rand is in a millennial satire, but
Freiman has taken that idea to its fullest and most hilarious expression."
                              —*Newsday*

"An epic hero's journey through New York, Los Angeles, and Lesvos;
a Künstlerroman of a novelist in a midlife crisis; a picaresque quest for
meaning."   —*The New Republic*

"Thanks to Freiman's unique ability to meld ferocious irony with heartfelt contemplation, *The Book of Ayn* goes beyond just another indict-
ment of millennials as narcissists and offers a fresh glimpse into how
21st century artists have to negotiate their sense of selfhood."
                              —*Esquire*

"The artist, Freiman implies, uses her 'I' as an alloy, creating a material both durable and porous, blending what she has felt to be true with what she imagines might be true for others . . . By the end, her 'I' has been vastly expanded: other people live in her head, whether she wants them to or not, shaping the innermost contours of her self. This vision of identity as plural means that self-assertion does not necessarily come at the expense of the rest of the world. It could even be a declaration of life on another's behalf."   —*The New Yorker*

"Freiman's sharp new novel puts modern life under the microscope, satirizing everything from cancel culture and cringey hookups to misguided meaning quests and ridiculous content creators. Beneath the book's surface-level hilarity, its eccentric cast of supporting characters add surprising emotional depth to Anna's story . . . While Anna's lack of self-awareness is easy to laugh at, her story draws tears, too."
                                                                —*Nylon*

"A joke-a-minute satire."   —*Vulture*

"*The Book of Ayn* Is Lexi Freiman's dangerous and cutting satirical odyssey . . . laugh-out-loud funny at times, and housing sentences so effortlessly constructed, I was reaching for my phone to take pictures of every page."   —*Shondaland*

"The funniest novel I've read in years . . . A comic work laced with extremely sharp insights and keen wisdom on our culture's hyper-sensitive sore spots (cancellation, greed, the need to be seen as empathetic, etc.). It's the best kind of writing: utterly fearless in the face of caution, a touch dangerous, and ferociously clever . . . An instant classic."   —*Interview*

"Beneath its comic surface, and for all its gleeful sleaze, [*The Book of Ayn* is] about the shrinking of horizons and the foreclosure of dreams, the endemic tragedies of failing democracies and middle age . . . Freiman's sentences are swift and vivid, her paragraphs precision machines . . . *The*

Book of Ayn . . . finds genuine pathos and imaginative empathy in the absolute last places you'd think to look for them or, frankly, hope to find them. Lexi Freiman shitposts from the bottom of her heart."

—*Bookforum*

"I'm no Randoid, yet Lexi Freiman's playful ribbing of our oh-so-human, moralistic inconsistencies is a lifeboat on a stormy ocean, where there is at present no safe harbor for a dangerous sense of humor."

—JIM CARREY, actor, comedian, and author of *Memoirs and Misinformation* (with Dana Vachon)

"*The Book of Ayn* is an exquisitely wicked prosing of the reality-cancellation that now passes for reality by pretty much the funniest writer of a generation that has forgotten to laugh."

—JOSHUA COHEN, Pulitzer Prize–winning author of *The Netanyahus*

"I had the rare experience while reading *The Book of Ayn* of slowly realizing I had stumbled onto something so good that it was changing my taste. So funny, so clever, so alive to the absurdity of contemporary life without reverting to the boring cynicism that would be so easy. I loved it."   —MEGAN NOLAN, author of *Ordinary Human Failings*

"Infuriating, perverse, contrarian, scandalous, nihilistic, and very, very funny."   —TONY TULATHIMUTTE, author of *Private Citizens*

Catapult
New York

The Book of Ayn

(a novel)

Lexi Freiman

This is a work of fiction. All of the characters, organizations, and events portrayed in this novel are either products of the author's imagination or are used fictitiously.

Copyright © 2023 by Lexi Freiman

All rights reserved under domestic and international copyright. Outside of fair use (such as quoting within a book review), no part of this publication may be reproduced, stored in a retrieval system, or transmitted in any form or by any means, electronic, mechanical, photocopying, recording, or otherwise, without the written permission of the publisher. For permissions, please contact the publisher.

First Catapult edition: 2023
First paperback edition: 2024

Hardcover ISBN: 978-1-64622-192-9
Paperback ISBN: 978-1-64622-240-7

Library of Congress Control Number: 2023936799

Cover design by Nicole Caputo
Cover illustration of ram head © andreyoleynik / Deposit Photos
Book design by Laura Berry

Catapult
New York, NY
books.catapult.co

Printed in the United States of America

10 9 8 7 6 5 4 3 2 1

Part One

New York

could trace my contrarianism back to age three, when I'd painted the walls of my parents' bedroom with my own poop. As a kindergartner I had usurped my birthday party clown by smacking him in the balls with a balloon animal, and in middle school I'd hoisted myself on the comic petard of a sexual obsession with my first cousin. Maybe the verboten felt more alive; maybe it just got me more attention. Maybe they were the same thing. Whichever it was, the culture had now changed. And after nearly four decades of bad behavior I'd finally gotten myself into some serious trouble—writing a satire on the opioid epidemic that *The New York Times* had called "classist."

Truthfully, I'd known that scatological humor was now banned from descriptions of the rural poor; that you were no longer allowed to write about the working class if you'd gone to a Manhattan prep school; that "Mountain Dew" was an unacceptable punch line. But there were so many new rules—all

set by college students paying two hundred thousand dollars for
their humanism. It was clear to all of them that I—having experienced no personal hardship—had failed to give my characters
enough economic pain.

Contrary to popular opinion, I didn't believe that people
were products of their circumstance. That a person could only
be understood by their historical or childhood trauma. In my
book I had made certain characters selfish without explaining
why. I had simply put them in their adult lives with a puppy
and a bag of heroin. It seemed wrong to me that people were
only worthy of compassion when we knew all the details of their
past. Why should empathy only work when you recognized that
someone had been hurt like you'd been hurt? Wasn't that sort of
more about you?

But I wasn't trying to change the world here. I was just
trying to write humorous fiction; trying to bring a little slap-
stick to the ongoing national tragedy. Comedy was meant to
transcend dreary morality and unite people in a mutual understanding of truth. The bad haircuts and misspelled tattoos and
how the main character shat his pants three times in one chap-
ter were all penned with a higher literary intention. It wasn't
funny to say the wrong thing because you could; it was funny
to say the true thing because it was wrong. I had honestly believed I was writing a book so good it metabolized its own
badness, a book that achieved the sublime self-canceling act of
artistic moral transcendence.

The New York Times reviewed Gwyneth Paltrow that same
weekend and found my book just as classist as a two-hundred-
dollar jade ball for a postpartum vagina. The review accused me
of under-contextualization and excessive moral nuance. It said my
characters lacked emotional credibility and fiscal-psychological

depth; that the only believable one was the amoral pharmaceutical rep sleeping her way around a devastated Appalachian town. Though even this character, it said, didn't seem convincingly horny. The review claimed that I was economically insensitive and had exploited the working class for my own selfish ends. Most upsettingly of all, *The New York Times* had called me a narcissist.

I had never considered myself one before. I'd always thought narcissists were very attractive people who couldn't admit when they were wrong, and I possessed neither of these qualities. I had a pale, downy face with the poppy black eyes of a threatened marsupial. My figure was squarish and saggy-bummed and I covered it in dark, shapeless layers. I also had no problem admitting when I was wrong. Willful naivete was part of my contrarianism and, I thought, lent it a disarming charm. I was never obnoxious, always curious—just usually about the other, less verifiable side. Being wrong didn't worry me; it was more embarrassing to be the same.

Still, the insult bothered me. One of my girlfriends (single, with eight eggs on ice) was a self-diagnosed "connoisseur of narcissists" who gladly lent me a book on the subject. Apparently everyone born after 1982 was a narcissist, which meant that my reviewer was at least technically right. The book said that narcissists were selfish, arrogant, and insecure. They were grandiose and fragile and incapable of handling any threat to their identity, which, the book said, was just an inability to metabolize shame. They were self-promoting and exploitative and experienced themselves as both specially destined and uniquely condemned. Narcissists saw themselves reflected back everywhere, made grand narratives of their lives, but felt at their core that they were empty. They also tended to pronounce everyone who'd ever hurt them a narcissist.

It was a terrible summer. My book had not transcended and there was a strong possibility that I was not brilliant or even very good. Twitter wanted to kill me or put me to work with heavy machinery. All social invitations stopped. My publisher dropped me and then I couldn't get a job. Even my old high school rejected my teaching application; all the prep schools were now, at least rhetorically, anti-capitalist.

Some part of my cancellation felt inevitable; I had always had a sense of myself as banished. Reading my work aloud in graduate school had been like stepping off a ledge and seeing who fell with me. Only one person ever did: a large, midwestern virgin who said my jokes made her tummy tingle in a way she didn't understand. To me, that was literature. You couldn't argue with the ineffable.

I suppose my punishment felt total because writing was my life. I never binged or scrolled; I only read what was relevant to my next project. Nothing went to waste; every social interaction was for gain—be it informational, vocational, or to fill some imaginary quota for "healthy socialization." Everything I did had to count toward this abstract notion of success; had to be adding up. And inside this sense of accumulation was real enjoyment, or at least a sort of pleasurable relief. Happiness was coming, I assumed. So was life. I would be forty next year but life was still coming, was still on its way.

And then it wasn't. That summer I spent all my days prostrate in the apartment. Mornings, I lay in bed or on the soft gray carpet in the bedroom, so that it wasn't rest, wasn't recuperative, but was rather a deathlike stasis. Making jokes that close to the floor had no buoying effect. Sometimes I cried but then that began to feel productive, like catharsis, and so I stopped mid-gape and just lay there. Something in me was rebelling. Trying to abort my momentum, my sense of life. At midday I would drag myself up and go make packet ramen and a cup of weak tea, which I took into the living room and slurped, prostrate, while staring out at the Murray Hill high-rises.

Gazing south, I could still picture the Twin Towers charcoal in the silvery skyline, and it filled me with nostalgia. You were supposed to hate those two buildings and everything they'd stood for, but I missed them. Life had been so simple then, so rich with possibility; I, so full of potential. I sniffled for myself. All alone, basically destitute, eating 7-Eleven soup cups. Though the optics, I knew, were slightly skewed: I lived on the forty-eighth floor of a Midtown skyscraper.

Perhaps unwisely, I had written my satire of the opioid epidemic in a Madison Avenue pied-à-terre. It belonged to a family friend who had left her Manhattan law practice to die at home in Connecticut. When the Edelsteins had offered me the apartment, in their somber chrome kitchen over a Shabbat takeout of General Tso's chicken, I'd burst into tears. I felt I couldn't accept a proposal so generous and under such tragic circumstances. But Magda Edelstein said that my book sounded like a timely and important story. A satire on white, working-class Americans with a *male* statutory rape at its center—it seemed to combine everybody's interests. Perhaps even Oprah would like it? Sitting there, I could already picture the dedication page—*To my beloved Edelsteins*—and had wept all the way home on the train.

Even now, the Edelsteins supported me. Having fled Soviet Hungary in the early eighties, Magda loved freedom in all its forms, and she applauded me for both my contrarianism and my classism. The last time we'd spoken, I had sat in the formal living room on the Natuzzi leather sectional and we'd talked about death. Not Magda's, but my own. How it was approaching fast because after thirty-five time really galloped and I mustn't let one bad review get in the way of my grabbing life by the balls. Magda loved the casual misogyny of the American vernacular; she'd never tired of the term "cocksucker" and refused to retire "son of a bitch," even when the feminists had asked her nicely. She wasn't my mom's type, but because they had met as young mothers and because Magda had been there the day my baby brother stopped breathing and because Americans were hopeful even about death whereas the crass, godless Hungarian had agreed that life was all merciless suffering, my mother had kept her around.

Life is merciless, Magda had repeated that last time in her living room. Not because she had stage-four cancer, which had taken her ovaries as a young woman and then returned in late middle age for her breasts, but because I had been canceled. We'd sat on her expensive leather couch surrounded by modernist sculpture and all the objects of stark beauty that America had given her, and Magda had told me that I had to fight for my life. The past didn't matter, she said. Not mine nor anyone else's. Life was always, for everyone, a present-tense struggle.

On the Italian travertine coffee table beside the tall stacks of architecture and design books, I'd noticed *The Tibetan Book of the Dead*. It seemed misplaced in this atheist's temple to American aspiration. I'd understood then that Magda was, maybe for the first time in her life, afraid. She'd taken my hand; her dark eyes glossy, the fat, tragic lips pinched with feeling, and she'd tried to give me some hope.

"It's what the Buddhists say, darlink. Believe in nothing but yourself."

—

That fall, there was only one event on my calendar. A long-standing invitation to a women's luncheon at the Upper East Side mansion of a conservative socialite rumored to be hiding an Islamophobic Muslim authoress with a fatwa from the liberal media. The guests were a sprawling mix. There were conservative media personalities in primary colors and pumps, grungy Gen X feminist professors, reformist Muslim commentators in hijabs and comic book tees, a disgraced former legend of the downtown punk scene who insisted on calling her old drinking pals "trannies," and a handful of young, ambitious media types seeking finance for their magazines. What everyone could agree on: female genital mutilation was bad.

I had decided to attend the luncheon knowing that Catherine Biggs would be there. This was my one ally from graduate school—the big, kinesthetic virgin who had gone on to publish a successful dogoir and then, when the editor of New York's premier literary magazine was fired for flashing an intern at his standing desk, had assumed his job.

For moral support, I had invited my old friend Vivian. Despite the fact that Vivian identified as "the urban poor," she had stood by me throughout my cancellation. She thought Marxism was elitist along with cancel culture, transgenderism, and conditioning one's hair. Vivian saw ideological censorship as merely another tool of elitism and was a proud lesbian, mocking of bisexuals and other "grabby" kinds of queer. Also, Vivian's own social circle had shrunk these last four years thanks to a mysterious illness that kept her largely housebound and complaining. Some days it was the black mold in her crumbling pre-war apartment; other days it was the mice who'd brought Lyme disease in from the Cloisters. Vivian's symptoms were vague and constantly shifting. She had described one of them as the feeling of being slapped by a large, male hand.

We entered the mansion on Forty-Ninth Street and immediately Vivian refused to hand over her coat. She jerked away from the preppy young woman, pulling the ugly windbreaker tight around her chest. As the coat check murmured anxiously into her earpiece, Vivian whispered loudly to me.

"You realize this is the house where they hid Cheney the morning of 9/11?" She combed a hand through the greasy noodles of her hair. "These fuckers aren't swabbing my DNA."

The windbreaker remained in her possession.

Upstairs, the lounge room was all dark floorboards and radiant white upholstery. Small cliques of women were scattered about the space. The skirt suits stood together picking at the sushi bar and showing off their fabulous legs. The professorial types huddled in fervent discourse around the fireplace. The magazine people scuttled cravenly between the groups. I glanced around for Catherine but couldn't see her. The familiar sense of alienation crept up and over my shoulders, sheathing me like winter roadkill. There seemed to be no group Vivian and I might slide casually into. No conversation we could graze on politely from the sides. At events like these, I seemed to lurk dimly at the outskirts until I was suddenly up close and flashing red. In group conversation I always felt myself come into being as a sort of social shock. Adding Vivian to this was like supplying the faulty hair dryer with a full bathtub.

She was hungry, so we made our way toward the sushi bar. Beside the dishes of yellowtail and bluefin was a deep glass bowl of grayish tusks. On the wall above hung a huge wheel of indeterminate animal bones. I vaguely recalled that our host's ex-husband had been extradited from Zambia for killing a lion.

By the seared scallops a coiffed woman in a red power suit was telling her little squadron how she had challenged their host's no-shoe policy at the front door. She'd said she didn't care that the floor was made from a rare Japanese elm that lived only four years before rotting: a woman should *never* be forced to remove her footwear. As the group tittered, I sensed Vivian begin to animate beside me. Then she lunged toward them, snatching up a nigiri.

"The *gall*," she said, "of asking women to remove their high heels at an anti-clitorectomy event."

Vivian's sarcasm tarred right over the buoyant mood. The skirt suits looked out at her with the round innocence of slimed animals. Even I felt soiled, and annoyed. I didn't want to dig her out of this. And then I saw that Red Power Suit was actually smiling.

"Not to mention the faux pas of serving *pink* sashimi," she said.

The skirt suits cackled, saved by their gracious leader. I felt a surprising warmth toward Red Power Suit. She probably thought I was Vivian's partner and just another aggrieved lesbian, but I appreciated her sense of humor. That she was trying to meet Vivian halfway. Vivian, of course, just became angrier. She glared back at the women and then her gaze dropped to the floor at their feet, and she appeared to almost vomit.

"Whose Kate Spade bag is that?" she demanded.

The women glanced between them, confused. But I knew what my friend was thinking. Vivian had a rousing and incomprehensible theory about the demise of Manhattan that involved 9/11 and Mayor Bloomberg's secret pact with both Russian oligarchs and the kinds of women who wore Michael Kors flip-flops. Vivian believed that Al Qaeda had worked with

Bloomberg, who had worked with Kate Spade to rid the city of all its urban working-class grit. I knew that my friend saw the devil's wink in that handbag logo. Vivian pointed an angry finger at the group.

"*You* gave New York its clitorectomy."

The skirt suits pivoted window-wise in distaste. I felt my own face wincing into a sour expression. It was only a subtle wince but enough for Vivian to feel psychically slapped by a large, male hand.

"Oh fuck this, then."

"Viv."

"Sorry but it's *satanic* in here."

I pointed hopefully to the schlubby academics. "Those people probably like Germaine Greer?"

Vivian cringed at the sight of them. "My skull hurts."

This was one of her symptoms. We stood there as Vivian massaged her temples, pretending she wasn't about to do what she always did.

"I think I need to be lying down."

I sighed and dismissed her and, immediately, Vivian developed two more symptoms and basically limped out the door. But I couldn't waste energy mollycoddling my friend. I had to find Catherine. Her singular encouragement had given me the confidence to persist with my unpopular fictions and publish my first book—a collection of stories about bad sex in my twenties. In early drafts for workshop I'd shared a story about the moral ambiguity of an aggressive blow job that had injured the owner's foreskin. Catherine had defended me, rebuking the class's outrageous claim that the fellator could never be guilty of sexual violence. She was a learned, sensitive reader and my forever champion.

When I saw Catherine now—stalking the seafood platter

across the room—large and pink with a tote bag on each arm, I became emotional.

"Cath!"

I moved toward her, smiling with outstretched arms. But as Catherine turned and saw me, she raised her paper plate, blocking the hug. Rattled by the obstruction, I dropped my arms and said hello again.

"Hey, Anna."

Her tone was subdued, and, nervous about this, I gushed. "You look amazing, Cath! You haven't changed a bit!"

Though this was more wishful than true. Catherine had very obviously changed. Her style was more severe and asymmetrical and she wore big, blocky statement frames that split her face into several hard, geometric shapes. She had lost that soft amorphous quality of a person truly open to ideas.

"I mean, you look really good," I said. "Really *young*."

But this, too, sounded wrong. Unfeminist. Though I felt confused about what was actually considered feminist now. Anxious, I asked her. Were we women meant to flatter or else console each other? Did we celebrate female successes or memorialize female defeats? The old winners were now the new losers and the old losers were the new heroes and suddenly International Women's Day seemed to get a whole month.

Catherine was frowning. And now I had to move fast. There wasn't time to stoke the old flames of affinity. I had to make my pitch.

"I've actually been thinking about a piece." My mouth was dry. "For the magazine . . ."

Catherine raised her eyebrows so they sat like scare quotes above her glasses.

"It's about opposites," I continued. But already the ideas felt formless and goopy in the way of things still trying to be born. "You know, how everything good is evil and everything bad is . . . suddenly virtuous."

Catherine squinted. "Define good and bad?"

"Well, it's a literary essay so I plan to keep it pretty ambiguous."

"Surprise, surprise."

She was mocking me. My face blazed as the whole room squeezed in around me. All the different shapes and shades of feminist pushing into my physical space. All angry and inflamed about the clitoris. In my periphery, Red Power Suit looked like a long, lean strip of sashimi. And then words began to exit my mouth.

"Like just because the clitoris is in pain doesn't mean it's necessarily good."

Catherine blinked. "You're saying the clitoris is bad?"

I was mostly joking and clarified this with an ironic inflection. "More like . . . *privileged*."

And, finally, here it was: the laugh in Catherine's eyes. The old openness.

"The clitoris is privileged?"

I nodded carefully. "Right now the clitoris is the loudest voice in the room."

Catherine rebalanced her tote bags. "You're at a female genital mutilation fundraising event and you think the clitoris is taking up too much space?"

I nodded, grinning evilly. Catherine was smiling too. It was a relief to feel this again. The old mutual understanding, and how it seemed to lift us up together, high above the others. Catherine chuckled and her glasses fogged up. She removed them so that I could see the soft contours of the old smiling face just before they tensed and went dangerously purple.

"I get it, I get it," she said. "It's just a joke. You don't have a stance. You don't actually care about anything."

I felt myself thud back to the ground, then sink straight through it. My voice was small. "I care."

"I honestly can't believe you're still trying to be original about things like female empowerment and financial inequality and freaking climate change."

"I've never said an original word about climate change!"

"No, but you would. You'd find some way to make it good because it's bad. Or cool because everyone says it's too hot or whatever."

"I feel like you've misunderstood my thesis."

But I couldn't say any more; my voice was cracking. I watched as Catherine restored her glasses and glared at me. They immediately fogged back up, and this time she kept them on, unperturbed that the windows to her soul were closing.

"Finally there's some real positive change happening in this country and you could be a part of it." Her large jaw jarred cynically open. "But you'd hate that, wouldn't you, Anna? Because then you'd just be like everybody else."

The next few moments blurred by as I sailed across the room, held inside a cold cone of persecution. Had I said anything or just walked away? My brain was all hot throbbing blood. My one lucid thought was that the word "freaking" did not belong in the mouth of a high-powered literary editor. I made it through coat check and out onto the street, where I began to fight silently back. I had overwhelming evidence of my own empathy. The period after college when I'd visited the World Trade Memorial nearly every afternoon, streaming tears over the granite ledge with all its engraved anonymous dead. Weeping mostly for bankers, I assumed, which only proved my heart was large and nondiscriminating. Then there was the homeless man who slept outside the Sleepy's on Eighteenth Street—an irony that had sent my empathy receptors into overdrive, prompting me to buy him a coffee and toasted cheese sandwich every day all summer of my first publishing internship. Even when he complained that the coffee was cold, and another time when he didn't say thank you, I had nursed my wounds and returned the next day bearing gifts. Catherine was wrong about me.

She was also wrong about jokes. Jokes cared, just in a different way. They were a natural and necessary thinking-through-of-things. A thinking that had to go barrelling straight through consensus to see what was on the other side. Even if that thing was just laughter. Just the useful acknowledgment that things were never solely good or bad; sometimes they were also, mercifully, funny.

Turning onto Lexington I was surprised by a small group huddling at the corner. The six bundled figures were looking up at a telephone pole where a hawk was tearing into the body of a bloody pigeon. Below, in the clearing at their feet, lay the bird's pristine head. The sight jolted me; the ground seemed to rock beneath my feet. Everything looked suddenly sharper and more fragile.

"It's considered good luck in Japanese culture."

One of the men was addressing the small group. He wore yellow Patagonia and had a broad, creaseless face that could have been anywhere between thirty-five and sixty. Around his neck was a ratty lanyard with the words "Official Ayn Rand Tour Guide." The six of them appeared to be in late middle and older age and all were grossly overdressed for the mild fall weather. They wore thick coats and some had gloves and hats and neck warmers. Though the more striking commonality was their unsentimental appreciation of the avian murder scene. I stood with them, staring at the hawk. Their peculiar unity was palpable, hedging in around me, holding me like a net. It felt cozy.

"Ayn would have approved," said a woman so bundled up she resembled a burn victim. There were hums and chuckles and nods of agreement. And then the guide clapped his hands together as if trying to bring sensation back to his body.

"Who's freezing their tail off?"

He lumbered to the front of the pack and they all started shuffling off down Lexington toward the Starbucks. Watching them go, my inner compass gave its gentle nudge. I never knew when this was a sign to listen for life's teachings or to simply pursue a subject for my writing. In graduate school we'd been told that these were always the same thing. I took off after the little group.

They sat at a table by the restrooms. It was small and greasy but farthest from the swinging door with its arctic draft. I took a seat at the espresso bar behind them and angled my stool so that I could watch discreetly from my side-eye. It was oddly comfortable in the presence of these quiet, stoic people who appeared to believe that the planet was actually cooling. They seemed vulnerable to the rest of the world and sweetly, helplessly bound to one another. The air around them was tickled—reality's grip just slightly looser.

I knew nothing about Ayn Rand. Just that she was the godmother of American libertarianism who had written two very long, didactic novels. I had always considered her the gateway drug for bad husbands to quit their jobs and start online stock trading. But aside from that I was ignorant.

The guide pointed to the street perpendicular to Lexington, where a slim brick apartment block stood mulish between the

condos. "That's where she lived." His eyes cinched on the structure as if on a rare, exquisite bird. It really was an interesting
building, and also a striking coincidence. I had walked past this
apartment block every day for two years and marveled at its brutal, almost Soviet ugliness. There was something grimly defiant
about it that I liked.

"She lived there for thirty years," he continued. "It's where
she wrote *Atlas Shrugged*, and the Objectivists had their meetings in her living room." He glanced up at the building, pursed
his lips, and gave a little nod.

"Very different from the Richard Neutra house." A neat
white-haired man in a plaid shirt and chinos smiled smugly at
the guide.

"Well, that was California," he responded. "If she could've
had a moat in New York City, I'm sure she would've."

There was hearty, unanimous agreement from the others.
And then a younger Indian man spoke up from the back. He
wore clear Perspex frames and was unselfconscious about the
AirPods hanging like pearl pendants from his ears.

"But living here in Midtown was always Ayn's dream." He
crossed his arms over the thick ribbing of his Uniqlo puffer
jacket. "She believed that skyscrapers were the highest expression of man's genius."

He told the group how Ayn had believed that collectivism
would return the world to a primitive state where all achievement, invention, and the material manifestations of man's rational mind would be seen as hubris and thus destroyed. Then he
gave an angry little smile. "And she was absolutely right."

The others looked quietly dazzled and Puffer Jacket continued. The latest casualty in the crusade against Western progress,
he said, was Linnaeus, the father of taxonomy. He had invented

the modern naming system for all animals, including humans, but because the Homo sapien he had examined was himself, the "primitive, Kantian deindustrialists" now wanted to unname the whole human anatomy. The others nodded, a little lost. But I felt my whole body leaning toward Puffer Jacket and his deflective aura of contrarianism.

"They want the whole Western world to be ashamed of who they are and where they come from."

"Ridiculous," said Plaid Shirt. His bundled wife nodded, her beady eyes blinking above the swaddling.

Puffer Jacket recrossed his arms. "Ayn would've hated cancel culture."

"What would she have said about it?"

I was surprised to hear my own voice, thin and shyly inflected. The group angled around to face me. Puffer Jacket looked hostile.

"I'm sorry," I said, "I know I'm not part of the tour."

"It's quite alright, young lady." The guide was smiling at me. "I'm always happy when someone shows an interest in Ms. Rand."

Plaid Shirt hobbled up and offered me his seat.

"Oh." Heat plumed in my throat. "That's very kind of you."

I joined them and even accepted a mini cinnamon roll from the plate of shared pastries. It seemed un-Randian to share, but so much of their culture was obscure to me. Puffer Jacket was the one to finally answer my question. Ayn would've hated cancel culture, he said, because it was about sacrificing the individual for the whims of the group. He then launched into something called "Roark's Speech," the legal defense that architect Howard Roark gives at the end of *The Fountainhead* for blowing up a housing estate. Roark, he explained, designed the housing estate but the construction company built it wrong. Which meant Roark was fully justified in destroying his own work: it was his creation, the manifestation of his genius, his life, and no one had any rights to it but him.

"So he was kind of canceling *himself*?"

Puffer Jacket eyed me with twinkling new interest.

"Nietzsche says true power is enduring injury without suffering pain. The German is *Aufheben*. To remove and thus preserve."

I had always been a sucker for "the German." And loved the brain numb of a good paradox. I now felt an affinity with Puffer Jacket, which made me want to open up.

"*The New York Times* tried to cancel me for writing a satire about the working class."

He grinned. "What did they say?"

"That I hurt people's feelings."

"Hurt feelings are not your responsibility."

"The *Times* also gave Ayn's first book a bad review," consoled the guide.

"It sounds like they hurt *your* feelings." Puffer Jacket was smirking at me. "Which means you let yourself be owned by your enemy."

The guide nodded sadly. "Property of *The New York Times*."

It was astonishing. This group of Columbia-wearing sexagenarian Beanie Babies were giving me some sound therapeutic advice.

"So what should I do?"

"You just need to act like a human being," said the guide.

"You mean forgiveness?"

"Heck no." He frowned at me. "You need to use your reason."

"*Think* about it." Puffer Jacket was impatient. "Anger is a response to powerlessness. When you stop giving someone the power to hurt you, you stop feeling angry."

"That's very rational."

"It's not called Objectivism for nothing." And he was suddenly on his feet, holding his hand out to the guide. "Thank you, sir. A fascinating afternoon."

"Glad I had something to teach you, pal."

"Oh." He zipped the jacket right up to his chin. "You didn't."

I watched the strange, imperious man march out of the Starbucks and into the street. The rest of the group seemed disoriented. They muttered over their steamy beverages, resettling themselves. I decided it was safe to ask them now. They seemed to like me.

"Guys, what's with the jackets?" They looked at me, confused but patient. "Is it a climate change thing?"

The guide took a small, warming sip of his hot chocolate. "It's cold outside," he said. "So, the rational thing to do is wear a jacket."

Back on the street, I checked my phone and saw that Vivian had left several texts and voice mails. I didn't want to relive the scene with Catherine. I wanted to savor this bolder, brighter, happier new feeling. At home I googled Ayn Rand, and was surprised to see that I bore an uncanny resemblance to the severe, bug-eyed woman whose face smirked pridefully out of a small square on the author page. Immediately, I ordered Ayn's two major novels and *The Virtue of Selfishness*.

It was only October but at six o'clock that evening, it started to snow. The Randians were right about the weather, though they seemed less interested in the ideological abstractions of politics and more concerned with the moment-to-moment realities of actual life on Earth. I watched the flakes spear down outside the window and imagined Ayn observing the same phenomenon from her own apartment windows, just two blocks south. How the city got gray and shaggy in a storm. How it hunched over and withdrew into itself. The silent stillness. And how just afterward, the sidewalk was a fresh white page awaiting footprints.

The books arrived twelve hours later and I started reading them straightaway. Upright. In the Saarinen wing chair by the Empire State–facing window. Ayn Rand said that most people submitted to the moral code of a social group or to God, meaning that one's moral behavior was almost always an obligation to others—to society, humanity, the poor—but never to oneself. Whereas Ayn believed you could live only for your own sake, in the service of your own life, and according to your own moral code, choosing values in alignment with rationalist principles. Being your own raison d'être resolved all questions of meaning and purpose; your physical and spiritual flourishing were the goal, and when you lived by a strong, rationalist code, this didn't actually lead to hedonism and greed.

But it also didn't lead to altruism. An ethical choice that Ayn believed was totally unethical. I'd always felt suspicious of altruism myself. Peter Singer and the consequentialists with their Don't Save Your Drowning Child Save That African Village computer logic just felt like a trigger for my childhood OCD. How could you ever do enough? Ever get it right? Consequentialist altruism seemed to want you dead; not wasting resources, not taking up space. The altruistic life purported to be meaning and purpose enough; an end in itself. But to me it had always seemed to push you into a religious way of living without any of the spiritual or communal benefits. Ayn Rand said altruism created a world in which people were either self-sacrificingly empty or else dependent on others for their own self-fulfillment. Both sides, she said, were existentially unfree.

I read for six hours straight. Occasionally I looked up from Ayn's rousing words to gaze at the Empire State Building or at a plane cruising eerily close to the downtown skyline. At all the evidence of human progress. What had got us into this mess, and, according to Ayn, the only thing that could get us out. She said that selfishness was a form of care; that self-responsibility was the ultimate freedom. Her ideas had the uncanny chime of paradox. The dizzy zing of the counterintuitive. She wasn't funny but I enjoyed her thoughts like I enjoyed jokes. Like anything audacious; true because it's wrong. Giddy with my new heresy, I FaceTimed Vivian.

I didn't tell her about Catherine Biggs. Instead, I told Vivian I'd left the party and run into a group of strangers calmly observing a hawk decapitate a pigeon.

"They were the Ayn Rand walking tour." I chuckled and then felt immediately traitorous and atoned. "But they were actually really nice."

"Sorry, but isn't Ayn Rand something rich psychopaths use to justify their greed?"

I thought of the guide and his shabby Patagonia. "Poor people like her too."

"Poor people also like the Bible."

I decided to try a different tack. "You know the women in Ayn's novels are all brilliant, high-achieving tyrants?" Vivian raised an ungenerous eyebrow. I forged on. "She even wrote a story called 'The Husband I Bought.'"

"Huh."

"She thought women could do literally anything."

"Really?"

"Except be the president."

"Why the fuck not?!" Vivian was yelling.

"Because if a woman were president of the United States there would be no man powerful enough on Earth for her to sleep with."

"Goddamn idiot straight women. Why couldn't she just fuck the president of China? Or Russia?"

"I think that might be treason."

"Then she could fuck Bill Gates! Or Zuckerberg! Or Musk!" Vivian had somehow missed the larger point.

"What Ayn says about self-esteem is actually really energizing."

"Anna, this is about as cool as getting into Nietzsche in your forties."

"I'm thirty-nine."

"It's evil trash. Like the Kmart in Astor Place."

I stared out the window and sulked. As usual, there were people marching below in the streets. I couldn't read the placards from up here but I could tell they were essentially protesting the social and material conditions of life. I knew the young people wanted to ban Virginia Woolf for elitism, Shakespeare for racist slurs, Picasso for sex crimes, and Freud for all three. These clever young girls with their angry pink hair and huge, tenty T-shirts and stunningly muscular bottoms. I missed the waif. I missed my bland, pacific girlhood touting heroin chic and The (gentle) End of History. It was frightening to see it now: History returned. Young and pink and marching down Fifth Avenue in cheeky shorts.

"Ayn Rand isn't as bad as you think."

"I don't want to think about her, Anna. She's the devil: she literally wore capes."

It was time to drop the topic of Ayn Rand and return to Vivian's favorite: all the confused young heterosexuals of Twitter.

"Straight girls are too porny," she groaned. "They want to cum *all* the time."

"Right."

"But *actually* straight men just want to jerk off alone, then pass out in a pizza box."

"To be fair, I think straight women also want to eat pizza."

"Well, everyone wants to eat pizza."

But I didn't. I didn't like food and only cute young boys made me horny and even then it was less horniness and more a bright cerebral amazement that one of them was actually paying attention to me. In other words, I was a lot like Ayn Rand, who had spent her whole adult life lusting after young men. Even once she was married, Ayn had seduced her male students and found herself in emotional and sexual relationships with attractive and aspirational younger men. They found Ayn's mind so formidable and her attention so validating that even in her sixties she was getting regularly laid. This was the part I didn't tell Vivian. That Ayn Rand had a workaround for the sexual conundrum of a female president. The trick was to value men not for their brains or power but for their youthful optimism, innocence, and physical beauty. In other words, to treat them like men treated girls.

For several years now, I'd been finding men my own age deeply unappealing. I'd noticed myself choosing dark restaurants and keeping the bedroom lights off and trying to look at them only in profile or other obscuring angles. I asked to see photos of them in college. I closed my eyes during sex and thought of Harry Styles. The men my age smelled old. They were balding or had hard white wires in their hair that made them look malfunctioning. They were always exhausted and eager to share their failures with me—something I doubted they did with younger women. Maybe they wanted to know me; they definitely wanted to be known. But I felt like a vessel for their broken dreams and disappointments. Like something their therapists had told them to try. Men my own age had nothing to give me. Or nothing I wanted, the main reason I found them so sexually moot. It was the transactional nature of sex that made it exciting, the power dynamics that lent sex definition and form. Which was why, in recent years, I had drifted casually and with surprising success toward boys.

Most were male literary interns who enjoyed my irreverence and were horny for my career. These boys were cute-faced and thick-haired and very anxious about the future of the straight male author. I let them rant, nonsensically. I let them make edgy jokes and express their fears about punitive feminism, their grief over dwindling debut novel advances. My heart rushed up to meet their bad opinions with its soft cushion of understanding. And these boys seemed to see me more clearly, more holistically. Or at least they looked at me with bigger eyes. Ayn Rand agreed that love should be transactional. Brains for beauty. Moral wisdom for nice big arms. She had even developed a whole philosophy and written two epic tomes in pursuit of the "Ideal Man." A passionate doer possessing the intellectual daring and physical beauty of a teenage boy.

—

A few days after the Ayn Rand walking tour, I learned that someone had in fact liked my book. I received an Evite to a "dissident soiree" at the West Village town house of a famously contrarian female columnist. I had read some of the woman's

work and knew that she'd contributed much to the rich scholarship on the politics of victimhood. She was sure to disagree with
The New York Times's harsh character assessment. Plus, some of
her guests were probably fans of Ayn Rand.

I waited patiently in the vestibule for the host to receive
me. She was greeting everyone here with a privacy waiver, her
interns topping up her champagne as the greetings got slop-
pier and more tactile. She wore a gold slip that accentuated her
spectacular breasts, and with her auburn tresses and perennially
sun-kissed face she resembled a painterly subject from the Third
Reich. When it was my turn, the host put a hand on my shoulder and leaned in very close with that tamped, chaotic energy
that made her pieces so fun to read.

"You were robbed," she said, rocking forward on her dagger
heels. It appeared she had mistaken me for somebody who deserved some sort of literary prize.

"Thank you," I said, burning with inadequacy.

"To cancel a debut author for a few poop jokes is inhumane."

I decided not to correct any of that. It was flattering to be
recognized and my instinct with this woman was to deflect pity.

"I'm feeling much better about it now." And then I took a
gamble. "Probably because I've been reading Ayn Rand."

The host frowned deeply, though her face remained uncannily
unlined. "I suppose Ayn Rand was a kind of . . . proto-feminist?"

There was a way to make this true. "Sure . . . she cared about
the rights of the individual. And women—ungrouped—are
definitely individuals."

"So then more of a postfeminist feminist who preceded the
feminist movement?"

I had no idea. "I think she just wanted *everyone* to have high
self-esteem."

"Right, so she basically thought that men and women were 'the same'?"

The host was being sardonic. I had read her infamous essay linking empathy in men to a sharp rise in lesbianism, and knew that she believed in gender difference and the importance of sexual polarity; that sex was a power game between players of different but equal means. But so did Ayn. I shook my head.

"You can tell from her descriptions of necklaces that Ayn thought all women secretly wanted to be strangled."

"Oh really?" Her eyes widened.

"And she wrote that famous rape scene, which she called a 'love scene' . . ."

"I should take another look."

The host smiled, then mouthed a silent hello over my shoulder as a tiny, southern concert pianist came mincing down the floor runner. They embraced beside me and the host seemed to forget my existence. But I was happy. She would take another look. I moved on down the hall.

In the living room, a vast table was laid with cheese and wine and an abundance of sliced, skewered, and brazenly heaped meat. The lights were too bright and I kept seeing the Francis Bacon brushstrokes of open mouths masticating prosciutto. I watched a very tall, beaky man try to balance a hunk of cheddar on a paper-thin cracker. He looked disgusted at everything. The thickness of the cheese; the thinness of the crackers; the shortness of everyone around him. I knew he had said something controversial about nonbinary people. I wasn't sure what he'd said, but I could see in his disdain for the cheese that he held strong opinions.

Most of the guests I recognized were centrists. There was the slow-talking bro who invited nuclear physicists onto his podcast and asked them about aliens. I recognized furloughed boomer editorialists, Black libertarian Substackers, ex-models with sleazy sex-positive memoirs, bisexual Zionist frat girls, and socially dysfunctional moderates out for a good time. They faced one another but all seemed to be in their own imaginary arguments with ex-bosses or coworkers or reviewers at *The New York Times*. Padding around in their socks, they seemed slightly desperate.

I moved off into the parlor and took a seat on an apricot chaise longue. On the other end two young women sat vaping in frilly pinafores, ironic sneakers, and ghoulish green eye makeup. One was raffish and elfin while the other was curvy with a shameless monobrow. I recognized them from a downtown scene that was vaguely socialist and acutely nihilistic. These two had a podcast and were famous for cooking spaghetti for war criminals and speaking the word "retard" to power.

"A lot of soft cheeses for a 'revolution.'"

The monobrow appeared to be talking to me. I was afraid of her. These girls were smarter than me, better read, and knew exactly which kinds of transgressions they could get away with. I glanced back at the living room. "*Those* people are trying to start a revolution?"

"Lol, no," said the elf. "They're too rich to start a revolution."

"What's wrong with being rich?" I said, surprising myself.

The elf pulled at the corners of her dress and I saw the red, lacy flash of her underwear. It was probably sexist but I didn't believe these two were actually socialists. The elf leaned right in over the chaise, observing me closely.

"I know you," she said. "You wrote that book about opioid addicts."

I nodded, staid. Whatever they said, I could take it.

"Your cancellation was retarded," said the monobrow.

"Super shitty," agreed the elf. "I mean *we* say 'retard' more than you."

I smiled, trying to accept their flattery with grace. "I didn't actually use that word."

"Well, I didn't actually read your book," said the monobrow.

"I read your first book in college." The elf spoke with a beguiling mix of boredom and reverence. "It was cool how you let the rape victim just be a total fucking douche."

I hadn't known that the bad sex I'd written was considered rape. Masochistic, yes, but still a choice the character was making.

"You were challenging victimhood." The monobrow commended me. "Before the Victim Caliphate even existed."

I felt light-headed. They were very hard-core. Pastiching consent culture with ISIS; I was out of my league. But also, they seemed to respect what I was doing. To align themselves with it, even. Now I had to ask them.

"Have you read any Ayn Rand?"

The monobrow frowned. "Isn't Ayn Rand a bit basic?"

"Lol, didn't she believe in free will?"

I hadn't realized you weren't supposed to believe in free will and it made me feel suddenly helpless.

The elf adjusted her pinafore. "Oh and like didn't she kind of hate women?"

"And poor people?"

"She hates everyone," I said carefully. "Who hates themselves."

The girls looked at each other and snorted. But I could feel their interest, even if only because it was wrong. I continued.

"Ayn hated anyone who resented people who'd had success.

And professional victims. And moral slaves. And *The New York Times*."

"Dope."

The monobrow seemed unsure. "But she was all about greed. Like, she believed in billionaires."

I could feel the word "freedom" elasticizing in my mind. "She believed in anarchy."

"Oh shit. So, she was basically the godmother of anarcho-capitalism?"

I demurred, not entirely sure what anarcho-capitalism was. It sounded Randian. But cool. "She just wanted everyone to be proud of themselves."

"Lol, *pride*," sneered the elf. She folded her fabulous young legs. "But it's kinda hot that she was such a psycho."

I understood these two. I knew the numb leap of provocation, the cool sparks of deflection, that cozy dark penumbra. These girls didn't want a socialist revolution. They just wanted attention. We were the same, or similar, and the thought was instantly deflating. The elf passed me her vape. I took it and inhaled and realized too late that it was weed.

"Can I get a hit?"

Standing opposite us, at the big bay window, was a short, rotund man in a steel-colored suit smoking a cigar. He was bald and shiny and made me think, uncomfortably, of an anti-Semitic stereotype. The elf shrugged and passed him the vape. I was almost immediately stoned and sat back, listening to the three of them talk. Cigar Man ran a tech investment firm in the city and Balenciaga had just designed him a ski suit for a disruptor summit at the Californian resort where chewing gum was banned. The girls were enthralled. They kept asking him for an intro to Peter Thiel, and Cigar Man kept saying they were only acquaintances. When he started showing them photos of his daughter horseback riding at Jewel's ranch, my thoughts drifted to Ayn.

The two of us actually had a lot in common. Ayn Rand had also been raised a middle-class Jew in a big, cosmopolitan city. In 1917, the Bolsheviks had seized her father's pharmacy and twelve-year-old Ayn had stood by impotently, witnessing his humiliation. Here, I saw a parallel with my own father—the hard-working orthodontist—where the Bolsheviks were his two fourteen-year-old daughters, my half sisters, who mocked him relentlessly for being bourgeois and accidentally misgendering their friends.

And then I began to wonder how Ayn's Jewishness had shaped her thinking. There was a strong sense of both individualism and collectivism within Jewish culture. If the Jews weren't being blamed for capitalism, they were communist agitators. And, undeniably, for a people who'd been consistently reduced to ashes, the material conditions of Jewish life were pretty damn good. Did Ayn see that as proof of the self-made individual? Or did Jewish achievement speak more to the idea of collective traits—an idea that Ayn rejected as cultural predestination and anathema to individual freedom. On the boat from The Hague to Ellis Island, Alisa Rosenbaum had changed her name to the raceless, genderless Ayn Rand. In this way, the most Jewish thing about Ayn seemed to be her secularism.

Later, Cigar Man and I stood outside the apartment building waiting for our cars. Mine was a very un-Randian Uber Pool still zigzagging through Flatbush, and his was a private car stuck on the Williamsburg Bridge. He asked me about my novel and I told him that *The New York Times* had said I wasn't allowed to write about people with missing teeth when my father was an orthodontist. Cigar Man laughed and shook his head. He told me that America had become European. Cowed by guilt, lacking self-esteem. It aligned itself with victims; attempting to reclaim its own innocence. He puffed deeply on his cigar. And because of Israel, he continued, the Jews no longer fit that profile, and so anti-Semitism was on the rise. Israel was a tech state driven by innovation and self-sovereignty that made it more American than America, with an implacable political conflict that made the world see it as more White than White. It was sad but true, he said. Whenever a culture set its sights on eradicating inequality, the Jews were the first to be blamed.

I was happy to talk about innovation and self-sovereignty. But I didn't want to talk about the Jews. Instead, I told Cigar Man that, in the seventies, Ayn Rand had waged war on the ecoterrorists for trying to abolish all technology and return the Earth to a primitive state.

"She was a huge defender of the electric toothbrush."

Cigar Man chuckled, and then the Escalade pulled in. I realized I liked him, but just in a fatherly way. He seemed, for whatever reason, to be on my side. As the door slid closed behind him, Cigar Man leaned forward so that all I could see was the oracular moon of his disembodied head. The moment felt a little bit messianic.

"You must be writing about her."

And, just like that, I was.

Ayn's political awakening had occurred on the train fleeing Petersburg for the Crimea. Out the carriage window, the aspiring young writer had seen beautifully illustrated propaganda posters papered to the city's facades. The regime's enemies were sketched below imperatives for the proles to fight the oppressors and brush their teeth. The posters were painted by artists, most of whom had joined the revolution (even the city orchestra had incorporated factory steam whistles into the wind section), and young Ayn was horrified that artists—those tasked with expressing the highest possibilities of human existence—had given themselves over to an ideology that sought the destruction of that very potential.

But trying to write this scene, I found my prose was flat. The sentences lifeless. I couldn't find the edge, the spark of interest. Writing historical fiction was like trying to masturbate to Michelangelo's *David*. I quit 1920s Russia but struggled to bring 1930s New York to life. Or 1940s Los Angeles. Or 1950s New York. My descriptions were broad and clichéd; all the dialogue sounded like a B-grade Billy Wilder movie.

Dejected, I closed my laptop and decided to walk up to Grand Central Terminal. The man-made miracle of industry had been such an inspiration to Ayn. I wanted to understand it. To know how it felt to get amorous for a train. She loved machines rabidly and even just oil, which she described as "life-giving black blood." Where other people saw dystopian concrete jungles, Ayn said cement had the texture of satin and the "friendly white radiance of a smile." Seeing through her eyes was like seeing the ruined world inverted. Hell was heaven and heaven was hell.

But I only made it down to the foyer, where I heard the familiar wailing of a street protest. They were coming down Fifth Avenue. A small army of black-clad boys holding signs with triangular symbols that I at first mistook for Stars of David. What, I wondered, were all these Jewish goths protesting? Or were they Black Israelites—that most unpleasant of religious groups, who terrorized tourists with plastic swords in Times

Square. And then I remembered: they were pentagrams. Now I felt silly, my own collective identity subconsciously swaying my thoughts.

These boys belonged to the violent anarchist group that had been so contentious a couple of years before. They aligned themselves with social justice, but now I wondered if anarchy actually had more in common with Randianism. Like Ayn, they believed that people were capable of running their own lives without the aid of government or religious morality; that individual freedom was the most important value. Mostly I was noticing that many of these boys were cute.

I followed them all the way down to Washington Square Park, where the setup was not unlike a farmers' market. People sold vegan snacks and yelled about the climate and waved flyers in my face. Off to the side was a small encampment. I understood that anarchists hated property, but their sprawling tents and just the way they slunk around, blobby and usurping as Saturday morning teenagers, made them seem strangely entitled.

I moved toward the mob in front of a small stage where furious little men growled chants into the crowd. Once the chorus reached me, key phrases had become nonsensical mumblings and I felt embarrassed incanting along with the group. The boys down here were less attractive, more pungent. I stopped chanting. And then I felt the person beside me turn to look.

"If you get closer to the front," he said, "it's easier to understand."

The boy was lithe, square-jawed, and adorably dimpled. His hair was a greasy flop and there was grit in the corners of his eyes. I smiled, coyly, taking in the strangeness of his outfit: a toggled black jumpsuit with low-heeled clogs. Perhaps, I thought, he works with highly specialized machines.

"I can take you down there," he continued. "I know the organizers."

It was easy to follow him through the crowd. He was tall and fair-haired and had one of those asymmetrical cuts with an underside shaved. Paired with the jumpsuit and his fresh, Aryan face, the boy looked like a queer Nazi plane mechanic. He glanced back at me frequently, introducing himself in three unintelligible syllables. It was probably Anthony but I began to think of him as Antifa.

"It's called 'horizontal democracy,'" he called back over his shoulder.

"Is that when everyone talks at the same time?"

Antifa nodded. "It's so that no *one* person can be in control." He glanced around, it seemed, for wider approval.

When we reached the stage, he swung his hand out and high-fived the small, bearded man yelling from the podium. Now that I could actually hear the words, I found it even harder to repeat them. They felt thick and potatoey in my mouth. It didn't feel like no one was in control. Or rather, I felt the dizzy pressure of coercion.

"It's so loud here," I said. "Maybe we could hear each other better at a bar?"

He nodded uneasily and now I worried that I had misread our interaction. The skin around his eyes was taut as a white cherry.

"How old are you?" I asked him.

"Twenty-two."

The protagonist of my opioid novel was a big-boned, potty-mouthed, graying pharmaceutical rep sleeping with a young opioid addict and talented amateur comedian. I had mostly used my imagination. But I had also attended a dozen open mic nights across the five boroughs, seeking inspiration for the boy. One of the young comics had taken me to his parents' house on Central Park West. On the way we'd walked past a film set and a crew member had whispered that it was a new Woody Allen movie. I'd joked that we should be careful not to get canceled, but the irony was lost on this boy; he'd never heard of Woody Allen.

Now I grinned at Antifa. "That's actually quite old."

He smiled proudly, and led me out through the mob.

Antifa walked us up the road to an old Irish pub. Inside it smelled moldy and dank, though the young crowd gave it a lively, animal heat. I immediately set off for a quiet booth in the corner, beneath the portrait of a portly Irishman. From here, I watched Antifa order our beers, then leave two quarters as tip for the barman. Taking the glasses, he loped back toward me, sloshing drink down the front of his playsuit.

When he was seated Antifa explained Žižek's concept of the phantasmagoric something, punctuating his points by pressing the sides of his hands into the table, as though confirming the size of a small fish or a large penis. The movement was like Occupy, he explained, in that it was about bodies placing themselves in corporate space. It wasn't really violent; it was just about being physically there, like a tree or a rock.

"We shared a bran muffin," he said, grinning.

"Who did?"

"Me and Slavoj Žižek."

I made my face a big round O of amazement though I couldn't remember who Slavoj Žižek was; he sounded like a war criminal.

Now Antifa launched into a spirited address on worker-led modes of production. The anarchy was all starting to sound rather *organized*. But I let him talk. Something about my large, round eyes and high Elizabethan forehead made men want to pump me with data. I didn't mind it. I liked learning new ideas, watching the world tilt in through a new perspective.

"Do you want another beer?" he finally asked.

I wanted a vodka martini, but the fifty-cent tip made me worry that he was only equipped for beer. It would be more feminist to offer my wallet but also, possibly, emasculating. Then again, I wasn't even sure what emasculating meant anymore. Was it forcing a man to divest himself of ancient, misogynistic values? Was it a way to redefine maleness? I supposed then that I *should* emasculate him. But, honestly, I liked a bit of force. It had often flipped my own uncertainty into full-blown desire. The few times I had been asked for consent, I'd felt the heat between us die, as the air thickened with moral smug. And I just couldn't help thinking, *loser.*

"I'd love a beer."

Antifa stood over the table. I realized with a sting that he was waiting for my money. I pulled my wallet out and gave him a ten. He took it and jogged happily back to the bar. Sliding my purse away, I saw a group of older, suited men sitting in the opposite corner, observing the strange occupation of their drinking establishment. They made me feel self-conscious. What was I doing with this young Marxist anarchist who seemed to be wearing an ironic gas station uniform? One of the men eyed me with a smile that scooched back into the soft leather luggage of his face. He seemed to be daring me to defect to their side. I looked away from him to the bar, to the asymmetrical back of Antifa's haircut.

When he sat down again, I nodded at the men. "Are they the one percent?"

"Definitely."

But they weren't. They probably lived in Williamsburg and took the train to work.

Antifa shook his head. "Anyone with a Chase account has blood on their hands."

I had a Chase account. In fact, I had three. Two credit cards and a debit. One was called "The Freedom Card." I'd used the points to book a flight to Mexico that March. These details slid together in my mind, arranging themselves into a forensic crime scene.

Antifa was seething. "Look at those gentrifying fuckfaces."

I looked but I didn't hate them. The smallest one reminded me of a cousin on my father's side. He was balding but combed it forward at the temples so that his face looked like it was clawing back up his head. These men were just more perspectives on the broad spectrum of human existence. They only knew what they knew. They only saw what they saw.

"Maybe they don't know about gentrification," I said. "We're all in our social media bubbles."

"They know, they just don't care." He crossed his arms smugly. "They probably think redlining is like not getting into a nightclub."

I didn't know what redlining was. My Instagram feed was mostly other people's kids.

"Where do you live?" Antifa asked accusingly.

"Midtown."

"Do you feel guilty about that?"

"For living in Manhattan?"

He sighed, as if it was obvious. "For being part of a racist, classist, murderous system?"

Heat pressed in on the backs of my eyes. The system probably was murderous, and my Chase cards were very likely smeared with blood, but, like Ayn Rand, I was done being blamed for every problem on Earth.

"I'm borrowing a friend's pied-à-terre," I said brusquely, disclosing my class and destroying any possibility of sex. Antifa sat back, stunned into a petulant silence. I sipped my beer, noticing a faint revulsion at the white blob of my hand clutched around the glass, the sensation of my throat working down the liquid. There was no philosophical reciprocity between us. No respect for my mind. Ayn would have said that no sex, no matter how cute the boy, was worth sacrificing one's self-esteem. I chugged the rest of my beer.

"Does it have a crazy view?"

I wasn't sure how to answer. I had whiplash. From a pile of steaming feces to someone with a coveted door fob.

"Yes," I said finally. "Very crazy."

But of course it wasn't crazy. It was exactly how a view from that height should look. For most people, it was just an uncommon sight. Something rare, special. Some things had to be inaccessible. Or else they couldn't exist.

We sat in silence for a few moments while Antifa stared into his glass. I couldn't tell if he was angry or embarrassed. When he spoke again his voice was soft.

"Can I see it?"

Standing in my living room at night was like being inside a decadent piece of jewelry. Despite this, I saw no oppression in the city's diverse topography; each structure a unique shape and shade of chocolate or charcoal. Antifa stood at the window in silent amazement, taking in the glittering panorama. It made me feel almost bad, like I was tempting him into material aspiration.

Up here, you couldn't see the Citibanks or the Starbucks or the Starbucks inside the Citibanks. From this height, the world was sparkling and blameless.

But as soon as we sat on the couch Antifa began to talk about corporate oligarchy and the billionaire boom. The high-rises blinked around us like gagged witnesses. He was starting to annoy me. But I kept listening, to protect him from embarrassment. In that way I was the charitable one—giving my total attention to this person who seemed to barely notice I was there. He was now eyeing the Empire State Building with a look of vague disgust.

"You know how many people died constructing that thing?"

I didn't know the answer to this, though I knew that thirty-six people had died jumping off the top. Perhaps the numbers balanced out? Ayn would have said that progress giveth and progress taketh away. Though not quite in those words.

"Five," said Antifa, and I couldn't help it; I laughed. His face puckered in contempt.

"Sorry," I said. "I was just expecting something higher."

"Five lives isn't enough?"

"Not that . . ." I considered my words. "It's like the building is more of a *symbol*, you know? That *transcends* human life."

Antifa recoiled. It was time to give up. He didn't like me and it had become impossible to imagine how sex might materialize between us. I apologized and told him I had to be up early.

"But we just got here," he whined.

This was a surprise. Though I sensed he just wanted to argue, to keep making me wrong.

"That's kind of *pushy*." But I could hear an odd, hollow flirtation in my voice. "You must really want to stay here . . ."

Antifa spread his arms across the seat rest. "It's warmer than a tent."

Now I was insulted. I walked all the way across the room to the front door and turned back around. But Antifa hadn't budged.

"Sorry, I've got a big writing day tomorrow."

Again, he whined. "The trains take forever at this time."

"Come on," I said, smiling. "I'm asking you to leave my apartment."

"Lol, you don't even pay rent."

I walked back into the center of the room, then tilted my head pleadingly. "I need to sleep."

"So do I."

This was absurd and I snorted. But Antifa just stared at me. Exasperated, I glanced out the window and silently communed with the whole city, imploring the Empire State Building to come crashing through the glass and transform the moment. Make it real.

"Do you make a lot of money on your books?"

I understood from his tone that he was trying to insult me, and so I said yes. Antifa looked nauseous.

"You don't think writers deserve to make money off their art?"

"Only as much as janitors. A universal basic income would liberate art from the market so that *everyone* could be creative."

But art was different from creativity. Art involved self-torture, and self-torture required incentive. I searched Antifa's eyes for some trace of humanity. "But you were born in the nineties. Haven't you ever wanted to be special?"

"*Special* is what's killing the Earth."

He crossed his arms and looked at the floor, all the energy pooling darkly around him. To my right I sensed the warm white gleam of the galley kitchen. All the appliances shining their sturdy encouragement. Antifa probably hated technology. He probably wanted to erase the electric toothbrush, burn down my building. I scanned the countertop. Could I actually wield a knife at someone?

I felt a soft blow to the head. He'd donked me with a throw pillow.

"Not funny," I said. But a strange chortling sound was coming from my throat.

Outside the window, the whole city rose toward me in rumples of twinkling velvet. It was like those last moments of suspension before you hit the tarmac. The uncanny lull as you wait to see whether your plane is landing or crashing. When I couldn't bear the tension, I knelt at his feet. Antifa's thighs tensed as my chin came to rest on his knee. If I did this, it was my choice. My will acting on the world, not his. And the closer I got, the easier it felt; as if the worst was already over. My body slid into a familiar pattern of movement. Pressed against him I felt protected from the possibility of violence. From humiliation; mine or his or both. My lips softened into his thigh and he seemed to take this. Not like the gift that it was, but like a man might take an iron branding.

"What are you doing?" he said quietly.

I drew back. The shame was numbing. "You don't want this?"

Antifa slumped forward, as if experiencing some sort of structural inner collapse. He remained hunched over, staring at his knees. I felt like poking him.

"So you don't?" I repeated.

"Now *you're* being pushy."

My laugh cracked loudly through the room. Antifa lurched off the couch. Dazed, I watched him jam his feet into his shoes.

What was happening? What did you call this? The phantasmagoric blow job? My whole body was burning. I sprang up and marched him to the door. Antifa paused in the vestibule.

"I think there's been a misunderstanding," he said, his sexless little eyes darting away. I watched them lock on something at the other end of the room: the book spines on my shelf. Their titles seemed to electrify his being, as if he beheld the spitting flames of some hellish volcano.

"What the actual fuck."

The heat pressed in again on my eyeballs, and my vision got starker. I saw the dark shape of him in the light of the doorway, standing on my carpet. Suddenly I was bending toward the shoe rack and then a sneaker was flying through the air. Hard into his chest.

"Get out of my apartment!"

He yelped and doubled over, hobbling out into the hallway.

"Randian psycho."

The walls absorbed the sound and held it over us. As if Ayn herself loomed. I leaned out the door and saw Antifa standing at the end of the corridor, helpless before the elevator's steel refusal.

"Press G," I ordered. "Not LG or B."

The doors opened and he stepped in, then turned back to look at me, eyes small with hatred.

"I'm going to give your book one star on Amazon."

Only once I'd sat down again did I notice I was shivering. The whole room looked ruffled and strange. As if the smooth stones of reality had been upturned to reveal their dark, squirmy undersides. Like my childhood home had appeared the night we returned to a broken window and stolen TV. I tried to be rational. Nothing had, in reality, actually happened. I hadn't been harmed. I hadn't survived anything. I might have gotten paranoid and then humiliated but that was just bad sex with strangers. I had even written a book about it. You couldn't be traumatized by someone questioning your right to a pied-à-terre.

—

A few days into January, I received an email from Cigar Man's son. Someone called Jamie who signed off with the puffer fish emoji. He said his father had told him I was writing something about Ayn Rand. I checked the signature; Jamie's management company had no website, only an Instagram that featured photos of their clients' purse dogs. I googled the dogs and found them to be legitimate. Then I wrote Jamie that I was happy to talk. He responded immediately with "RN?" so I googled "RN" and wrote back "K." Ten seconds later my phone was ringing. I hadn't given him my number.

Jamie had big plans for me. His wager was that cancellation was about to become cool. It was definitely, he explained, what the culture wanted RN. Or definitely in the next six to twelve months. He also said it would be cool AF to have more controversial women in Hollywood. Ayn Rand was a bad biyatch, he commended me. Bad, like capitalism itself.

I told Jamie I was open to getting re-canceled, though I was only in the early stages of drafting a book.

"Could you make it a TV show?" he said seductively.

I hated television. The corny, bloated hackery of it. Watching a TV show I always felt somehow duped; the neat, structural formulas depressed me and made humanity seem simple and doomed. Even when it managed to move me, from behind coerced tears, I still felt locked into a helplessly predictable species destined for historical failure.

But I wasn't a fool: TV meant money.

"Could somebody else make it a TV show?" I asked him.

"Nobody else would dare."

I wondered for a moment if he was cute. If he looked like his father but with hair. If this really was some sort of messianic intervention.

"I guess I could try," I said. "But I'm not making fun of her or of capitalism."

"Absolutely not. That's the getting canceled part."

"And it won't be like *Succession*," I warned him.

"Of course not."

"So less like satire and more like . . . funny homage."

"It will be whatever you want, Anna. It's your show."

A *show*. It would be a show. I felt light-headed, a dizzy pull toward the window. It came from the west—not New Jersey, but the final amoral frontier. California. And now I wondered: Could you really be canceled into a career? Could reputational suicide actually work in the service of one's life? Jamie seemed to think so. And the good thing about paradox, like suicide, was that it contained all argument.

The phone call ended with an awkward sequence of hyperbolic compliments and abstract promises. I watched the phone number recede into my home screen and remain there for a minute, the concept still emanating from the faded 213 area code. *Los Angeles.*

Ayn had also gone to Los Angeles at age thirty-nine, to adapt *The Fountainhead* into a movie. This was a few months after the book had been mis-advertised by the publisher, slammed by the press, and deemed a commercial failure. The book's selfish ethos was denounced by the media but the public were quietly, satisfiedly reading, and word of mouth accelerated after Warner Bros. bought the rights for fifty thousand dollars—affording Ayn a Richard Neutra ranch in the Valley with a moat and a pride of peacocks. In Los Angeles she lunched with Barbara Stanwyck and attended movie premieres and cocktail parties with Hollywood royalty. She bossed King Vidor around set and wrote acting notes for Gary Cooper. She bullied Warner Bros. about keeping every word of her script, and she won.

Los Angeles possessed a glossy soft focus in my mind. An easier, looser, more morally ambivalent place than New York. I knew it was a town that worshipped youth and beauty. But at my age perhaps I could live there less as an ingenue and more as Ayn Rand. That is, the kind of Hollywood woman formally known as a Hollywood man.

—

Despite their proximity to the city and the fact of their divorce, my parents insisted on a monthly family Zoom where they pummeled me with questions and discussed the downfall of the American empire and impending demise of the Earth.

My mother, Jackie, was a beautiful, fragile woman who hid her wealth behind a rustic cottage upstate and a chic horsey aesthetic that had no functional relevance to her actual life. Over the last four years, Jackie had found meaning and purpose in political canvassing. Winters, she argued with strangers on the telephone. Summers, she argued on porches and front lawns.

My father, Mark, was a lovable schlub under the orthorexic thumb of his pink-pussy-eared wife and their tyrannical spawn. Once every six months I sat at their dining table, watching my half sisters bully our father and wanting to punch them in their Marxist-private-school throats. They felt entitled to an elite education that taught the value of dedicating one's life to self-sacrifice, and my father was their financer/punching bag. All through my cancellation Mark had remained quietly and abstractly proud of me. But late in the summer, even he had turned slightly against me: developing a fixation with my fertility that obviously meant he no longer believed in my career.

It was a comfort to think that biological kinship had meant little to Ayn Rand. What she valued most was philosophical mutuality. Ayn believed that one had to choose people, along with every aspect of one's life, moment to moment, unburdened by the past. True freedom, she said, lived in this untethered sense of forward momentum, in the breaking of bonds and the severing of ties. It was only through selfishness that one could ever be fully and authentically oneself.

During the monthly family Zoom I usually listened with a soft, unfocused mind and retained little information. The discussion topics didn't rouse me but I often cried when I got off the call. For the three of us. That this was what having a family had amounted to.

But today I had an agenda. I hadn't borrowed money from my family in years. It was humiliating and un-Randian, but I told myself I had no choice. If I was going to get enough bad attention to support myself, I had to be in Los Angeles. On the call, I told them about Jamie and the tight schedule he'd set. I had three weeks to write the pilot and series doc and already he was setting meetings with producers and networks and private-equity people. Jamie believed I could use my penchant for wrong ideas to my advantage. He had prophesized the imminent rising of my star. And I trusted him, I told them. He was very, very young.

As usual Jackie seemed skeptical. Of both my plans and my morals. Ever since the poop incident, it seemed, my mother had been suspicious of my character. It wasn't my fault, of course, that my baby brother had died for no reason in his sleep, shattering everyone's sense of good and evil and the meaning of life itself. But my behavior had not been helpful. I had rejected the pall of grief, the hush of speech, the new moral sensitivity imposed on our home. I hadn't cared for my parents' feelings. Acting out was so much easier. Jokes were fun and also useful. They smoothed the edges, consisting, as they did, in the soft stuff of moral subtlety. I had started with practical jokes involving poop and then moved on to other ones—with bad words or ideas that made people feel funny in their tummies. Like they, too, were getting away with something.

Unlike Mark, Jackie was resistant to my humor. She was always sending me articles about sex-trafficked women who'd started their own yoga studios or texting me Thoreau quotes. She made diagnostic allusions to the fact of my being an only child, and maybe she was right and I was spoiled. But so was Thoreau. Everyone knew he'd left Walden on weekends so that his mother could wash his clothes.

"And this manager guy thinks your book will make a good TV show?"

Mark sounded hopeful. I explained that I was not in fact adapting the opioid satire but rather writing an original show about an iconoclastic woman who had been mislabeled an "anti-feminist."

Jackie's face lit up. "Jane Fonda?"

"Ayn Rand."

And now my mother shook her head woefully. "Mark, we failed."

I was quietly thrilled that the family Zoom was starting to resemble Ayn Rand's own combative departure from St.

Petersburg. Ayn's mother had become a kind of Soviet darling, an underpaid teacher and beneficiary of the State's meager rewards system who disapproved of her daughter's stubborn ambition that dismissed both feminine roles and egalitarianism. Whereas Ayn's father, having renounced the totalitarian State, had encouraged his brilliant daughter to pursue her dreams, her freedom, and a better life in America.

"Puppy," said Mark. "I understand that you're trying to transition to a more lucrative industry and I understand that you were canceled and that it's not easy these days being from a wealthy family . . ."

I thanked him for seeing these things, for seeing *me*. Unlike dismissive, unfeeling Jackie, who had now jerked right up to the camera in a great, quivering pink blur. When I'd told her that they were going to publish my first book, Jackie had congratulated me and then begun almost immediately to describe the migration habits of a subspecies of tern that flew amazingly from Alaska to New Zealand, shutting down one side of its brain and then the other, in order to remain awake for the yearlong duration of its flight. I had let her rhapsodize; I couldn't compete with a creature of such genius and economy.

"But lending you money at your age," Mark continued. "Really isn't good for your self-esteem."

I completely agreed. Dependence was a trap; I had to be self-reliant. That was the only way to inner fulfillment and existential freedom. But I didn't have time to wait tables; Hollywood had literally just called me.

"It's an urgent matter of the zeitgeist," I said.

"And I want to help you, Pup. I really do."

I beamed at my loving father. Only he cared. Only he believed in me. Even when he disagreed he still accepted me; still laughed at my jokes; still made the choice not to be offended. Because it was a choice. Every moment of our lives, a choice.

"But I need you to make an appointment at the Murray Hill clinic."

To freeze my eggs. It was a bribe and definitely his wife's idea. A woman whose mind couldn't stretch beyond the cul-de-sac rat maze of their Westchester neighborhood. A woman who could not imagine a life without children like she couldn't fathom a female hand without a manicure. Whereas the thought of producing a child frightened and depressed me. I could barely care for myself, let alone a tiny, screaming organism with its own needs and ambitions. With its own thoughts and politics. Its own guilt and innocence and impossible-not-to-hurt-feelings. Having a child felt like the least fun way I could destroy myself.

"Please, Dad. I just want to make a TV show."

"And after that you might want to have kids."

"I won't." My voice was resonant. I believed myself. Or I believed what Ayn said: to be a full-time genius, there simply wasn't time for progeny.

"But what if you meet someone," Mark persisted, "who wants to do that with you?"

"I won't."

"Not if you keep dating young boys." Jackie was smug.

"I date *young men*," I clarified. "Because the ones my age are all married. Or old."

Mark blinked at me with glassy eyes. My failure to be loved was suddenly his failure, and Jackie's fault. Now I had to prove them both wrong. But I was going to cry, and before the call was over. I selected an emoji filter and swiped it on over my face. A sunny yellow avatar filled the frame, swallowing down a mighty sob.

"Puppy. Just make the appointment."

I nodded. I really could just make the appointment. Whatever they told me there I could probably spin into bad news. Too many hormones; too few eggs.

Jackie looked annoyed. That I had won. That I was heading to LA to get myself canceled. She hated my ambition. As if true art poured only from selfless people who'd been purified by their suffering; magical horse-whispering women who'd borne their own father's children and lived to start a yoga studio.

"Well, I'll miss you guys," I said to my parents. "Till next month."

Then I got off the phone, and cried.

When I spoke with Vivian that night, she was in a bad way. Her symptoms had worsened; medievalized, really. She was now experiencing a sharp pain—*like an army of tiny, spiked wheelbarrows*—and a weird swelling sensation at her temples. I was sorry for my friend, whatever was happening to her. Vivian was broke, uninsured, and basically squatting in her five-flight walk-up. I offered to lend her some of my father's money.

"I'm actually okay."

I was stunned. Vivian had never described herself as "okay." She explained that a young couple had just moved into the building and offered her support through their mutual aid organization. They brought her groceries each week and all she had to do was vlog her symptoms for their patrons.

"You have patrons for your Lyme disease?"

But Vivian didn't find it funny. "They're good folks, Anna. They were actually just tweeting at me not to kill myself."

I felt ill. Not because my friend was potentially suicidal but because she'd tweeted about it. Vivian was torturously herself, and I loved that about her. But this new platform felt like some kind of capitulation. Neither one of us liked being told what or how to think, but now, it seemed, Vivian had sponsors to answer to. I was also a little bit jealous. No one on the internet had asked me not to kill myself; in fact one of them had suggested I take my book out onto the penthouse balcony and use it as a parachute. It didn't matter that I lived twenty floors below the actual penthouse. These people cared nothing for nuance.

"You tweeted you were going to kill yourself?"

"I was mostly kidding but they took me seriously."

"How *good* of them."

I was joking but it seemed to provoke a cool, mutual silence. I looked out at my view. The city skyline signified money and pollution and various forms of supremacy—evidence of all the systems that had failed us. But that, too, was capitulation. Not every problem was the fault of some failing system. Human beings were not so weak and susceptible. Individuals could still think themselves into better futures. If you didn't believe that, how could you ever be anything but a victim?

"Caretaking will just keep you in need of care."

"What's that supposed to mean?"

It meant that these friends of hers were vampires; sucking Vivian's anemic blood for their own spiritual strength, using her for their pseudo-religion of altruism. They would get so much more from her than she could ever get from them.

"You need to find a way to look after *yourself*."

"Oh you think so, Ayn Rand?"

And now I was angry. Vivian didn't just hate cape-wearing, libertarian pro-industrialists; she hated artists. Many times, I'd heard her denounce our grandiose self-exemption from societal concerns. Our treasured moral relativism and allegiance to the sublime mystery of art. That we believed in the supreme importance of an ineffable thing that produced opaque ethical results. It was part of her general hatred of elitism. But in despising art she lacked discernment, and expertise. Recalling Antifa's toilet-cleaning novelists, I felt myself ice over.

"I'm actually moving to LA for a while."

"Perfect!" she spat. "You can practice your self-help yoga pants Randianism out there."

I didn't wear yoga pants and it was one of my most redeeming qualities. I could feel it; there was no explaining the concept of selfishness to a person whose identity was built on their own physical disintegration. I couldn't help Vivian either, and ended the call.

I got a blood test and then, a few days later, I had my appointment. The fertility clinic was a large, minimalist space painted in rich, coercive pinks with glossy wall prints of Buddha and Ganesh and gigantic, vaginal close-ups of unfurling lilies. I took a seat in the waiting room opposite an enormous print of the Madonna and child. The world hung darkly over the two figures; her face was lit the sad, lonely blue of screen-gazing as she beheld her pudgy infant Christ. A pensive baby like a balding adult man trying to hold in a fart.

It was a long wait. When I finally went up to inquire with the receptionist I was ushered apologetically down a long pink corridor to the doctor's office. The door opened on another pink suite with more religious art. The doctor sat at her desk. She was tan and curvy with tight shiny curls and gave off an aura of nubile neatness. Removing her earbuds, she greeted me with the slow, blinking eyes of a ruminant.

"I like to do a short *guided* after lunch." She smiled at me, remorselessly.

On the desk was a photo of two red-faced children with the doctor in between; the three of them squashed together, exhausted with happiness. I wondered where their father was. Or if he was merely sperm in a vial. I couldn't tell—was the photo an admission of failure or an advertisement for single parenting? Whichever it was, I felt a tart little glee that the doctor's family was so untidy. She was now fussing with the computer; clicking and scrolling, her face growing tense. The meditative calm receding as she read through my file.

"Your test results are quite . . . surprising."

"How do you mean, surprising?"

"Just for your age."

I had heard of this. Women in their late thirties, even early forties, who had the ovaries of sixteen-year-old girls. *Dangerously* fertile. I took a moment to wonder if this held some deeper meaning, was perhaps an arrow pointing me toward an unexpected fate.

The doctor leaned toward me, while something inside seemed to tug her back. I saw the strain in her body, like she was evading some dangerous edge.

"It looks like you're in the early stages of perimenopause."

My first thought was doom. That something medically terminal had happened to my body. But this quickly changed, spun into a coldly ascendant, vaguely spiritual feeling; that I had been right about myself all along.

"With the depression," she said. "And irregular periods and disturbed sleep, it does make sense."

So did, I'd thought, the stress of my cancellation. But infertility made more sense; both of my symptoms and of my life's Randian trajectory.

"Freezing is still an option but with your egg count so low . . ."

"No, no." I waved her away. "I don't even want children."

"Oh!"

"I only got the test because my dad made me."

"Ah." She nodded, smiling but wary. Her gaze fell over the family photo and she took a greedy little sip.

"And anyway," I said. "The planet is dying so their lives would just be misery and chaos."

"Right . . ."

I was mostly joking and really hadn't meant to become an anti-natalist eco-warrior, but the doctor now seemed to fear me. She withdrew behind the safety of her monitor, and this, along with the print above her desk, pissed me off. The painting depicted another homunculus baby Jesus glaring up at its doting mother. It was an image that, in the context of this office, implied that a child should be the whole meaning and purpose of one's life.

"You know your wall art is kind of evangelical."

The doctor flinched. "Beg pardon?"

"Never mind."

I was embarrassed. Why was I giving this woman—this bureaucrat of the unquestioned ordinance to keep women in babies—the power to hurt me? The doctor's fingers scuttled over the keyboard and a paper tongue purged from the printer.

"Just in case you want to see someone." She handed the sheet across the desk. "These are the counselors I recommend."

"Thanks, I'm good."

The doctor looked down into her lap, shifting in her chair. I was making a scene. I could feel the omniscient gaze of my stepmother, who knew the doctor from Pilates and who would, no doubt, learn of my transgression and report back to Mark, who would certainly tell Jackie. I could feel the weight of their judgment already. As if I had done it on purpose: made my own body an inhospitable place.

"I'm sorry," I said gruffly. "I just *really* don't want a family."

She looked up again with nervous, hostage-y relief.

"Well, it's great to know exactly what you want!"

It was, obviously. And crucial to living life for oneself, and on one's own terms. But I found that I couldn't, for some reason, return the doctor's enthusiasm.

Los Angeles

I arrived at LAX with "INT. ROSENBAUM KITCHEN – NIGHT." and my hope. As I flew down the freeway, even the landscape looked optimistic; the luminous pinks and hopeful greens and the palm trees all bending toward some great, unnamed prize. I was relieved to be in Los Angeles. Unlike New York, it still seemed to be a place where magic happened to people who absolutely didn't deserve it.

I had found a roommate on Craigslist. The ad I'd answered was for a one-bedroom apartment at the bottom of Beachwood Canyon. The Hollywood sign was visible from the kitchen window, which was important to me as a visual person without a car. I would be sleeping in the large living space, which had a futon and a room divider. In photos, the apartment looked beautiful and light and my roommate, Raffi, was young and had perfect facial symmetry. If his boundaries were bad, at least there might be sex.

When I buzzed the door, there was no answer. I texted Raffi and waited. After a few minutes, a muscular woman in athleisurewear let me into the building and I sat in a beanbag chair in the foyer for forty minutes until Raffi finally responded. He didn't apologize; he just informed me that he would now proceed to head back from the gym.

The foyer décor was disturbing. By the fake foliage–covered back wall was a narrow, abstract water feature surrounded by swinging cabana chairs. The ceiling was high and beamed and industrial chandeliers hung anachronistically above brightly colored beanbags. I couldn't tell if it was Children's Nursery Posing as Sex Dungeon or more like the reverse. Whatever the aesthetic, it didn't bode well for the intellectual life. But that was okay, I told myself; literary history was full of iconoclasts like Ayn who had thrived in enemy territory. In the 1940s, Ayn had shared the city with the Frankfurt School exiles. Those ill-fated, socialist intellectuals fleeing the Nazi regime—Adorno, Horkheimer—along with her least favorite author, that pretentious do-gooder, Thomas Mann. Poor Ayn had come all the way to America, to the final western frontier, only to discover that all her Marxist enemies were living just down the road.

I decided to leave my bags behind the beans and take a quick stroll around the neighborhood. The sidewalks were clean and the streets were leafy. People walked big-boned pure breeds and sipped coffee from pastel-colored reusable cups. I found the affluence calming. Looking back up the hill I saw soft pink and orange mansions wafered into the cliffside. The sun was setting. It burnished the pale concrete and gave the garden foliage a dark iridescence that seemed to deepen the great, alluring mystery of having. Being in Los Angeles I wanted, for the first time in my life, to own property.

I walked all the way down to the main road, where I noticed an unusual billboard. It wasn't the standard splashy boast of celebrity names and Emmy nominations, but an extreme close-up of a boy's face with the glistening snout of a puppy. There was no text. Just the blurred features, tongue protruding slightly out the side. It was a sweet, blameless face that seemed to be saying "duhhh."

Returning to my building, I now noticed that there were a lot of young, attractive women in residence. They hurried through the foyer in luminous sweatpants with contoured orange faces that made them look like sunburned cats. A few practiced dance steps while waiting for the elevator. One girl filmed herself walk in, then out again, then in again; like a man with OCD I often saw on the Fourteenth Street subway platform. They all seemed to be around twenty-three. I couldn't quite imagine what they were doing with their lives.

When Raffi arrived he took my suitcases but made no acknowledgment of his lateness. Following him through the lobby, I felt my whole being pull back, putting a cautious distance between us. I had never trusted people who couldn't be wrong, even before I'd read the literature. And then more disappointment: riding up in the elevator I began to feel the dead, amiable air between our bodies; Raffi was gay.

The apartment was modern and light but in every corner I saw neat piles of Amazon boxes and folded Postmates bags. There was a small citadel of LaCroix cans on the coffee table, surrounded by a tiny cemetery of joint butts. Above my futon a huge square of pink fabric was pinned to the wall. On the floor beside it was a pile of expensive-looking camera equipment. Raffi had described himself as a "creator," which I assumed meant he made advertising content. But all the mess on shameless display now made me think he was actually self-employed.

At the kitchen table—a round high-top more suitable for bar snacks—Raffi explained that he created content on a video-sharing app. The app was new and I had never heard of its one-syllable name, which I immediately forgot, recalling only that it sounded a bit like "Jizz." What set Jizz apart from all the other user-generated micro-content apps, said Raffi, was its animal avatar feature. It seemed that some Silicon Valley savant had decided that what the culture wanted RN was to see itself as animals impersonating the kinds of people who were annoying IRL. Disguised as a shy panda or an affable giraffe, you could behave in ways that were off-limits to human beings. Raffi showed me a thirteen-minute YouTube compilation of his work. His animal avatar was a vivacious marmoset with the vocal tics of a gay beauty guru. In any other universe, it would have been both misogynistic and homophobic. But Raffi had nearly a million followers.

I had by now noticed that there wasn't a room divider. Only a loose dump of exercise equipment in the middle of the floor. Weirdly, above the flat-screen was a single, impractical bookshelf. I glanced over brightly colored business and self-help tomes. And then, at the far end, I saw the novels of Ayn Rand.

"You like her!" I pointed gleefully at the books.

"Ayn Rand?"

My heart sank. He had mispronounced her name. Anne, instead of Ei-en.

"My old roommate left them here. He was a stock trader who cooked steak for every meal."

"Gross." I felt light-headed, acting so hard.

"But his books take up shelf space, which is good for me because I don't read."

Raffi smiled, shamelessly. His unapologetic lateness now

took on a different sheen. His mess attained a dignified aura. Raffi appeared to be a person living fully and uncompromisingly in the service of his own life. An unwitting Randian. I had a good feeling about Los Angeles.

Ten minutes later, Raffi's female guests arrived. All four of them were stunningly beautiful and had evidently reclaimed the track pant, the potato chip, and the word "thick." They immediately began talking about how they all regularly farted on their boyfriends' heads. *Yes of course you can*, I thought, *when you look like that*. There was something both slovenly and aggressive about these four. They had suddenly somehow occupied every piece of furniture in the room.

"Raffi says you also make satire?"

It seemed that one of them was now talking to me. Though her eyes had not left her phone. *Did* I make satire? Lately, the word was making me cringe. Like everything else, satire was too concerned with power. "Punching up" meant there had to be a good side, and a bad one.

"Yes," I said. "But I don't punch up."

The girl's eyes flicked up from her screen, while the rest of her face remained downcast. "So which way do you punch?"

I thought about it. "Sideways. Like, at whoever happens to be standing there."

Another girl pointed at me. "That's funny," she said, unsmiling. "You're funny."

The others agreed, then almost instantly lost interest. Raffi emerged from the kitchen with more LaCroix. He handed them around and then perched on the edge of the sofa and told me about his "girlies." Three years ago these four had met online and formed a band based around the concept of their ADHD. They'd written one song—"Can't Do My Homework"—that got them a small following, but had quickly learned that lip-syncing and micro-dances were far more lucrative. Soon after that they'd discovered Jizz and the jaguar face filter and that their true talent was micro-satire.

"What do you satirize?" I asked politely.

One of the girls stopped punching her friend in the boob. "The patriarchy."

I felt a wave of exhaustion. The fact that they were all hot and their boyfriends greeted their farts with applause didn't help. I wasn't famous for my intersectionality, but these four were hardly being oppressed by the patriarchy. Women who got to poop in front of men were always outrageously good-looking. Ayn probably would have said that having masses of sexual currency meant you could afford to lose some shares in the toilet. She and I weren't that kind of woman. I had always instinctively known to hide all evidence of my digestive function from men.

Soon after, I excused myself. Once again the girls instantly forgot me, but I saw Raffi make a little face. He knew I'd been silently judging them. And that my satire had nothing to do with the patriarchy.

Jamie had set two production meetings for the following month and the producers were going to need to read a pilot. The first draft was due in a week. I was finding it hard to write jokes for someone who took life so seriously. To see absolute evil in a socialist architecture critic or trade union leader, as Ayn herself had done. But I also didn't want to make fun of Ayn; that was too easy, what everyone else would do. To write her, I figured, I just had to understand her better, though my methods—reading all her biographies—seemed to undermine Objectivism. People weren't the products of their pasts. They were what they said and did. The life force animating the choices they made in the present moment. And yet, taking someone at their word felt too easy, like bad television. If I was going to write something nuanced, I had to dig deeper.

When I got downstairs I lowered myself onto an oversized beanbag and tried to read my biography with some semblance of dignity. I was quickly immersed in the story of Ayn's first stint in Los Angeles. Delivering her unsolicited story samples to Cecil B. DeMille's studio, Ayn had encountered DeMille himself in the parking lot. A low, torpedo-style Tourer pulled up alongside her and a bald man with large doughy ears squinted out. He thought she looked hirsute and exotic and offered her a lift down to the Culver City set of *The King of Kings*. DeMille let Ayn shadow him all afternoon, and by the end of the day she had a job as an extra in the Palm Sunday scene and a brand-new name: "Caviar."

The insult of playing a sackcloth-wearing plebeian in a biopic about Jesus Christ was challenging. But Ayn had high self-esteem. Her first day on set, she marched straight back to wardrobe and said she refused to play a slave. The head of the department was a man known only as "Adrian." He seemed to understand Ayn at some deeper, almost spiritual level and poured her a glass of champagne, then dressed her as a patrician. Returning ennobled to set, Ayn had spotted her future husband. A handsome legionnaire in a very short toga. She knew faces like his only from the movies; the thick jaw and broad, leonine symmetry. Ayn Rand believed that her own intellect and courage had earned her a hero in the classical mold. She moved stealthily toward him, avoiding his gaze, acting the part of a dignified noblewoman. As the crowd pressed in behind them,

Ayn parted the folds of her dress, stretched out her leg, and tripped her destiny over.

Too tired to absorb any more of Ayn's early years, I returned to the elevator. But before I could press the floor number I was already descending to the basement. The small detour felt punitive. I didn't believe in God or haunted machinery but somehow moments like this always felt deserved. As if I had earned a lifetime of small punishments for something I'd once done. For the person I was. Ayn, of course, would have rejected this; reality was only what you made it.

At the lower level, the doors opened on a big, handsome boy with floppy hair and ridiculous sneakers. My heart pounded. He was exactly my type. And, for some reason, holding two trumpets.

"It's for a challenge," he explained, stepping inside. "I have to drive my car using these instead of my hands."

The big boy spoke with a deliberation that made him seem almost remedial. I was beguiled. "Are you also a creator?"

"I'm a Labrador."

The elevator rose.

"Does everyone in this building make micro-content?"

The big boy shrugged his large, powerful shoulders and then stared at me with his big blank face. "Did you just move in with Raffi?"

"How did you know?"

"He has *a lot* of roommates."

I felt concerned and then, standing beside the big boy, I had the heart-thrilling thought that he could kill me with one hand and yet was choosing to spare my life. The most unfeminist and sexually exciting idea I'd had in weeks. The doors opened again on my floor.

"What will you do with the trumpets now?"

He looked down at the two curly instruments in his hands, like a man suddenly transformed into crab.

"I have no idea," he said in adorable bewilderment.

I stepped out of the elevator, jokes circling in my head. I wanted to leave an impression. Something about shoving a trumpet in my ass. And then I thought of Raffi's girlies with their feminist ass triumphs, and lost my nerve.

"Salad servers?"

The doors closed on his laughter. Which was bright and bouncy and which I caught to my chest like a ball.

When I got back to the apartment, Raffi and his girlies had vanished. I took the LaCroix off the coffee table and deposited them into an empty Amazon box in the kitchen. Then I thought of breakfast and opened the cabinets. There was nothing but protein powder. The fridge was also bare aside from two takeout containers and a small container of CVS strawberries. I slammed the door in disgust.

The bathroom was even worse. Every surface was dusted in beige powder and there were fleshy smears of concealer on the vanity, the sink faucet, taps, mirror, and even the flipped-down toilet seat. The room smelled fruity and synthetic. I felt nauseous and then, flipping the seat up, I saw the turd. It curled against the bowl, bereft of paper. A middle finger to the notion of civility. To my presence in the house. What kind of person used the toilet and had the gall not to wipe their ass or flush? I knew that narcissists enjoyed the smell of their own waste but was it possible to be so narcissistic that you left a turd there, stinking up the bowl? Or was Raffi's narcissistic self-absorption so extreme that he had simply forgotten to flush? Was he fucking with me? Was he just living his life? I flushed the toilet and started reorganizing the cabinet to fit my toiletries.

But the turd stayed with me. Getting into bed I sensed its dark presence there, under the covers, and quickly yanked them back. No turd. But when I switched off the light, it was everywhere. Like a miasma that filled the apartment or rather the apartment inside my mind. I could still smell it. And feel its rough, slimy texture; its will to soil, to structural disintegrity. I did not believe in evil. But this paperless turd had a terrible power I couldn't understand.

I woke the next morning to Raffi jumping rope in the kitchen. His thuds vibrated through the thin futon. He had also opened the blinds and a shocking white light was creeping along the carpet, already licking at my toes. I dragged myself up and into the bathroom. The air was thick with hairspray and deodorant and the sink was coated in that musky-smelling beige powder that made me want to gag. Thankfully, this time there was no turd.

When I stepped back out of the bathroom the blender was jackhammering in the kitchen. But at least this let me know it was safe to dress in the middle of the living room because Raffi was engaged. The blinds, however, were open and operated only by a remote control, which was missing. I performed a cruel contortion below the windowsill to get myself into shorts and a T-shirt. There was no desk to work at. Only the tall kitchen table dominated by Raffi's two laptops. Now I could hear the television playing loudly from his bedroom.

But it was my responsibility to handle any negative emotion I felt toward the material conditions of my own life. It was my choice to endow Raffi with evil intentions, with the malicious desire to inflict suffering on me despite the obvious obliviousness of his actions. I had to treat Raffi's turds like an unconscious accident, like the unforeseen outcome of a major pollutant or of globalization. Like it was the 1950s and nobody knew any better; like the world was a happy and innocent place. It would all be fixed later.

I took my laptop and left the apartment. Exiting the elevator I saw that the recessed area where the beanbags usually sat was now occupied by three rows of muscular young women stretching on yoga mats. In the center was their stocky, bright-eyed instructor performing cow pose with a small white goat balanced on her back.

Slinking along the side wall of the lobby, I observed the scene. The women were told to contort themselves into postures that both built gluteal tissue and enabled a safe human staircase for the goat to ascend. I watched the women perform something called the Bulgarian Split Squat—holding a painful lunge while waiting for the goat to mistake their juicy thighs for a tempting mountain outcrop. This didn't look or sound like yoga, and yet the instructor assured them that it was. Over a pumping dance track she yelled inspiration at her students. Shrieking that the presence of goats bestowed a conscious awareness! A gentle alertness! An attunement to all of existence! The goat would get them in touch with their deeper spiritual selves. Which was, she told them, the only place from which to positively impact the world.

One of the yoga women had a mat with the maxim: "God Is Dead. Be Kind to Yourself," but I found I didn't hate this; Nietzsche had become important to me. As a younger woman, Ayn had kept a copy of *The Genealogy of Morals* in her purse and read it unabashedly at cocktail parties. And now I wondered if Vivian was right. If yoga people did have a slightly Randian bent. They feared government intervention (especially when it came to medicine), and they seemed to take responsibility for their emotions by putting their own spiritual fulfillment above everything else. Personally, I wasn't trying to make a positive impact on the world. I hoped not to make things worse, but I was suspicious of those in the business of world-impacting. Aside from the hubris, it also hinted at a secret aversion to death. A denial of the hard fact that Earth would ultimately return to stardust and life's meaning would remain illusory, if not moot. But the yoga women's desire to world-impact didn't bother me that much because, quite frankly, I didn't believe them.

Three blocks from my building I passed a homeless encampment. Walking between the grungy tents and battered furniture I could feel the low sonic vibrations of deep distress. I moved fast; from fear but also the hot squeeze of shame. I knew Ayn's unsympathetic argument: people were educated into low self-esteem. They were taught dependency and grievance and despair. This felt a little generalized, and it didn't address the factor of mental illness. But then again, the reality of mental illness seemed to be in dispute. Was it neurochemical or trauma symptom, or just the unconscious manifestation of cultural dysfunction? Ayn would have said the whole culture had an objectivity problem.

I found a café two blocks past the encampment where everyone was enjoying a full brunch on a Tuesday morning. Did I agree with this? Was it freedom? And wherever there was a flagrant burst of it, wasn't there always someone in a dark storeroom or walk-in freezer being horribly oppressed? I took a seat in the sunny center of the room. This morning I was reading

Ayn's essay on the Contemporary Left. "Contemporary" being the 1970s, and "Left" being the progressives disappointed by the failure of the cultural revolution. Ayn said these progressives shared a personality disorder that made them irrational and ruled by feelings. They lived in a world of pure subjectivity, with no distinction between past and present, where every historical injustice was happening *right now*—in language, symbols, and nebulous concepts like "the establishment." She called them "psycho-epistemological barbarians" and appeared to blame the whole phenomenon on Immanuel Kant.

According to Ayn, American culture had been poisoned by guilt and resentment. People imagined they were confined to powerless groups striving for collectivist ideals, which Ayn said only dehumanized the individual and always led to things like totalitarianism and genocide. She had developed a theory of the Spiritual Parasite—a person who rejected the responsibility of judging things for themselves. Movement without an internal mover. I could see evidence of it right now at the opposite table, where a young woman in a fedora was compulsively photographing her huevos rancheros.

The idea of the internal mover intrigued and troubled me. What exactly was it? A will to live and a drive to conquer that were somehow divorced from one's own psychology? At age twelve Ayn had watched a group of Bolshevik thugs shove her father to the ground as they seized his pharmacy. Before her young, impressionable gaze, patriarchy had fallen to its knees beneath the crumbling pillars of capitalism. I didn't want to contradict Ayn, but it was hard not to link this story with her lifelong battle to destroy the Left.

Somewhere just behind me, I could sense his large, Labradory eminence. I turned discreetly and saw Big Boy standing in the doorway. He didn't see me then or as he went bounding from the register to the bar, where he took a tiny stool behind the espresso machine. The waiter immediately brought him a coffee, which Big Boy downed in one long gulp before flipping open his laptop. He attached a webcam, sank two AirPods into his ears, and hunched closer to the screen. I had a clear view of Big Boy's reflection in the chrome side panel of the espresso machine. Something he had obviously not accounted for.

Big Boy talked softly to the camera, and every few seconds he pulled an extraordinary face—collapsing his chin and slacking his jaw so that the tongue bulged out, while the eyes made a slight but unmistakable crossing. And now I recognized him. Big Boy was the big *duhhh* from the billboard. I watched in astonishment. What was he doing? Was it courage or impunity? And how did he get away with it on a major social media platform? Embodying idiocy in pursuit of one's own enjoyment felt Randian. I could think of no purer form of self-pleasure than making funny faces in the mirror. Or maybe one, but that wasn't an ideal way to advance a career in the arts.

After a few more minutes, Big Boy took a book from his satchel and made his bounding way toward the restroom. Such confidence: to sit on a toilet in a stylish restaurant and take a long, leisurely shit. My whole being radiated with admiration. And then, as if he could sense me glowing there in the middle of the restaurant, Big Boy glanced over. He smiled and came straight to my table, holding up his bathroom reading material. The cover bore the loud, officious font and dreamy sunset pinks of the self-help genre. *Understanding the Borderline Personality.*

Big Boy wagged the book. "Do you think Raffi's a borderline?"

I disapproved of his generation's obsession with diagnosing people you didn't like as chronically delusional, along with a tendency to excuse their own bad behavior with exotic neuro-divergencies. But Big Boy's hair looked so thick and floppy, his shoulders so broad.

"He definitely lied about the room divider."

"Bad boundaries," Big Boy affirmed, and flipped the book open to a dog-eared page. "*Borderline: a person whose self-absorption is so acute they can't empathize with others.*"

"Oh . . . I thought that had a different name?"

Big Boy shook his head and his recitation gained force: "*Borderlines punish people who upset them and dehumanize anyone who challenges their point of view.*"

I wasn't sure that Raffi had points of view. But my heart flew out to Big Boy; I recognized this. "Did someone call *you* a borderline?"

He eyed me nervously. "How did you know?"

"A similar thing happened to me. *The New York Times* said I was a narcissist."

Big Boy's jaw dropped, though it made scant difference to the quality of his expression. "Isn't it kinda narcissistic to call yourself 'the paper of record'?"

My insides melted and all I could produce was a soft sort of mewling sound.

"I'm just lucky I bought this book." He eyed it tenderly. "Otherwise I would never have figured out that my ex is wrong."

I tried to picture Big Boy's horrible dehumanizing ex-girlfriend. She was probably very young and attractive and thought Chekhov lacked moral clarity.

"She said I have no empathy," he continued. "Because I'm too irreverent and my animal impressions are just mirror neurons, which she says don't count. And because I wanted to watch different TV shows."

"Let me guess," I said. "Borderlines love to call other people borderlines?"

Big Boy broke into the wagging smile of his breed. We grinned at each other for a long dizzy second and then he winced and brought a hand to his belly.

"Coffee just kicked in."

And he was off.

I immediately pulled up Jizz on my phone, found his handle, and watched some clips. Big Boy's doggy avatar was a barely verbal impersonation of a hot football jock in a state of semi-concussion. But the character was magnetic. He misused words and mangled meanings and seemed to be rebelling against the concept of linguistic specificity itself. Jizz loved it. There were hundreds of comments below his clips from young girls with pouty thumbnails and angry colored hair, declaring their love and begging to be his "wife." I understood both the semantic irony of this and that they actually meant it.

Back home, waiting for Raffi to vacate the bathroom, I watched more creator content. I wanted to understand Jizz better, to reach some sort of truce with its culture. I learned that Jizz creators were given challenges by their followers, who paid them to do things like hoverboard through a car wash and slap their own mother's ass. It was vaguely sickening but also, essentially, a cultural stock market without regulations. In fact, it was a better argument for Randian philosophy than the stock market itself. You didn't even need capital to make capital in the micro-content space. It was a free country operating on its own meritocracy. As long as you possessed Great Something. Great Beauty or Great Talent or even Great Stupidity: the free-market attention economy didn't mind. Jizz, with its subversive caricatures hiding in plain sight, seemed to be the ultimate manifestation of laissez-faire.

When he finally emerged from the bathroom, Raffi was painted like a geisha. He saw me and covered his mouth, uttering a coy Japanese schoolgirl *heeheehee*.

"You're allowed to wear that on the app?" I asked him.

"A marmoset beauty guru is allowed to wear it."

Raffi bowed and glided away into the kitchen. And so, at last, I was able to shower and brush my teeth. For a few moments afterward I stood in the cleansing steam feeling optimistic about my decision to live in Los Angeles, among these beautiful people and their micro-talent. And then, without thinking, I raised the toilet lid. The force of my shock threw me back against the shower screen. This one was larger and more aggressive than the first. It nosed up out of the water, cocked like a missile. Raffi's poop seemed to have its own will, to be will itself, a blind unbending will pitted against my own. Perhaps it was innocent and unintentional, but the poops were beginning to impede my ability to live.

That afternoon I finished reading the chapters on Ayn Rand's early years in Los Angeles. They were sad and lacked triumph and made me sympathize with her in a way I hadn't expected to. In LA, Ayn had been socially isolated and artistically underappreciated by DeMille's story department. She wrote treatments where women rescued their husbands from Siberian prisons or bought their fiancé's debt with their own inheritance. Ayn's superiors said her work was ideologically unfashionable and commercially unviable and she was eventually laid off. There was also a strange lost year that the biographer mostly skirted over. Destitute, Ayn was forced to get a job at a department store in the Valley and became seriously depressed. It was unclear how she had pulled herself out of this funk but there was one diary entry, heavily footnoted, that seemed to set her on a new creative course.

On the 23rd of March, 1927, Ayn had come across a news article. Nineteen-year-old William Hickman had kidnapped the twelve-year-old daughter of a well-known Los Angeles banker. After a week of fraught negotiations, the aggrieved father had agreed to Hickman's ransom and his terms. The banker had delivered the money himself, through the open window of the kidnapper's Ford. But instead of handing over the man's daughter, Hickman had snatched the envelope and sped off down the road. He'd stopped at the corner, flung the car door open, and hurled the girl's body onto the sidewalk. Minutes before, smiling at her father from the passenger seat, she had looked alive. But Hickman had just wired her eyes open and sewed her lips up into a thin, bruised crescent. He had also cut off her legs, removed her organs, drained her torso of blood, and stuffed it with bath towels.

In her diary, Ayn had been careful to avoid too much description of the crime. It was Hickman's police interview that she couldn't help praising in superlatives that the book's editors had obviously tried to play down. She'd also relayed in swooning detail how Hickman had played the Victrola as police searched his house, smiling and offering them cold beverages. She'd described him as a "bad boy with a very winning grin," admiring his "calm defiant attitude" and "inhuman strength"—joking in the face of his own death sentence. Ayn had gushed repeatedly over his pithy defense: *what is right for me is good*. But more obvious than that, she had written a thirty-page treatment for a book based on Hickman, called *The Little Street*.

It was about a young man called Danny Renahan with a

brilliant, sardonic sense of humor who shocked and amused people with his cynicism but had the "clear ringing laugh of a sunny soul; the laugh of life itself." Danny had no social instinct, no feeling for the herd; he knew himself and that was all he needed. He embodied Ayn's antireligious belief that Eternity didn't matter—to exist was glorious enough.

Danny had also murdered his town's beloved pastor. A cleric described in great fulminating detail as a giant baby with a soft pink head and comically fat fingernails whose belief in equity made him a despotic zealot of mediocrity. This is what "the little street" meant to Ayn: the glorification of smallness; the wrecking of man by teaching him ideals contrary to his nature. It was a metaphor for humanity's love of mob rule and the "heavy, dumb, jail-like monotony" of family life.

Reading about Danny Renahan, I felt heartened. More than that, I felt hotly adrenal. The psychosexual pieces, aka the fun parts, were starting to fit together. Ayn Rand seemed to have a thing for sadists. She had described *The Fountainhead*'s infamous rape scene as "rape by engraved invitation," and the paragraph on Dagny Taggart's diamond choker was the most erotic description of jewelry that I had ever read. I didn't mind that Ayn Rand had been inspired by a psychopathic murderer. In Europe, that was normal. That was the artist's special privilege. In fact, most of my favorite Northern European auteurs had produced at least one work of semi-veiled enchantment with Hitler.

And so it felt like kismet that I was drinking that night with Ming—an unrepentant cinema snob who had recently lost a teaching fellowship for screening the films of Lars von Trier.

I met Ming at an old run-down bistro in Santa Monica. My friend had been writing her great McLuhanesque horror film for the last nine years—"The Medium Is the Monster." Each time she finished a draft the technology changed and so over the years Ming had developed a hatred of youth and trends that I found immensely comforting. A good thing when everything else about my friend made me feel stupid and afraid. Ming had a screwy intelligence and a ferocious contempt. Her clothes were purplish and shaggy and always seemed to be unraveling, which—paired with her porcelain skin and roped black mane— gave Ming the spooky menace of a Tim Burton heroine. Pavel, her much older Ukrainian husband and a professional clown, had moved them to Los Angeles three years earlier and Ming had been contemptuous ever since. Or more contemptuous than she'd been in New York.

Whenever I visited LA, Ming took us somewhere conspicuously dumpy; protesting the city's obsession with appearances. Once she'd sat us at the La Brea Tar Pits and made me stare into the bubbling brown morass as she mused on the city's unconscious desire to shit itself in public. "It's an earthquake town," she'd said. "And no one lives at the edge of calamity without secretly wishing to be destroyed."

Ming had described the Santa Monica bistro as dim and roachy and attracting the kind of local scum that had once made the neighborhood "real." Also, she taught nearby. When we got there it was clear that the joint had undergone a modest upgrade. Our waiter had the artificial appeal and uncanny friendliness of an actor, and there was an industrial kitchen aesthetic evocative of chic public urinals. Ming was appalled and shared her disappointment with the waiter, who apologized for the upgrade and seemingly his own existence, flashing a bright, self-erasing smile. Satisfied, Ming ordered our ironic piña coladas and shooed him away.

Tonight I wanted to talk *formally* about television. I was still struggling with the limitations of historical fiction and now also with the constraints of the half-hour form, and Ming always gave excellent advice. It seemed easy enough to start with the most common question in the human conversational repertoire. I smiled at Ming and asked her what she'd been watching.

"You know I don't watch television."

"Not even prestige?"

"Great art transcends its own form, whereas television is constrained by the demands of the market and so, unlike cinema, is unable to transcend the structural bounds of capitalism."

It was a bad start: the Marxist reading. We hadn't even gotten to the part about Ayn Rand or the fact that I was trying to depict her as a relatable protagonist. Ming leaned back with professorial gravitas and continued.

"Television functions much like psychotherapy. A medium designed to unravel a subject's trauma, drawing them into endless sessions that only amplify the issues and rake in the cash."

This seemed to make sense of my struggle with the form. Television dictated that, in the space of thirty minutes, a character had to exhibit an escalating sequence of behavioral flaws that precipitated a reckoning wherein those flaws were exposed and a resolution reached; at least until the next episode. I had been finding it impossible to do this with a character who acted only according to rationalist principles and denied any connection to her past. But maybe Ming had a workaround. I took a long sip on my drink, then told her I was trying to write a TV show.

"It's okay, Anna. *Everyone's* writing a TV show."

"Are you?"

She took a stiff suck on her vape. "I've got a series doc for 'The Medium Is the Monster.' I'm not a fool."

Her vulnerable admission aroused such feeling in me that I, too, was suddenly confessing.

"My show's about the life of Ayn Rand."

Ming looked concerned. "A biopic?"

"Yes," I said quickly. "But don't worry, there won't be any trauma. Not really even a character arc."

"Smart. People are about as interested in sympathizing with Ayn Rand as they are with making psychological excuses for Hitler."

Ming didn't care what people were interested in, but I sensed she was trying to protect me after her curricular misstep. I continued, telling her that there would be no psychological backstory, only an exciting psychosexual tendency, as I had by now deduced that Ayn was an intellectual top and a sexual bottom. Ming's eyes brightened.

"This sounds promising." She took another long, contemplative drag. "But I think it needs to be a film."

"My manager says half-hour comedy."

"And what does *he* know about form?" Ming's face was suddenly vascular with contempt. "You punish Ayn for two hours, then kill her suddenly at the end. Lean and brutal with no character development. Like actual life."

Even as I said it, I knew it was wrong. "So that the audience sympathizes with her?"

"No." Ming was glaring. "Sympathy has nothing to do with art."

I nodded, obediently, though none of it had solved the problem with my TV show. I was not a European auteur and no one was going to pay me to write a punishing script about Ayn Rand that didn't involve psychological growth. The conversation was starting to make me feel both grandiose and insecure.

And then, staring into the frothy white dome of my drink, I saw the dark outline of Raffi's turd.

"I think my roommate might be a sadist."

"How so?"

"He leaves his turds unflushed in the bowl."

"So then, a masochist."

"Aren't his turds hurting *me*?"

"Depends. If it's intentional, it's the sadist's gift. If it's unconscious, he's a masochist seeking annihilation via shame."

"I think he might be borderline."

"Oh the whole *culture* is borderline."

"I thought the culture was narcissistic?"

"No, that was the boomers. We live in a society of boomer-abused borderlines. The culture is victimy, punitive, and suicidal. Borderlines are always threatening to leave or die because they love to hear their own eulogies. The scholarship says that boomers are narcissists, Gen Z are borderline, and millennials bridge the gap. How old is your roommate?"

"It's hard to tell. He's always wearing makeup."

The waiter was suddenly smiling over us coquettishly. He held out a small black tablet.

"Excuse me, ladies. Would you mind if we took care of this now? My shift is ending."

It was a perfectly reasonable request but something about the technology unsettled Ming.

"So we have to pay you *right now*? *Right* at this very moment?"

The waiter straightened his shoulders. "No, you don't have to." He smiled, handsomely. "I would just really appreciate it."

Ming fixed him with her tar black glare. "Don't misunderstand me. I don't mind paying you before your shift ends, but I don't enjoy the fascism of that little machine you're holding.

Leaving a bill on the table and giving us a few minutes to consult with each other is the humane thing to do."

"I totally agree with you," he said in a collusive hush. "I'm sorry, we just got these tablets and management really wants us to use them."

Our waiter had no way of knowing that evoking the management would force Ming to summon them.

"Well, I'd love to speak to management."

"Certainly. I'll go get him for you."

The waiter's relief was euphoric and I wished him well on his flight through the swinging kitchen doors. Waiting in tense silence for the manager, I wondered if the monster was this little black tablet—exerting its ideological pressure on Ming and transforming her from a brilliant, articulate woman into a roving missile of senseless aggression. Or was Ming the monster? Aiming her rage at the small, round man in ovular leopard-print frames who now stood over us, wringing his pudgy hands.

"Ladies, it has been brought to my attention that our new gadgets left you with an impersonal service experience. Is that correct?"

"Yes," said Ming. "If I wanted to be harassed by a screen for my credit card details I would have stayed in and ordered online. I come to this place because despite the mirrored wall tiles, it's still a regular old dump. I've always come for the dumpiness and that's what I expect to get."

The manager nodded, politely. I felt for him. Ming had a talent for putting congenial people in impossible binds.

"Absolutely," he said with saintly restraint. "I understand that you are one of our older customers and the new owners want to keep some of that older flavor. I will bring you a paper bill on a small plate and you can pay at your leisure. Thank you, ladies."

He gave a brisk, tortured smile and whisked himself off to the kitchen.

His emphatic use of "older" felt humiliating to me, but Ming knocked her drink back sprightly, reenergized by the conflict. She took out her vape and enjoyed it gazing off into the kitchen, presumably reliving her moral triumph. When she did finally look back at me, her anger had receded all the way to her ears. Ming appeared to be smiling.

"Read some Sade," she said.

"For my roommate?"

She shook her head. "For your monster."

The next afternoon Jamie rang. He had set up a meeting. With an actress my age; a gummy-mouthed, button-nosed bland biscuit of a blonde whom I always confused for two other actresses. Tammy had spent the last decade contracted to a network drama as the wholesome Christian neighbor and was now apparently desperate to do something gritty. She had read Ayn Rand in high school and only really remembered that she was "a bit of a badass." At the meeting, Jamie explained, it was my job to assure Tammy that Ayn Rand was indeed a badass and in all the right ways.

"But I thought this show wasn't afraid to get canceled?"

"It's not." His voice deepened with authority. "But actresses spook easily."

"So I need to lie?"

"You just need to assure her that Ayn Rand's philosophy has been updated for contemporary audiences."

"But it hasn't."

"In that case we'll need to make it an animation."

I thought of Big Boy's doggy billboard and felt a rush.

"And what about Tammy?"

"She's open to voice-over."

"Okay . . . so it's now an animated, half-hour historical comedy?"

Jamie sucked saliva hard through his teeth. "Yeah, so, people are actually looking for hour-lengths right now . . ."

"That's a lot of historical comedy."

"The more the better."

"And only the women can say 'cunt'?"

"Correct."

I sighed.

"Lol I'll send you the restaurant reservation."

I didn't see Raffi at all that week. Through the veil of sleep I heard him showering or rushing down the hall, but by the time I roused myself he was always already gone. It was an uncanny ability he possessed, to slip away. He continued to leave me turds that I refused to flush. They'd be gone by the afternoon but the bathroom stank. The houseplants looked unwell. The air seemed yellowish.

When my copy of *The 120 Days of Sodom* arrived I took it straight down to the lobby and commenced reading. I was almost instantly struck by the similarities between de Sade and Ayn Rand. Both of them were imperious determinists who wrote relentless tomes in defense of personal liberty, full of philosophical rantings and aggressive atheism. Ayn was not a hedonist but she agreed with Sade that people should live for themselves and that the pursuit of freedom was an almost religious commitment that shielded one from the ideological tentacles of the State; even if you were in prison, as Sade was for most of his adult life. Ayn, too, seemed to live in a kind of mental prison, where Soviet collectivism haunted her until her death, despite her physical presence on American soil, and even under President Reagan.

Ayn Rand, I now understood, was an intellectual sadist with a masochistic sexuality. All her love scenes having been written before the sexual revolution, it wasn't surprising that the sex was male driven and coercive. But Ayn had taken it much further. Not only did the rape scene where Howard Roark forces himself on his boss's daughter reveal erotic titillation at the transgressive act, but their subsequent love affair insinuated its moral justification. Maybe for Ayn, being a fascist on the page meant you had to play dead in bed.

As I read on, a large, oval-shaped shadow darkened the text. "What the Markwiz be so sad about?"

Big Boy's cranium had eclipsed the industrial iron chandelier that hung above us. He was pointing to the book's cover, which had a cheeky illustration of a bald mustachioed man aiming a fire poker at the naked bottoms of two young girls. "He don't look so sad."

I beamed at him. I couldn't help it. "I really like your micro-talent."

"Thank you," said Big Boy, making the face, and then making it twice as hard.

I wondered if he really was a radical. Conversant in the language of downtown dissidence and covering it behind a face of intellectual incapacitation.

"Are you a socialist?" I asked warily.

"Sometimes." He crossed his arms sensitively over his chest. "But I can also be pretty introverted."

Now I wondered if he was just a genius. "Is the idea that stupidity can be a type of childlike wisdom?"

"You mean like Billy Madison?"

I couldn't remember the movie but Adam Sandler definitely felt like the ballpark. I nodded but Big Boy was suddenly looking down, distracted by his phone. I watched his big beautiful jaw slacken insensibly.

"Wanna come up for N64?"

For a wonderful hopeful second I thought this was a sex position. Then cold comprehension sank in. "You want to play video games?"

He smiled at me. Blank and handsome and wagging. But I felt nervous. Ayn Rand said a man always preferred the hunt—that he didn't want his prey delivered directly to him, already twitching and bleeding from the neck. Then again, she'd tripped a man over in a very short toga and he'd loved her for fifty years.

I nodded and followed Big Boy out to the elevator.

His apartment's décor was sophomoric. All the fundamentals of adult existence were there—a sectional sofa, coffee table, easy chair, giant flat-screen—but interspersed with these bland upscale pieces was evidence of a childish rebellion. Two gigantic orange beanbag chairs sat inches from the television, Nintendo consoles poised on indented squish as if their teenage wranglers had just been zapped into a fifth dimension. The shelves were lined not with books but with colorful Japanese monster figurines. There were two inexplicable gold beach balls in one corner of the room, an air hockey table in the other. Big Boy tossed me a Nintendo console and walked off into the kitchen.

Now I noticed that the television was already on. Paused

on a YouTube video with the title "Dad Fails." Recalling a recent family outing, I felt queasy. The twins squinting at their phones while our father asked in his most hopeful and wanting-the-best-for-his-children falsetto for the restaurant's "signature dish." Immediately, their little mole heads had wheeled around to commence lecturing on the evils of fine dining. I'd watched my father's face pinken as he'd looked down, mocked and defeated.

Dads were one of the few phenomena toward which I felt almost unfailing empathy. Watching a dad walk his child around a playground or push a stroller down the street, one could sense the weight of his spiritual sacrifice. The sexual defeat evident in the curvature of his spine, the watery melancholy basined in his eyes. In the act of procreation men seemed to lose something fundamental of themselves. They seemed permanently cowed, fractured; a living breathing break that never fully healed.

It was different, I felt, for women. Having birthed a child, mothers seemed to possess the smug satisfaction of a physical fait accompli, their own somatic arrival tethering them to the Earth. Remembering the fertility clinic, my blood boiled. If I'd been a different kind of person, the kind who worried deeply (and not just with vague, erratic dread) about the planet's fate, I might've called these fertility doctors a certain brand of Hitler. Populating the world with needless babies for the satisfaction of female wombs. But I didn't call people Hitler, just like I avoided acronyms or anything else large swathes of the internet were doing. Still, the biological selfishness of women never ceased to amaze me. Dads, I felt, were sort of haplessly roped in, then blamed for all the world's problems. When Big Boy reentered with two pamplemousse LaCroix, I asked him what Dad Fails were.

"Wow. Have you been in a coma?"

But he looked excited. Big Boy bounced down beside me and scrolled to a video called "Dad Fails Best of 2019." I accepted the flavored water and settled in to watch the twenty-seven-minute compilation. There were dads falling off roofs; dads stepping backward into swimming pools; dads crashing through birthday cakes and making their children cry. I winced all the way through. Big Boy also appeared to be both amused and in silent pain.

"Poor dads," I said.

"Poor dads," he agreed.

"Poor men," I added with deeper feeling.

Big Boy stared at me, open-mouthed.

"Women are very borderline." I made the correction: "Right now."

"They are?"

I huffed at the screen, where the vast phantasmagoric something of borderline women seemed to reside. "They might want to be your wife but they also want to kill you."

Big Boy's eyes got very round. I was throwing the sisterhood under the bus but the sisterhood had never been kind to me. As a younger woman I'd been a middling sexual threat and now I was just a black cape that went around saying things like "consent is complicated." But whatever. I was a product of my generation. The heroin waif. The Spice Girl. Hillary Clinton Version 1.0. Just because I was perimenopausal and Philip Roth still made me wet did not mean that my life was over. There was still such a thing as the wisdom of experience.

"It must be hard for men," I said. "To be dehumanized all the time."

Big Boy seemed puzzled. "I love being a Labrador."

"Yes, but you're also kind of hiding behind a filter."

He shrugged but I knew he was just scared; I had seen his art and it was subversive.

"I know you don't actually like 'Wet Ass Pussy.'"

"That was just a bit." He blushed. "You know, dogs hate cats . . ."

But I could feel it now. The sly undercurrent of flirtation. I gave Big Boy a knowing smile that strove to communicate the breadth of my sexual understanding without coming across as a world-weary slut. His borderline ex-girlfriend had obviously made him gun-shy, so I went slowly; coaxing him out like a battered animal with morsels of bloody meat. I told him that all power imbalances belonged in the bedroom. That according to Ayn Rand, sadomasochism was healthy sexual roleplay, and how even strangulation had a rich history that preceded porn.

Big Boy still seemed apprehensive. "What kinda feminism do you call that?"

"I think it's proto-feminism. Or I guess it could be post-."

He nodded, thoughtfully, and then picked up his phone.

"What else does Ayn Rand say?"

He was watching me through the camera lens, the highest compliment of his culture. It made me nervous but also felt like a kind of mating behavior. And so I told him. About the empty moral center of altruism, the self-sacrificing impulse at the heart of socialism. The death drive, which I knew almost nothing about. Big Boy cackled silently behind his phone, thrilled with his capture. He hadn't asked for permission to film me but I didn't want to spoil the moment or emasculate him. Still, I was paranoid.

"Please give me a filter."

He gave me the big, bobbling head of a horned sheep. The filter modulated my voice so that it had a low, braying quality while my gestures got jagged and hoofy. The ram was funny. But still likable, I thought, and intellectually convincing.

"Ayn Ram," he announced.

I couldn't hold myself back, and hugged him. "I love her."

Inspired, I made a few quick notes in my phone while Big Boy powered up the N64. Perhaps he wouldn't kiss me tonight. Perhaps that was better.

"*Mario Kart* or *1080*?"

"The tax form?"

He liked this. My natural talent for the misuses of language. We agreed to play *Mario Kart* and then Big Boy told me I was playing Princess but actually assigned me Toad so that I spent the first lap believing I was zooming around in my little pink buggy while my actual avatar butted repeatedly into a rainbow. I liked this. Its promising sadism. I played Nintendo until my legs went fizzy and my mind began to snow. Big Boy didn't make a move but he was mercilessly competitive, which had the exhilarating whiff of sexual domination. This was clearly a man who so revered my mind he had to own me with a digital go-kart steered by a tiny pink princess. When night fell, I left the apartment feeling mentally used and physically spent and deeply, deeply satisfied.

—

My struggle with form meant that Jamie had had to push back my production meetings, which was good but also meant I was definitely going to run out of money. The two thousand dollars my father had loaned me would be gone in a week. I needed something fast and probably menial, though I feared drudgery and more so, I believed, than most people. I had spent so much of my life being opposite, avoiding normalcy, that capitulation felt annihilating; the sense of failure crushingly existential. Normalcy only got harder with age because I had nothing to show for myself—no family I had sacrificed for, no partner, not even a pet. Those things were, in some way, the already-made sacrifices. To sit in an office and fulfill someone else's dream felt even worse than the small-*d* death of my cancellation, because it was an acceptance of that death—a death beyond death.

But Ming had an idea. She said it was a job that allowed maximum mental freedom and none of the pettiness or indignity of workplace politics. No asshole bosses, no bored, colluding coworkers. In this job, she assured me, my pride would be left intact. Dog walking, Ming explained, was a very respectable occupation in Los Angeles and often led to industry connections. This immediately made me not want to do it. I didn't want to get work because people liked or pitied me. Ming backpedaled—honestly, you made almost no contact with the owners; it was all lockboxes and door codes and finagling side gates and fences. She had done it two summers ago and while walking had come up with the whole ninth draft of "The Medium Is the Monster." It was mostly just you and the dogs and your own ambling thoughts.

I found a woman on Craigslist who owned several dog-walking vans. She greeted me in pajamas while holding back four demented-looking pit bulls and yelling at me to get inside and close the door. The dogs growled and whimpered at my feet as she began to race through the instructions, stopping every few moments to check the loud dings coming from her Apple Watch. In her fifties, she had a fatigued, bitter beauty and her home's cozy squalor gave off the aesthetic abdication of a college rec room. I assumed she'd come to LA to be an actress and had instead spent the last decade raising four canine sons.

But it was worse than that. These weren't even her dogs. Her home, she explained, was essentially a kennel. And this made her aesthetic even sadder; every surface was covered with a filthy blanket or mangled pillow. All the décor was functional. As we walked out to the garage, she handed me a list of dog addresses to type into a delivery service app that would optimize my route. Optimization was key, she told me, and now I saw it. Her pajamas were mud-stained; not the product of one lazy morning but the daily uniform of a dog concierge. The van itself was a hollowed-out shell, bereft of upholstery or radio or anything that might detract from getting ten stinking beasts from point A to point B. She continued to blast me with instructions as I reversed the lurching van out into the street, before slipping a contract in through the open window. I was to read, sign, and return it by the end of the day, but I wasn't allowed to stop for lunch. Or I was, but it would be a misuse of my time. I was being paid per dog, she informed me, which meant I had to race the clock to make anything over minimum wage.

Flying around Mid City, I became enraged by other drivers. I swore at trucks and trailers and called a bus "fat cunt." I sped over humps and took corners like a stunt driver. The pickups were also stressful. I knelt outside doggy doors, trilled names like "Cheeto" and "Whopper" and "GIF." I rattled and rammed side gates, hauled myself over garbage cans, and futzed with temperamental lockboxes until I shook them, swearing. Once I had collected all my canine charges, I sped to the nearest dog run. Seeing the open field, the dogs all immediately began to howl. Their sad chorus boomed through the van's metal shell and made me feel insane. I parked erratically, hurled myself from the van, and hurried around the back to free them.

At the park gates, I became flustered and couldn't figure out how to get my dogs in without letting the other dogs out. But I was assisted by a young woman in an over-accessorized track suit with poop bags parachuting from the pockets. She calmly herded my dogs into the run while blocking the hopeful escapees with her large left thigh. Once they were inside, all five of my dogs trotted off in opposite directions to take a shit. I found the first three poops and then fled to the drinking fountain. From here I watched in shame as the gate-herding angel scooped up the last of my missing turds. She gave the weighted bag a little shake and smiled, as if she'd heard the tinkling of gold coins.

"Lola," cooed the angel. "Pepper, Chewie, Frog."

Now I understood. She was a fellow dog walker. And there were two more with her. Both young and ruddy-faced with a mix of joy and exertion. It took me another twenty minutes to approach them and once I did I learned that these gentle, serene walkers worked for a different company. It was owned by a woman named Shar who lived on an urban farm in Culver City, gave them free root vegetables, and paid them fairly. Shar did the driving for her walkers, dropping the dogs to each park and then retrieving them afterward. The walkers stayed in the park all day, playing with the dogs. Which meant the walkers' fee, unlike mine, was fixed. They couldn't speed like maniacs to earn more or accidentally get on the freeway and earn a whole lot less. They had nothing to strive for, no incentives, no hope. They were, I supposed, the communists of the dog run.

My day went on, humiliatingly. A Cavoodle stole my hat and I had to chase him around the park for ten minutes. Later, a Shiba Inu rolled in shit and I hosed her down while she shook shit water all over my pants. Dogs, I learned, really liked to do the wrong thing. I might've respected this, even identified with it, if I hadn't been losing money. Returning the van, I found myself emotionally depleted in a new and disturbing way. It wasn't just the degradation; it was something more banal and common and related, in an unnerving sense, to deregulation.

—

Jamie had booked a restaurant for Tammy and me on a narrow, winding street in a leafy hillside suburb that my Uber driver said didn't actually exist.

"Can't tack on a 'Heights' and give it a whole new zip code," he scoffed, dismissing my Google Maps with a brisk wave of his hand.

He dropped me off at the bottom of an incline, which I then trekked back up in precariously high shoes. Between the trees I could see the hill drop away to the sprawling concrete blocks and roiling freeways. And everywhere, popping up like rectangular polyps, were the billboards of big, friendly animal faces.

The café's entrance was ambiguous. I crept along the wall of bougainvillea, molesting the foliage for an opening, then pawed my way in through the prickly boughs, licked by waxy leaves, until finally lurching out into the chlorophyll light of a canopied courtyard. And there was Tammy. She was tiny and there was something slightly obscene about her smallness. The shiny smidge of gum, the bright corn-bit teeth. It made me think of a lifelike doll I'd once owned with a strangely ornate vagina. In Tammy's lap sat a tiny tan puppy. The dog shivered in the deep V of her sweater as Tammy told me all about its rescue. There was a flight from China, a second one from San Francisco, and then a two-hour ride in an Uber Select. It seemed to me that the puppy rescue mission had added a lot of fuel to the already flaming Earth. But I wasn't here to be contrarian; I was here to give Tammy a crash course in the nice parts of Ayn Rand.

I opened with a quote: *Wealth is the product of man's capacity to think.* It was a form of flattery to tell rich people this. But Tammy was immediately on the defensive.

"And *woman's* capacity," she said. "And nonbinary people's."

"Of course."

"But also." She screwed up her adorable little nose. "Isn't wealth systemic?"

"Systemic?"

"Like a product of a failing system?"

I bit my tongue.

"I mean I'm not a communist," she said. "But like I don't think capitalism actually *cares* about people."

"No," I said politely. "And that's why it's fair."

Tammy cocked her head left, then right. "But it isn't fair."

I was ready for this. Thanks to Ayn. "*People* aren't fair. Capitalism is totally without prejudice."

Tammy looked annoyed and then cuddled her puppy obscenely. I could feel that economics were not the way in. Neither of us really knew what we were talking about. I had to stir up some emotion.

"Did Jamie tell you much about Ayn's feminism?"

"He said she was sort of the original girlboss?"

"She was definitely bossy."

Tammy's tiny features engorged. "Jamie said she liked to tie men up and strangle them?"

I silently cursed him. Now I had to explain that Ayn had, in fact, been into the very opposite. That she was actually nothing like the kind of modern TV heroine Tammy was probably imagining. The flawed female protagonist who used men for

violent orgasms or loveless procreation. And then I glimpsed
Tammy's small hand. The woman may have been miniature but
she wasn't young. Tammy, like me, had come of age in the late
nineties, when the best a woman could hope for was Chandler
or Ross or David Foster Wallace. Tammy, like me, had suffered.
She had obviously pushed herself hard and managed to succeed
in a culture that believed Leonardo DiCaprio was entitled to
teenage supermodels until the day he died. Tammy deserved
better. Or at the very least, the same. She was a talented, ambitious, high-achieving woman entitled to all the socio-sexual
benefits of her kind.

"What if I told you Ayn Rand only dated male models?"

Tammy's eyes bulged. "She did?"

"No, but she *would* have. Had the culture been more in tune
with her sexual politics."

"Which were?"

"Ayn believed in transaction," I said. "In swapping value for
value. A powerful older woman deserves better than a balding,
insecure pussy hound."

Tammy squinted dubiously from behind her drink. "And
what about nice, secure men who are just happy for their girlfriends' success?"

But I heard the achy belligerence in Tammy's voice. This had
never happened to her. I continued. There was an untapped gold
mine to be plundered by perimenopausal women. This was the
antidote to the older man–younger woman dichotomy that had
been shattering mature females since time immemorial. Young
men loved older women. It was about power and it was fantastic.
As I told her this, Tammy began to smile, her tiny lips curl-
ing lustily. It must've been more painful for a petite, childlike
woman to get older. All her sexual currency depleting as she

moved from adolescent straight to crone. Tammy needed my help.

I told her how Ayn Rand had found equilibrium by combining mental self-sovereignty with letting a hot young stud ravage her between the sheets. Now Tammy commenced a low chuckle that she sustained all the way through my discourse. A low-grade hysteria that I found very encouraging. I enumerated Ayn's young lovers, including the brilliant student she'd taken in as a lodger, right under her oblivious, flower-breeding, and possibly bisexual husband's nose. Tammy's little feet swung gaily beneath the table. By the end of my speech, she was giddy and practically drooling. When I told her about the strangulation, she leaned in low over the table, smothering the puppy.

"You can do anything," she said, breathlessly. "In an animation."

Tammy loved the ram idea too and agreed that the animal was a powerful symbol of female strength and virility. It would be just like *BoJack*! she declared. I humored this, though in reality, our show would be nothing like *BoJack Horseman*. The comedy would be free from the countervailing weight of personal failure. There would be no pathos. No moral apologia. It would be a story about the triumph of the human spirit where swimming pools were not emblems of existential despair. A show that dared to celebrate private tennis courts and seven-car garages and people who read Nietzsche in their forties.

Lunch was a success. Afterward, I felt like I had just survived a severely turbulent flight—all the desperate promises forgotten once the seat belt sign had been switched back off. In a high new spirit I decided to walk home. Snaking down the leafy crescents, I sensed my place here among the huge, hidden bungalows. The neighborhood sounds filled me with the proprietary strangeness of déjà vu. The sultry whispers of tasteful water features, peppy smacks of tennis balls, the big gay oversplash of an infinity pool, and in the distance the soft humming industry of a mobile doggy groomer. I thought of my horrible day job and felt an airy, ascendant certainty that it would all soon be over.

When I got home I opened Jizz and saw that Big Boy had uploaded the video of Ayn Ram. My heart started speeding. I checked the likes. Eight thousand. Over ninety thousand views. This, I knew, meant that it had technically gone viral. My brain was tingling; my breath shallow. I checked the comments. They were mostly comprised of emojis—but good ones. Clapping hands, both tears-of-laughter faces, and an array of animals with the dollar signs for eyes. Each love heart went straight to my head, tingling into a micro-orgasm. There were also a few long, unfamiliar acronyms and some emoji syntax I couldn't quite parse, but the sentiment was clear: these people didn't hate me.

And now I became emotional. I had written two books of over eighty thousand words each, and yet it was the single minute of ranting with the head of a sheep that had given me all the love and attention I'd ever craved. These people were my TV test audience, and that audience seemed large and very enthusiastic. I thought of my parents and felt relief. I was going to produce something and it was going to be, at the very least, divisive. I watched the clip eleven times and reread all the comments and then I texted Big Boy.

He was at a party and told me to come; his friends were apparently excited to meet me. I felt elated. Were we seeing each other? Was I his girlfriend? How could so much good fortune befall someone all at once? And in their thirty-ninth year? Raffi was home but I didn't want to spoil my mood. I was still coiffed from lunch and so I called an Uber and ran downstairs without setting foot in the bathroom.

The Studio City house was a large white box whose "rooms" were delineated by beams and several illogical mini-staircases. In the kitchen I noticed a lack of refreshments. Despite the host's obvious wealth, there was only one cooler of beer, one bottle of vodka, and some red Solo cups stacked in three low towers across the kitchen island. Someone had put out a tub of hummus beside the potato chips. There were no crackers. I observed a bicycle hung up in the corner of the room and a lava lamp beside the flat-screen, and remembered that these people were not even thirty.

I found myself standing at the kitchen island with a group of Big Boy's friends. They all looked about twenty-five and had quiet, doting girlfriends who all looked about nineteen. Within this group, the boys were telling jokes, or rather giving micro-performances in response to verbal stimuli. The girls were paying sweet, handheld attention. I watched a pretty, pug-faced boy spill a drink into his lap, then tip himself backward off his stool. Three people filmed it.

Eventually Big Boy introduced me and everyone said they loved Ayn Ram. One obnoxiously handsome boy told me he'd sent the clip to his mother, who was such a die-hard Randian she'd named the family terriers "Who Is" and "John Galt." He wanted to know if I had any more content and I told him a TV show was forthcoming. Now I received high fives all around. It was a confusing feeling—inclusion. I could see the spiritual benefits but also how addictive it would be. How you might lose your edge trying to chase it.

When Big Boy went to the bathroom I started up a conversation with a bespectacled girl who had hot pink hair and a vast humble T-shirt (but possibly no pants) as she watched her date pretend to choke on an ice cube. I learned that the girl was a PhD candidate at Stanford writing on neorealist Italian cinema, and we exchanged a few banalities about *Bicycle Thieves* before I pivoted rather elegantly to billionaires and the antitrust laws.

With a little shiver of sadism, I told the PhD candidate that Ayn Rand had called billionaires "the most persecuted minority under American law." The laws were contradictory, I explained, and designed to ensnare these hated producers of wealth, jobs, and innovation. If they set prices too high, they were charged with monopolizing. If prices were too low it was "unfair competition." And when they tried to meet the prices of their competitor they could be jailed for collusion or conspiracy.

The girl had stopped watching her boyfriend's micro-choke and her expression was at once titillated and appalled. Enjoying this, I continued, telling her in a louder and more strident voice that anyone who cared about individual freedom logically had to care about billionaires. Because caring about billionaires meant caring about the smallest minority on earth: the individual.

But now the girl was cringing. "I'm sorry," she said. "I think I prefer it with the filter."

I was embarrassed by the failure of my natural charisma but flattered that she had recognized my work. "So you just prefer sheep?"

"Caring about the world doesn't make you a sheep."

"No, I was talking about the ram."

"And I disagree with every single thing you just said."

"Okay."

A spiky silence ensued as we both watched the boyfriend. I

felt rattled. Had this person really liked Ayn Ram? It seemed hard to believe, considering her university thesis and the fact that she seemed to hate me. Thankfully, an announcement was made for everyone to come take a seat in the living room. In the most sunken part of the large, open space I now noticed three rows of plastic chairs were lined up in front of a projector screen. Stanford and I glided away from each other and I was happily reunited with Big Boy. As we slid into our seats, a handsome Asian man with a milquetoast botanical tattoo sleeve gestured to the two unassuming people seated to either side of him.

"Everyone in this row has gone viral," he informed me.

I nodded, pride and fraudulence swirling awfully inside me.

We were now treated to an amateur comedy show. Something, apparently, that Big Boy's friends did often. It seemed there couldn't be a social interaction among these people without constant, low-level performance. The three comics stood in front of the screen on a slightly elevated section of the living room. They were all good-natured and physically attractive in a way that seemed to betray the physiological laws of comedy. I missed the mean, ugly schlubs and the angry weirdos. During each of their sets I noticed a sort of mild, low-stakes goofery, the kind practiced by bored teenagers where talent and virtuosity gave way to lazy impressions performed while maintaining one's sexual appeal. I didn't want to judge Big Boy's friends, but also, my livelihood now seemed to depend on them.

The headliner was a handsome white man who opened with satirical ditties about cis-het capitalism in shows like *Friends* and *Sex and the City*, and then just moved on to songs about annoying white women. I found his jokes prosaic, with too much emphasis on punning and rhyme. The lyrics were projected behind him so that the audience could sing along, which they did, with magnanimous laughter. I tried to be open-minded but the headliner was both mediocre and a feminist. Which just proved Ayn's point: that mediocrity always attached itself to virtue because it couldn't bear the inherent contradictions of vice. The headliner was certainly no provocateur, just an ordinary attention-seeker who was slightly more attractive and amusing than everyone else. Someone just like them, just a friend waving from inside the screen. It wasn't the remote alienation of the celebrity; this was the narcissistic embrace of the familiar. People were laughing because they liked this person.

And yet these same people liked Ayn Ram. The whole evening now had the bitter aftertaste of a Yiddish curse. *May you go viral on the internet and all your fans be cartoon dogs.* I tried to believe that these idiots contained multitudes, but I wasn't in the habit of giving people a chance.

When we were back home and sitting on his couch, Big Boy told me that he had a rare form of ADHD that meant he couldn't recline on a sofa unless he was watching an action movie. *Die Hard. Mission: Impossible. The Terminator.* I recognized the reticent Randian hero at the center of each story. Men of courage, purpose, and physical beauty. *Terminator 2* was Big Boy's favorite. It was the car chases, he told me, but also the emotional storyline. I couldn't quite remember what that was—something about a son teaching his father to feel or a boy teaching his robot to cry.

But before we could snuggle up on the sofa, Big Boy ordered outrageously spicy Thai food. From a local restaurant with flashing laser lights and blaring K-pop. I had walked past it the night before and felt old. There were many places like this in Los Angeles. Designed to assault the senses and keep people in an overstimulated state of hyper-consumption that presumably led to catharsis in the toilet bowl. Ming was right—Los Angeles secretly wished to shit its pants.

When the food arrived it burned my eyes. I had to keep the lid on as I dipped in and out of my container. I didn't want to be overly critical but I had been to Thailand and pad Thai wasn't even spicy. There was something punitive about eating food this hot. Ming might've called it a liberal masochism punishing itself for its colonialist past. I stuck the fork back in my noodles and closed the lid.

While we enjoyed dinner, Big Boy showed me a Useless Robots compilation. The clips featured simple humanoid machines butting into walls and falling down stairs and spraying ketchup into their own crude circuit-board faces. I didn't understand.

"Is it nihilism?"

"Nih-il-ism," he recited. "Is that when you *really* love the river?"

I laughed. But Big Boy was suddenly pensive over his chicken satay sticks. Behind the beautiful blank face I could feel a tortured new introspection. I pressed him gently.

"It's nothing," he said.

"Come on." I butted his shoulder with my head. "Tell Ayn Ram."

I felt vulnerable being Ayn Ram after our disappointing outing, but it seemed to get Big Boy talking. Frowning deeply, he told me that he'd shown the useless robots to his ex and she'd accused him of being like Phineas Gage.

"Who's Phineas Gage?"

I was now informed of the famous neuropsychological case study—a reserved railroad foreman from Vermont who'd accidentally shoved an iron rod through his ventral medial prefrontal cortex. Phineas had survived the brain injury to become a gregarious prankster who liked to flash his testicles and call people "cow dung." He was apparently proof in the personality disorder world that irreverence and lack of empathy were neurochemically connected.

"Well I think Phineas sounds like fun."

But Big Boy remained withdrawn. He picked up his food container and started shoveling the chicken satay into his face with a terrifying disregard for the sticks. I was frightened for him and found it hard to watch. He finished quickly and then immediately reclined. Down here the frizz of his memories seemed to calm. Digestion made Big Boy slow and contemplative and soon he was talking again about his ex. How, as a result of her accusations, he'd found himself deliberately empathizing with all kinds of people. Even bad, "selfish" ones (his scare quotes made me feel seen). But it was actually a good thing in the end, Big Boy told me, because he'd discovered he could empathize with anyone.

"I even did it with Hitler."

I felt sick and laughed. Big Boy stared back at me with unruffled innocence. And, really, what was he guilty of? Behaving like a European auteur? Being an artist? I made myself into a soft, feathery mattress of compassionate curiosity.

"And what did you understand about Hitler?" I asked him.

"That he was borderline."

"Not narcissistic?"

"I mean, probably both. His insecurity was off the freaking charts."

It wasn't much of a provocation, and yet I felt relieved. That, at the very least, Big Boy agreed that Hitler had a severe personality disorder. Restored to harmony by our shared interests, Big Boy and I sat there for a long, comfortable silence. Or at least it felt that way to me. Big Boy, I realized, was actually trying to release a large, voluminous burp. I pictured it traveling up his body like a giant pearlescent bubble, and felt that I would gladly receive its vaporous burst all across my face.

"I feel a real philosophical mutuality with you," I told him.

Big Boy pursed his lips, freeing the gas in a long, focused hiss before reclining further back.

"What's 'mutuality'?"

But before I could answer, he was asleep. I tapped him and called his name but he remained unconscious. Then I shook his shoulders and let a hand linger on the lovely smooth dip of his left bicep. I felt sympathy for the young men of Big Boy's generation. These poor boys were always being told to shut up and listen, to move over and step down, to quietly just disappear. But they weren't some big, insensate collective noun. They were individuals.

I gave Big Boy's hand a gentle squeeze. He'd briefed me on what to do. I was meant to play something loud and full of explosions from his list of action movies. Or I could just let myself out and let him sleep. Or, I supposed, I could just keep sitting here.

I stretched my legs out and reclined beside him on the narrow sofa. The skin where our shoulders met was hot, and sliding my hip in to where it naturally jigsawed with his waist I felt the same pleasurable burn. I lay like this for a few minutes, enjoying our synchronous breathing. And then, because I was already touching him, I let my elbow bend up and my arm rise to meet his chest—my hand falling lightly across his pectoral. I curled in to face him, pressing my mouth up against his bare arm, my breasts cushioning into his ribs.

It was weird what I was doing. I knew that. But also hard

to call it "doing" anything at all. It made me think of a night in college when I'd shared my bed with a friend. He'd spent the first forty minutes pressed against my back: cuddling, but with a boner. I'd ignored it. Pretended to be asleep. He was my friend and the easier thing was to not hurt his feelings. I'd written a scene just like it in my first book. And now, lying there beside Big Boy, I felt it again: consent *was* complicated. Especially with the Taoist riddle of whether unconscious boner-nudging actually inflicted psychic harm. My friend's dick in my back hadn't hurt me. I had never allowed these things to get in the way of a good story. That was my power: turning people into jokes. Antifa was the same, I told myself. Then realized I hadn't actually told anyone about that.

When I noticed that Big Boy was drooling, I lost my drive. Molesting a man in his sleep turned out not to be my sexual preference. In fact, it hurt my feelings. I wanted him to want it. To take it, even. Inconveniently for me, his free will was crucial to my arousal.

—

The danger with being so unconditionally accepting of young boys was when they started to see you as their mom. I had experienced this before. The limping penis and sudden contempt. But Big Boy didn't have mommy issues. His problems were very much daddy oriented. I believed I was safe. It was just a period of gestation. We were accumulating both micro-content and emotional trust.

To distract myself from the anxiety of what we were, I decided to go out. To remind myself that there was a world beyond me and Big Boy, one that included other boys, big and small, who might also find me appealing. Really, I wanted to inhabit a space beyond our confusing relationship, or just a space where he and I did not share a laundry room and plumbing.

And so I agreed to join my friend Terra at a TV premiere. These types of invitations were the only way I ever got to see Terra—holding her bag while she posed on a red carpet. Googling the TV show, I read that it was a half-hour comedy about four diverse New Yorkers in their mid-thirties, dating and having neurotic conversations about nothing. Early reviews were calling the remake "revolutionary." Though, from my understanding, to be revolutionary one had to change the fundamental structure of something—its actual *form*.

Terra had texted to fetch our tickets while she walked the carpet, but once I had them in hand she texted that she'd been held up and would just catch me inside. I drew my cape tight around my shoulders and moved unseen through the glamorous crowd. In the bright, buzzy theater I sat alone, nibbling at the complimentary popcorn and watching the exit doors hawkishly for my friend. Speeches were made, people were applauded, three of them said the word "revolutionary." Finally *Shinefield* started, without Terra.

Where the original had been vanguard for its meandering and conversational formlessness, the remake seemed to actually *impose* form. Each of the core cast—the eponymous lesbian comic with chronic OCD and her three neurotic millennial friends—did something selfish and then, for most of the thirty-minute episode, various plot points pushed them toward an examination of their behavior and its psychological causes. In other words, toward their trauma. It was neat and moralizing and very OCD. The writers had explained away every moment of surprise, all human mystery. However, this did make *Shinefield* formally different from the original and thus, technically, revolutionary. When the lights came back on, I stood quickly and rushed out to the foyer. There was a text from Terra that she'd missed the screening but would meet me outside the after party. I tried to stay gracious, calling an Uber to the upmarket pizza restaurant that was an inconceivable twenty-minute drive from the theater. But Terra wasn't outside the after-party either.

I hurried down the red carpet between a sea of limp cameras, my cape flapping in the wind like the wings of an enfeebled bat. Inside, I ordered a martini and went to drink it alone by the fireplace. The restaurant looked like a midrange ski lodge but served greasy pizza slices on paper napkins. I sat on a stool that may have been a side table, and stared into the fire. No one talked to me. No one even offered me a slice.

I got a second drink and moved toward the cold, treeless courtyard, where the attractive catering staff were nosing trays around and shining at all the guests. The cast were sitting at a banquette, flanked by small fawning men in tight suits who kept fist-bumping everyone in violent sycophancy. I snatched a slice off an abandoned tray and slunk into the adjacent booth. Here, the old feelings of isolation and despair swam in. I was physically and spiritually alone at the *Shinefield* premiere. There was no one to talk to about the philosophy of Ayn Rand. No one who might want to discuss the relationship between self-esteem and self-responsibility or catalogue the many historical examples of when collectivism had been dehumanizing to the individual. And so, feeling alienated and slightly mawkish from the martinis, I pulled *The Virtue of Selfishness* from my purse and began to read.

I was up to the part about *ressentiment*. Nietzsche's idea that the resentful person formed a whole identity from the negative space of their comparative lack. It was really a kind of masochism, I thought, draining my second glass, where you came into being by virtue of your own dejection. Despite my tipsiness, I was aware of the irony. I didn't want to sink into the negative space of Not Finding *Shinefield* Funny. I had to resist an identity forming around my rejection of its ideological premise. I knew I could do it—rise above the dull pain of exclusion and be more than just my grievance.

"Is that meant to be funny?"

I looked up and saw Jody Shinefield herself, peering down over the banquette partition.

"Is what meant to be funny?"

"Reading Ayn Rand." Shinefield rolled her eyes, then rolled them back the other way, presumably to make it even. "You've been waving it around at the whole party."

This was unfair. It was dark and so I'd had to hold the book right up to my nose. I felt misunderstood and attacked. The whole point was that, here, I was nobody.

"I didn't think anyone was watching me." My tone was more maudlin than I'd intended. "I'm not part of *the revolution*."

Shinefield swung herself around to face me. "What's that supposed to mean?"

I thought of Ayn, sparring with the red kerchief–wearing student council leaders at the University of Petrograd. The creators of *Shinefield* were also psychological determinists who didn't believe in the subversive mystery of life or art. I tried to remember Ming's argument. The medium was the monster and the monster was Jody Shinefield.

"I just don't think comedy should be 'right.'"

"Right?" Jody laughed and then her frizzy-haired, shoulder-padded friend turned to look over the partition.

"What did you just call her?"

My heart jumped. "I'm talking about comedy and form."

"I think she's calling a lesbian comic 'unfunny.'"

Shinefield was joking, but also, seemingly trying to get me killed. Shoulderpads laughed and now more people were turning around. The small army of managerial gay men eyed me hungrily like a speared bull.

"Did someone call a lesbian comic not funny?"

They were ganging up on me for something I hadn't said. I loved lesbians and the lay ones were some of the funniest people I knew. It was the professional comics who tried to make comedy out of virtuousness that I thought were misguided. It wasn't funny to say fuck the patriarchy; it was funny to say fuck the patriarchy then send our progeny to the best schools. But now someone else had made a joke about Ellen and they were all clicking their fingers in the air. Their pinched digits snapped at me like the beaks of angry insects. I felt besieged; this wasn't horizontal democracy, it was a mob.

"You know that snapping thing is kind of fascistic?"

"So now you're calling us fascists?"

This incited hoots of laughter that only infuriated me more.

"The snapping is fascistic but the snappers are actually slaves."

Even through my martini-fog I knew this was a mistake. I'd been referring to the Judeo-Christian *moral* slaves who sacrificed their mental freedom for the lie of eternal salvation. What Nietzsche said. I could probably just find the paragraph. But Shinefield was grinning with revulsion, like someone enjoying the smell of their own fart—a symptom, I'd read, of narcissism. She rubbed her hands together. "And now we're *slaves*?"

The blood shot to my temples and it stung, like Vivian's tiny army of spiked wheelbarrows. Jody Shinefield was trying to destroy me. She wanted a world in which everything was mapped, everyone psychologically and morally leveled. Television might've been shaped by market forces but it was the communism of artistic expression, and *Shinefield* was a perfect argument for mass psychotherapy, which ultimately, if you thought about it, led to the same charge aimed at Lars von Trier.

"Your TV show absolves the crimes of Hitler."

Shinefield stared at me. I could tell she now thought I was just insane. And I did feel lightheaded. Confused by my own logic. And then suddenly dizzy, as if knocked off center by my own hypocrisy. I had invoked Hitler's name to savage my enemy. I had called them fascists. Nauseous, I grabbed my bag and stood. Hurrying past the tables, my legs were weak and my gait unstable. It felt like the whole courtyard was glaring at me, willing me to trip on my heels.

But I made it outside, back to the red carpet's flaccid cameras. With thick, fumbling fingers I ordered an Uber Select, though it did nothing for my self-esteem.

———

I hadn't had a boyfriend in nearly a decade and the idea of it had become a kind of abstraction. I'd never been good at sharing a bed (anxious sleeper) or a meal (picky eater) or compromising my writing time. I didn't like sitting in restaurants and hearing about someone's day. The thing I'd most enjoyed about coupledom was probably the holidays. Being with The Boyfriend's family at a big house in the country. The whole weekend like one long, sleepy undulation. Waves of warm, rolling contentment that moved me from one room to another, one activity to the next; where everything was pleasantly aimless and I only had to be half present, half awake. As if between the two of us we were only responsible for a single consciousness. I suppose it was a type of self-loss, or unselfing of some kind. Sometimes it had frightened me but I had also really liked it. In fact I couldn't recall any other sustained periods of happiness in my life. Intense enjoyment, yes. But always brief, and often attached to a violent and slightly painful hope. Writing was like this. Cold and electric and so different from that warm, easy twoness I had almost given up on. Until Big Boy.

It was a risk, I knew. My Ayn Rand project was sluggish enough without the added complication of losing myself in love. But even Ayn had taken this risk. She'd found a man who respected her intelligence and let her work like a maniac, sacrificing his own middling acting career to follow her intellectual whims. Big Boy was as close to the Ideal Man as I could imagine. And the slowness with which we were taking things filled me with optimism for a solid foundation. Maybe the sex would come once there was more of a power imbalance; that is, once I had my own TV show. I didn't mind this. I found it motivating. It was a well-known fact that, historically, men had made art to get laid, whereas women received no sexual reward for their artistic labors, only for their looks. Thus, women had been denied the major egotistical incentive to make great art. *This* was how patriarchy continued to thwart female artists. Ayn Rand, on the other hand, had always wanted bigger female egos. Egos that lived for egos' sakes.

To make up for her absence at the *Shinefield* premiere, Terra invited me to a party. It would be mostly Black Broadway, she told me, and when I asked why she explained that they were all bicoastal now, thanks to the diversity quotas. In fact, Terra claimed, there was so much screen work for her fellow Black actors that all the good ones were having nervous breakdowns and sleeping in their cars between jobs. Ayn Rand had disapproved of affirmative action and all gestures of equity, which she said just sent disadvantage spilling over into someone else's life. Some undeserving individual. It made me think of Magda's words, spoken that last time, across the Italian travertine coffee table. *Life was always, for everyone, a present-tense struggle.*

Big Boy and I arrived deliberately late, but Terra wasn't there. We walked through the large, empty house and out to the patio, where most of the guests were gathered around an industrial-sized fire pit. As we approached the group it became clear that they were engaged in some sort of party game. A hush fell over the circle as a beautiful young woman with thick braids rose to her feet.

"I guess people kind of say I look like a young Alicia Keys?"

The group agreed in loud, mellifluous cacophony, and then their host threw his golden voice like a javelin. "There's Alicia but there's also some major Zoe K."

Now came a softer, more symphonic agreement. I took a seat on the edge of a divan beside Big Boy. He had offered the leggy young androgyne beside him some chips from his plate and the two of them were tucking in.

"What's happening?" I asked them quietly.

The boy with the beautiful legs smiled, batting his big frondy lashes like the regal bow of a peacock. "Celebrity doppelganger."

I had played the game many times before. Nothing seemed to be more enjoyable to a group of people born after 1982 than telling each other which attractive famous person they most closely resembled. If I was honest, I enjoyed the game too. But I was nervous. There were only two other white people in the circle and they both possessed the easy familiarity and physical relaxation of the Actually Invited. Knowing the other guests seemed crucial to a party game like this. The group's attention now shifted onto the bald, rakish man seated beside the Alicia Keys Doppel-gänger. He struck a few voguish poses as people conferred.

"RuPaul."

"Too obvious."

"DaBaby."

A great, shuddering hilarity rolled over the group. I had no idea who DaBaby was but the laughter was infectious. Big Boy giggled too, shrugging with that big transgressive idiocy that I loved so much. I leaned in close to his ear.

"Maybe we should go back inside now."

"But we just got here!" He placed a large paw on the shoulder of his divan-mate. "Plus I don't want to take the chips away from Jean-Henri."

We stayed and I remained tactfully quiet. Big Boy kept his own mouth full of chips as the game continued around the circle, and it began to seem that things might actually go well for us. Then the group's attention fell on a large silver-haired monolith in blue faux fur, and Big Boy came barking suddenly to life:

"Neil deGrasse Tyson!"

I stopped breathing.

"Mmm, I see what you're going for . . ." This was a patient DaBaby. "But I actually think he's more of a Cornel West. Or actually, Don King."

The circle thrummed with warm affirmatives. I felt relieved and squeezed Big Boy's hand: a gentle but stern request that from now on he please keep it zipped. As I released my grip, I could feel him wanting to linger. It was either that or he was trying to smear some of the chip grease off onto my palm. I decided to be hopeful.

When it was Big Boy's turn to be doppelgangered, everyone agreed that he bore a striking resemblance to Dave Franco, only bigger and with floppier hair. I was very pleased with this assessment. And proud to be there with this large, dopey boy who had somehow charmed his way into their circle and seemingly also their hearts. Everyone was being so friendly and inclusive. Despite Terra's absence, I was glad that we had come. And then it was my turn.

"There's shades of Cher," said the host.

I was shocked and delighted and hoped very much that Big Boy knew who Cher was.

"But there's also someone else."

"Someone smaller."

"Less narrow."

My face needled with the dread of being compared to Liza Minnelli. It had happened before. Things were delicate enough with Big Boy that I didn't want his lust for me poisoned by some cutting remark, some unseeable observation. I had to own the joke. So I slid the book out of my handbag and raised its back cover.

"I think I look like Ayn Rand."

The whole circle squinted forward. There was a moment of expectant silence, and then Jean-Henri pointed a long silver fingernail.

"Didn't she love billionaires?"

The whole group looked at me. It wasn't necessarily a hostile look. Everyone here was aspirational and they easily could have been my audience, but I'd been burned so many times. Without a filter I was scared to give my speech about the smallest minority on Earth. And then Big Boy was whispering in my ear.

"Do the bit about race."

He was talking about Ayn's views on racism: how it was just another form of determinism that denied people their faculties of reason and choice, imprisoning them in a cultural predestination. And how she believed that capitalism was the great liberating philosophy of the last two hundred years—abolishing serfdom in Russia and slavery in the American South.

But I didn't say that or anything else. Because the bit about race wasn't a bit. It wasn't meant to be a joke. The game moved on and I crouched low in my thoughts, frantically trying to make sense of things. Did Big Boy think I was making fun of Ayn Rand? Had he misread my homage for critique? A nightmarish jumble of emojis flashed through my mind. Did posting the cat with dollar signs for eyes mean you *liked* money or *didn't*? And were the high five/prayer hands used to congratulate someone or else beg them to stop? What if Big Boy and his fans had missed the nuances of my satire or, worse, what if I had missed theirs?

It was only in the Uber home that I confronted him.

"This whole time you were laughing at Ayn Rand?"

Big Boy nodded blankly.

"Meaning, Ayn Ram is satire but your Labrador is homage?"

"Homo-what?"

But this time his wordplay only frustrated me, divorced, as it now seemed, from any kind of dissidence. "So Ayn Ram wasn't meant to be in any way provocative?"

Big Boy shrugged. "I mostly did it for the rhyme."

"It's an off-rhyme, dummy."

I was instantly ashamed of myself. It wasn't Big Boy's fault. It was just a simple miscommunication. I had missed the joke and he had missed the whole point of Ayn Rand's philosophy. I knew I shouldn't join him for Nintendo, that I had to take stock. Something was wrong; our mutuality queasily lopsided. But loneliness clung to me like a wet T-shirt, and my reason lost out. I didn't want to be alone.

Upstairs on his sectional, Big Boy tossed me a console and plopped himself down at the opposite end of the L-shape. The geometry of our distance felt significant. It was self-hating, but I asked him anyway.

"Were you just using me for micro-content?"

Big Boy looked hurt. "I thought we were . . . collaborators?"

The word roused pangs of humiliation. I brought my hands up to my face, feeling the pain and breathing my own wet heat. In here, I seemed to become a feminist.

"And you think it's okay to compare strong women to rams?"

But Big Boy actually wasn't an idiot. "Since when do you care about that?"

He was right. I didn't care about that. I cared about nothing. Inside my hand cave I closed my eyes and tried to vanish from the whole awful scene.

"I'm sorry," he said. "But I think I need to go to bed."

I dropped my hands and looked at him. His big blank indifference.

"You're being like the Terminator," I said.

"T1 or T2?"

I couldn't remember. "Whichever one doesn't understand why people have feelings."

"T1."

I performed a perfunctory inner search for my will, but couldn't find it. My reason had now completely fled. I wanted to cry. And then, thinking how pathetic it would be, I did.

"This is so weird."

I blinked up at him. "Weird?"

"You don't even like me. You think I'm dumb. You just want to have sex with me."

"That's not true!" But my voice was strained. "I think you're funny!"

"Yes, but . . ." Big Boy gave me a sharp, intelligent look. "Is it homage or satire?"

And now I wanted to cry again. Because he did see me. Which made the whole thing so much lonelier.

"I'm sorry," I said, and made myself stand up.

Big Boy rose beside me and put his large paw on my shoulder. "It's okay, Anna."

"A borderline would never be this nice," I thanked him, tearfully.

He gave me a thumbs up. "And a narcissist would never say I'm sorry."

I had no time to wallow in self-pity. When I got home I checked my phone and saw a disturbing email from Jamie. Rumors were circulating that I had called the cast of *Shinefield* slaves. Jamie's friend in development at Amazon had informed him of the rumors, and now one of the production companies had postponed their meeting with me and Tammy. Jamie was scared that our star would hear of the controversy and bolt. I had to get the pilot to Tammy ASAP. She'd need something to get excited about, he explained. Tammy needed proof of concept.

But so did I. The concept was now seriously in question. The people who'd found it funny had been laughing for the wrong reasons. Because they thought the ideas were bad. It was also true that these people lacked discernment and had no feel for provocation. But maybe I had misunderstood the form. Did animal avatars speaking historical comedy just make everything absurd? Or was it my own turn of phrase always wringing out the irony, the opposite, the joke? I would have to find my answers on the page. But the writing had to wait; the next day I was dog walking.

I got up at dawn and took the metro across town. Everyone in my car was homeless and I felt paranoid that they could somehow see the libertarianism on my face; feel it emanating from my self-serving pores. I kept my head down and experienced a steady barrage of shame flashes from the night before; staring into my hot, red hands as Big Boy had asked me to please stop occupying his apartment.

Driving the van this morning, I was newly aware of time. That the two of us were in competition; me: a flawed and irrational human, and Time: a perfect, unbreakable machine. Every red light was a miserable failure; each waddling pedestrian my mortal enemy. Racing time my being was nothing but pure, chilling drive broken by short bursts of loathing. Existence itself became a constant panic. Every moment I wasn't winning, I was losing.

Dogs, of course, didn't care about time. They were always wriggling out of it. All of my loudly stated goals were thwarted by a dodging paw or a leaping body or a big slimy lick on the face. Play—their raison d'être?—was in epistemological opposition to time, and although I knew that surrender was possible, preferable, that everyone said dogs were God spelled backward, et cetera—I had much more important things to do. Rushing, I yanked their leashes harder than usual. I petted no heads. I cuddled nothing. And then, pulling in for the last day's walk, I saw a film crew. Three trucks and a catering tent dominated one corner of the park, where people marched around in practical shoes and important puffers. Maybe I should have tried to see it as a sign; that better things were coming, that my dreams were on their way. But I didn't believe in signs. And I really didn't want Hollywood to see me picking up dog shit.

I hurried the dogs across the field and into the dog run. Once inside, I felt better. I let the dogs off leash and sat on a bench, typing the pilot outline into my phone. Like Ayn had probably done at her empty perfume counter. Jotting notes for *The Little Street* and Danny Renahan, her psychopath hero. I didn't know how to revolutionize the form or how the form might be revolutionizing Ayn's ideas, but I did know that my pilot had to address wealth inequality. Ayn Ram had to make a case for why inequality was a sign of capitalism's health, and that of the culture at large. She had to remind us that people were different and would always earn differently; that social comparison was the disease, not individualism or ambition.

I was putting these ideas into a scene between Ayn Ram and an immigrant polar bear seeking a better life far from the melting ice caps. Greed was bad, Ayn would tell the polar bear, as it led to more desire and less satisfaction. But wealth was a beautiful thing. Not because it enabled ostentation but because it provided independence, autonomy, and personal freedom.

When I looked back up from my phone I saw two walkers playing with my dogs. One was rubbing the supine belly of my fat Labrador while tossing a ball for the deranged border collie. The other was in a cuddle pile with the two pit bulls and an adolescent husky. They seemed happy to do my job for me, and so I let them. They weren't aspirational like I was. Which was just how it was; people were different. Some people walked dogs; others paid for dog walkers.

When my timer went off I wrangled my dogs and hurried them back across the field. Just before we reached the van, the husky decided to take a shit. He made a real show of squatting and, once he had finished, kicking the grass up behind him in three earthy flares. I saw a few film crew people watching from the tent as they sipped their coffee. They were watching, I could tell, to see if I was going to pick up the poop.

And so I left it.

Loading the animals into the van I could feel the crews' eyes burning into my back. I slammed the doors and threw myself into the front seat, quietly cursing them. I jammed the keys in the ignition and wrenched the gears back, reversing and correcting in one vicious careen. And then I heard a crunch and the whole car clenched, everything holding its breath, even the dogs.

I sat there for a moment, resisting reality. Trying to take it back in my mind. Accepting responsibility for my irrational behavior and vowing to move forward with self-control. But, of course, that wasn't how things worked. I had hit another car and would have to pay the insurance excess, which was more than two weeks' wages, meaning I'd have nothing to give Raffi for rent. *That* was how things worked. In a week I'd be homeless. Or I could've been, had I been someone else. Someone without parents. Without Magda Edelstein or Ming. Still, I would need to borrow more money or else leave LA. My dreams were slipping away and I had no idea, in that moment, what Ayn Rand would've done.

I dropped the van back, got fired, and paid the eight hundred dollars. Then I took the metro back across town. Watching my fellow homeless riders I felt a new kind of dread. Not because I was like them, but because I was so obviously not. It was a literary dread; the nauseating shame of having produced a bad metaphor. And the sinking fear that all my ideas were somehow wrong, and not in a true way.

By the time I got home, anguish and fury had joined the dread in a violent leadership coup. My material conditions were, at least, partially to blame. I was now ready to scream at Raffi for the turds; for the gross indignity of making another human being erase your fecal matter. But outside the apartment door I could hear shouting. I paused and listened. It seemed that Raffi was actually being shat on by someone else.

I entered quietly and went straight to the bathroom. From his side of the phone call—yelled from every other room in the apartment—I gleaned that Raffi's girlies were accusing him of misogyny. He moved between flustered pleading and accusing them of homophobia. The conversation went in circles and I began to fret. I had to get my pilot done.

The solution sat in a blister pack in Raffi's medicine drawer. I'd seen the Adderall many times before, but only now did I make the connection. Ayn had completed *The Fountainhead* on a Benzedrine bender that lasted several months. And why not? Speed was just a strong dose of ambition. A shot of capitalism into the bloodstream. It was a rush of pure drive that narrowed focus, numbed feeling, and killed off all moral nuance. But maybe moral nuance was getting in my way. Ayn Rand had written pedantic, preachy fiction with no tolerance for human fallibility. Maybe that's what I had to do with my script—imitate the form, the monster. Do on the page what I rejected in life—make myself really care about something.

I took the pill and my laptop and fled downstairs. Sitting up unnaturally straight in a beanbag chair, I began to type. The writing came fast and forceful, and then I was stabbing violently at the keys. I wasn't delighting in the subversive nature of my ideas; I wanted to bludgeon someone with them. Every line was emphatic. Every parenthetical "with piercing look" or "yelling." There was no space for counterargument, yet I could feel a dark disquiet pressing at the sides of my focus. Ming was right; at this rate I'd have to kill Ayn Ram off within two hours. My protagonist was sadistic.

"Girl, your skin is *glowing*."

The yoga instructor was standing above me, smiling down with her big rubbery pasta bow lips. My skin probably was glowing: the pills were making me sweat.

"Thank you," I said, casting a generous glance over the instructor's Botoxed forehead. "So is yours."

"I'm forty-seven," she gloated.

"Incredible."

She patted the skin at her orbital bones. "You realize we've just entered the age of Aquarius?"

I glanced around for help. "Uh . . . is that a good age for water signs?"

The yoga instructor made a sharp whistle and her goat came trotting over. He stood reluctantly in front of us, presenting his flank for a pat.

"Aquarius is the age of self-love."

I felt suddenly, dangerously, thirsty. I smiled weakly, then sipped from my plastic Poland Spring bottle. It was a week old and smelled, upsettingly, of dog. The instructor appeared to notice.

"You're not a big self-care girl, are you?"

I shrugged. Long baths made me feel unproductive. I ignored the goat's healing hide and eyed my blinking cursor, but once again the instructor missed my cue. She seemed intent on having an impact.

"When we love ourselves," she said. "It's like a tap turns on and all that love starts pouring out onto others."

Yes, I knew this. It was the sentiment of Hank Rearden, Ayn's fictional industrialist, "who could forgive anything to anyone because happiness was the greatest agent of purification."

It was only ever through happy self-fulfillment, said Ayn, that genuine benevolence could flow. But where exactly was it? Where had all this free-market happiness actually spilled over into abundant generosity? My heart skipped and then a warm, dizzy wave broke over me. The yoga instructor was suddenly holding my forearm. She clicked her fingers and the goat kicked its front legs up gently into my side, supporting me like a tripod. The woman rubbed my shoulder. We stood like this for a few moments. Then I realized my bowels were churning and that a sharp pain had seized my abdomen.

"I'm sorry," I said. "I think I need to use the toilet."

The instructor clicked again and the goat kicked its legs back down, releasing me. A business card appeared from inside the woman's sports bra. It was for a goat milk exfoliating scrub called Scrape Goat. She squeezed my hand tenderly.

"What's your IG? I'm sending you some product."

In my weakened state I gave it to her. Then I grabbed my things and rushed for the elevator.

Raffi was still shouting into the phone, but the content was obscured as I went racing down the hall and into the bathroom. I had barely got my underpants over my thighs before a wild torrent came rushing from inside me. The conversation outside receded and then stopped. My exertions, at least, made the shame feel like a sound murmured from another room. When I was finally empty, I wiped and flushed and splashed my face with water. Then I looked down and saw that my waste had not been sufficiently swirled away. So I flushed again. But pressing the button I knew, even before the scum pond started rising, that *this* was why Raffi didn't flush. My skin went cold.

I grabbed the plunger and started stabbing at the hole as the sludge rose. No, I heard myself say. No, no, no, I repeated.

Fuck no. And then I was praying. Please no. Praying to God? To Dogs? To Ayn Rand? The sludge breached the toilet rim like a bellycrawling black beast, sliming down the sides and onto the white tiling. The shit tide bled across the floor, around the bath mat, and toward the door. I could picture it seeping into the hallway carpet. It would keep going, out the front door and along the corridor, pooling over Big Boy's ceiling and cataracting down into his bedroom. I dropped to my knees and reached around the bowl for the toilet filter tap. Wrenching it down seemed to halt the flow. I breathed. Breathed it in. And kneeling there the truth came down, black and roaring, like the will of a building.

It was all Ayn Rand's fault. The burning forests, the homelessness, the guns, the suicides, the drugs. Her bad ideas were behind everything. Big Pharma, the billionaire space race, the gig economy, Twitter, the emptiness of modern life, Jizz. Ayn was the root cause of all of it. That singular will converted into thousands—millions—of singular wills. In the fetid brown soup I saw my face reflected back and recoiled, remembering the strange, solipsistic thing Ayn had said in a final interview—*I will not die; it's the world that will end*. A paradox, though she'd famously hated them. Another inconvenient fact I'd been ignoring. That she hated the very thing that made art good and life mysterious and unknowable and, in a meaning-making sense, worth living. Finally, I let myself think it: Ayn Rand had no sense of humor.

I had to give her up. But it was worse than that; I had been yoking myself to bad ideas since I was three years old. Since my very first transgression: the bad idea of painting the walls of my parents' room with my own poop. Maybe I had always been too generous with the disreputable side, too indiscriminate and expedient with my philosophical alignments. And now, like an idiot, I had extended all that willful generosity to Ayn Rand.

When I finally emerged from the bathroom—having scrubbed it and myself—Raffi said nothing. An enormous kindness that made me instantly forgive the missing room divider and his bad boundaries. I had a strange new feeling walking through the apartment. Numb and floaty; a dissociation I recognized from the start of that summer. The week I'd got my review and first died my reputational death.

I got into bed and stayed there until the following afternoon when Raffi came in and sat on the edge of the futon. I told him about the dogs and the van and my disillusionment with capitalism, and he was sympathetic, though also unable to cover my rent.

"It's okay," he reassured me. "You were only in Ayn Rand drag."

As he smiled at me with his blinding teeth, I saw something pure and good in Raffi's perfect facial symmetry, and found that I actually liked him.

"Is your avatar satire or homage?" I asked.

Raffi shrugged. "I'm a gay man making fun of gay men. So who the hell knows."

The next morning I packed up my things and caught an Uber to Ming's place. She lived in a tiny, crumbling apartment in West Hollywood. It was all peeling pink walls and worn brown carpets and Ming seemed genuinely proud of its grim authenticity. She said it was essential in a city like LA; the cockroaches were an anchor to The Real.

I arrived to a scotch on the tiny balcony and Ming's eccentric brand of sympathy. She was thrilled that my Ayn Rand project had failed, assuring me that now my "real project" could emerge. I quickly changed the subject to my other failure, the romantic one; explaining how I had dehumanized Big Boy, overvaluing his physical attributes and missing the fact of our philosophical incompatibility. Ming replied that his wordplay did sound misleading and also that the whole thing was very banal. This was a painful accusation, but probably warranted. I had imposed a whole persona on Big Boy, a filter on top of a filter. He wasn't a contrarian; he was just a professional Labrador. And more pathetically, I told Ming, I'd believed he could be a libertarian lover. Ming sighed and I worried that I was still being banal, but then her eyes got that tortured glaze of introspection. It appeared that I had said something provocative.

"Yes," she said. "Because all sadists are masochists, and vice versa."

"That's a bit confusing."

"It's not confusing; it's dialectics. The sadist and the masochist switch psychic roles as they use each other to establish form inside the egoic void."

I didn't understand what she was getting at. It sounded like she was saying I secretly wanted to molest him in his sleep. I brought the scotch to my lips and watched an ice cube clink around, slow and imperious as an air hockey puck. So dense and shiny and full of itself.

"All romantic love is just an exercise in ego."

I must have withered then because Ming put her long, cold hand over mine.

"But it's okay, Anna. Everybody does it."

I stayed for a week, watching difficult European cinema and crying in the bathroom. On the third day, Raffi Ubered over a Scrape Goat product basket he'd found on the doorstep. Applying the anti-aging serum to my orbital bone, I became fixated on the fine lines beneath my eyes. I spent several hours reading beauty blog reviews, purchasing new creams and serums, reading different reviews, and canceling my purchases. At four a.m. I found myself in a chat room devoted to sun-damaged rosacea survivors. I identified with their plight. With the societal devaluation of their biological material. Whatever Ayn Rand had given me, it didn't feel like self-esteem.

At dawn, I ordered a cream from a defunct website and found myself the victim of a scam. I started to cancel my credit card but then worried that this might make the scammers mad. They had Ming's address. They could just come right over and murder me. For being myself. For being vain and having credit. Or maybe just because I hadn't said Thank You in my email. In the morning when I told Ming, she said that the scammers were probably in Nigeria and there was no way they were coming to her apartment to murder me.

"And you know," she said. "There's something beautiful about being scammed. A divine justice in the redistribution of global wealth."

I felt myself conceding to the gentle absolution of this idea. A soft capitulation to the cosmic justice of my credit card's theft and, with even greater relief, to my own divine bankruptcy.

That afternoon I sat on Ming and Pavel's balding brown sofa and watched a difficult piece of art cinema from the Caucasus. The film was about two young girls at a convent in rural Georgia. One was in love with the other one, who was in love with God. Unexpectedly, I found myself siding with the provincial Georgian church. I wept at the end of the film as the murderous nuns were hauled off in a police van. They had only tried, in the best way they knew how, to free the romantic girl of her delusions.

"I think you missed the point of the movie," Pavel said later.

He had a large, pumpkin-shaped head with silver side-tufts and pale, mournful eyes. For a clown, he was caustic. But I liked him. The three of us were eating a dinner of beef stew by monastic candlelight. Ming sipped scotch and Pavel had his glass of milk.

"No, she didn't." A string of brown dribble clung to Ming's chin, which made her defense of me seem somehow kinder. "Anna had a complicated response. That's the point. That's why it's a good film and not a mediocre movie."

Pavel frowned at his wife with a pulverizing, Ukrainian disdain. "We're supposed to feel the bad conscience of the priest."

His wife returned a crushing, Ural Mountains glare. "Well, maybe Anna felt the bad conscience of the filmmaker."

"What's bad conscience?"

Ming turned her glare on me. "I thought you'd been reading Nietzsche?"

"Just the first twenty pages."

"Keep going." Pavel chortled. "It gets better."

Ming flashed violently at her husband and then returned her attention to me. "You're saying that the problem with romantic love is the problem of individualism?"

"How can she be saying that?" Pavel was caustic. "She's a Randian."

"I've actually stopped that now . . ."

But Pavel plowed on; he'd obviously been burning to inform me:

"Ayn Rand testified at the McCarthy hearings! She *started* cancel culture!"

I looked down, my vision narrowing to the thick bulb of my nose as all my stupidity congealed around me.

"Enough," said Ming. "The medium is the monster and Anna's killed her now."

But Pavel wasn't finished. He brightened behind his milk.

"You know the German word for canceled?"

"Actually, yes," I said; recalling Puffer Jacket's description of Howard Roark. "*Aufheben*."

"So then you *did* read the Nietzsche?"

I considered confessing to my conversation with the Randian climate change deniers. "No," I said. "I must've just seen it on Twitter."

"'If you can endure injury without suffering,'" Pavel recited, "'that's when justice becomes mercy.'"

The Randians hadn't mentioned that word. I smiled at him. "Mercy sounds good."

Pavel smiled back. "*Selbstaufhebung*," he agreed. "Self-overcoming."

I stayed at Ming and Pavel's for another week, then I got an email from my mother. Magda Edelstein was rapidly deteriorating. She probably only had a few days left. I booked a one-way ticket to New York and from JFK I took a train straight to the house in Connecticut. It was a foggy January day and the air inside the living room was heavy with grief and the strange manic undercurrent of everyone else's contrasting survival. I moved past small groups of silver-haired women shawled in maroon wool; their bodies full and sealed like mountains. I could feel their eyes on me. They knew who I was: the scheming young novelist who had usurped the Edelsteins' pied-à-terre to write her cruel book about poor people. But I was used to feeling separate, a moon in cold orbit around the others. Grief only seemed to sharpen that sensation.

Magda lay in bed. She wore a neutral expression; not peaceful or serene, but medicated. The equipment looked invasive. All the tubes and liquid pouches seemed to be sucking the life out, not sustaining it. But perhaps these things were just hurting me. My mirror neurons. I didn't know anymore what was empathy and what was just a cunning form of self-preservation.

Seeing Magda's husband, my feelings rushed up in a big rude sob. I swallowed it back down and went to hug him. Martin was thinner but surprisingly warm. He explained that everyone was being asked to read a few pages aloud from one of the six books that Magda had been rereading. I wondered what use words and ideas could be to Magda now. She was slipping from consciousness toward a place where the mind no longer mattered. I didn't want to contradict Martin but I felt that Magda would have preferred to relinquish all knowledge. Believe in nothing, like the Buddhists said.

When the frizzy, birdlike woman reading from *Sabbath's Theater* blew Magda a kiss and moved toward the door, I stepped in to take her place. The books on Magda's nightstand were a mix of classic literature and religious texts. Martin had assigned me the *Tao Te Ching*. I opened the book randomly to a page.

> *I alone am muddled.*
> *Calm like the sea;*
> *Like a high wind that never ceases.*
> *The multitude all have a purpose.*
> *I alone am foolish and uncouth.*
> *I alone am different from others*
> *And value being fed by the mother.*

I tried not to make the message about myself. But it was hard. I wanted to be like the maroon mass of women in the other room, merged in their solemn purpose, nurturing their sorrow. But I didn't belong there. I barely even belonged here, beside this dear woman who had been so good to me and whose love I had largely taken for granted. I leaned in and kissed Magda on the forehead. The coolness of her skin was a shock. The hard unyieldingness. *I'm sorry*, I heard myself whisper. But even this was misplaced.

Out in the living room, a tiny Romanian woman in a dirty smock gave me a small plate of cookies and a cup of lukewarm tea. I took these things gratefully and occupied myself with them in an empty corner. The Edelsteins' vast bookshelf loomed overhead. The authors were intimidating. Nabokov. Céline. Rushdie. Roth.

They were not "good" people. And could you ever really separate the work from the personality? In modernist fiction the medium was the message, the consciousness, the monster themselves. But maybe that was always the case with art. Because the good stuff didn't come easy—that pure, clean channel between artist and muse. Perhaps the definition itself just had to sound less noble and more like the personality disorder that it probably was. *Artist:* a grandiose and insecure person who feels especially destined and uniquely condemned and, deep in their heart, fears that they must be empty.

New York

Magda died the next day. I had taken the bus to Woodstock and so, again, my mother delivered the news. We cried a little on opposite ends of the living room couch, then hugged and agreed it was good that Magda's suffering was over. I felt sad and also felt the fact of her death as a dissonance—an alien object adrift in my mind, snagging me all through the day.

Strangely, it was Martin's ongoingness that was most painful. His small, hunched figure alone in their house; eating takeout at the kitchen island; tucked up in bed, turning the pages. I couldn't stop seeing it. With Magda's death, her husband's life had ended and yet it went on. He was like the German word for canceled—*aufheben*: removed *and* preserved.

I followed my mother around for the first few days. It was just easier to say yes and drag around behind her like a depressed teenager. We went to the grocery store and I was introduced to various lively New Age sexagenarians. I smiled and said nothing and they received me with the delicate discretion befitting a princess returned from sanitarium. Wandering off to walk the aisles I felt a pleasant aimlessness. Meaning and purpose had receded and there were only cans and packets and bags of things I didn't want. I had no appetite. But that wasn't really new.

My mother's house sat on a wooded hill. Inside it was orange and crystally and I felt smothered in certain corners of the living room where the light was too warm. I spent a lot of time staring out the bay windows, through the narrow strait of glass uncrowded by river stones or scented candles, to the snowy hill beyond. When I became self-conscious that I'd been staring too long, I picked up one of Jackie's climate change novels or a photo essay on the life of Joni Mitchell, and flipped mindlessly through.

That first weekend in Woodstock, as Jackie dressed for a date, I found myself drawn to the busy warmth of the upstairs en suite. She flamed around the little room, dabbing on creams and drops of perfume—the whole second story lighter with the fragrance of hope. I sat on her big, lavishly pillowed and beautifully arranged bed, and watched the bathroom door. The way the light bent into the dark bedroom from a sconce over the sink reminded me of how it had felt watching my parents get ready for a night out. With the bathroom obstructed from view, all the erotic promise of an adult evening seemed to live in that single shaft of steamy light. It was there in the luminous contrast of the shaded wall and milky beam; the deep mystery of grown-up love and the dark ecstasies of sex.

And so it was strange to be nearly forty and not the beautiful, erotic adult woman to my own ten-year-old daughter. To be still the guilty, creeping child. I rubbed my cold hands and noticed the raised striations across my fingernails. They were the same as my mother's, only fainter. I had always thought of hers like tree rings, as experience carved into cartilage. But on my own fingernails they seemed unearned. I hadn't had or lost any children. I'd suffered no divorce. I was the other kind of survivor, the one who hadn't had to fight for its survival. The child who had arbitrarily lived, surviving for no reason, when the other child had just as pointlessly died.

Jackie left the house for her date that night and was home again forty-five minutes later. The man had apparently voted for the Bad President and then told her he'd gladly do it again.

"He was a brilliant architect," she said, disbelieving. "He taught over at the university."

Jackie had once dated a man who lived in a hole—an eco-therapist "getting back to nature" or "manhood" or both. Whichever it was, people who dated people who lived in holes oughtn't cast stones at architects or divorce orthodontists. Annoyed, I rose and went to make tea at the counter.

"Your date probably likes Ayn Rand."

"We all used to like Ayn Rand."

The air sailed out of me. "What?"

"Everybody had a moment of loving Ayn Rand. Especially in the sixties. We all thought she was very antiestablishment."

I felt an odd protectiveness toward Ayn. "She was. Just not your version."

"Yes, well, we made our own interpretations."

"Ayn would've hated that."

"I guess a writer can't really choose how they're read."

This felt like a dig. I poured my tea while Jackie pretended to be absorbed by the back cover of her new book. It was the latest *New York Times* bestselling novel about the impending environmental catastrophe. I could see the author's photo: the pale, guileless face above a neat floral-print shirt. One of those Brooklyn creatures with the husband and the kids and the deep existential ties to her community garden. A straight white affluent woman who had found a way to artistically matter, to linguistically belong, by yoking herself to the dying Earth. I sipped my tea while Jackie flipped open to her favorite part of a book: its acknowledgments page.

"Why don't *you* write something about climate change?"

"And why would I do that?" I was suddenly febrile behind the wall of steam. "To offset the carbon emissions of my own miserable progeny?"

"What miserable progeny?"

Jackie seemed startled by her own joke. I must've been too; my feet took me out into the hall before I knew what was happening. Here, I felt my heart beating very fast. It got faster and my breath thinner as I circled my mind looking for consolation. Another outcome to my life. Another vision of the future I could imagine myself into; somewhere I was going, someone who would be there. But there was nothing. I was old and my thinking was wrong. I wasn't going to make it in Hollywood, in publishing, in anything. And the reproductive option, the one I didn't actually have, suddenly stood like a sealed wall against my life and made me feel how all the climate change novelists probably felt: like I was living inside an ending.

In the reflective glass of a framed MoMA print I could see my mother in the kitchen, blinking and swallowing. *That* was who I was. That woman in the glass, blinking and swallowing down her shame. We had the same plump, guilty mouth, the same pinching chin. I watched the woman wipe her eyes, collect her spangly purse—a token of the night's failure—and walk slowly up the stairs.

Lying in bed an hour later, surrounded by my mother's salt lamps and angel cards and the faint, earthy smells of her, I imagined Jackie in the next room. The nicer room with its bigger window and wider bed and the shelf of photo albums with their cluttered pages and all the little sinkholes of grief.

Ayn was wrong. There wasn't a reason for everything. There couldn't be. Some things were just random and horrible, like the death of a child. Life was merciless, as Magda had said. Though it didn't seem possible to keep living unless you had mercy, even for life itself and what it had taken from you. Had my mother forgiven God? Or had she shifted her faith onto people? Onto social justice and climate action? Onto things that humans could control? Toward me, she still seemed merciless. She couldn't accept me as I was; couldn't acknowledge my achievements (getting canceled) or laugh at my jokes. Maybe she found them too nihilistic. Maybe she thought her disapproval was helping me, teaching me, being a parent. But didn't mercy have to be blind? Forgiveness was grace, not because you understood the mechanics of someone's behavior, but despite the fact that you didn't.

I pictured my mother in the next room, sliding in under the sheets and pushing in her ear plugs. Lying there small and vulnerable and acutely aware of herself as a woman, alone. I felt an almost unbearable tenderness for her, a sickening sweetness. As if I was merging with her pain, with my mother herself, like incest. I pulled myself back from the feeling and waited there in cold, thrilling loneliness. Clear of sorrow's undertow. Alive to everything else.

The next morning I watched Jackie sit in bent abjection over her coffee and considered owning up. To how care felt like death, like disappearing. Meaning that my sense of life must've lived inside the *opposite* of care—in making a joke to show that I didn't.

—

Two days later Vivian's name was in my inbox. I was surprised by my own emotion and read eagerly. Vivian had written a group email to a long list of people whom I had mostly never heard of. In it, she explained that she was going to Greece. To the island of Lesvos. Not because she was queer (I noted the new designation) but because there was a meditation center where they taught you how to kill your ego. She described it as the next step in the evolution of her consciousness. You couldn't be a good ally, she wrote, or truly care about anyone else, until you had killed yourself.

At first I wondered if I'd only been accidentally added to the recipient list, but decided not to let that stop me. Whether she'd meant for me to read it or not, the content resonated. I'd tried several kinds of artistic suicide, but ego death sounded new and exempt from the pressures of failure. On the path to killing your ego, failure even sounded like a part of the process; like a type of success. Ego suicide also seemed like the last stop before you attempted the real thing. I wrote straight back.

I told Vivian that I'd had a terrible time in LA, that Ayn Rand had failed me, that I'd gone viral but it hadn't brought me love or money, and I was now living upstate with my mother. I said I was sad about our friendship and curious about Vivian's decision to go and kill her ego. Surprisingly, she FaceTimed me right away.

She was wearing a basketball singlet, her hair was short, and her face had lost its gaunt, angry beauty. Vivian had filled out. She looked soft and pink and almost happy. With her usual disarming frankness, she explained how the community actions and mutual aid work and all the queer activism she'd fallen into had been helpful, but not quite enough. Something was still getting in her way.

"What do you think it might be?" I asked.

"Oh, I know what it is." She made a pistol grip and cocked it to her head. "It's this fucking guy."

"You're trans?"

"No, Anna." She jammed her index finger hard into her temple. "*Me.* This idiot right here. My ego. My self."

It sounded like the opposite of Randian philosophy and this was a relief, an arrow even. I wondered if it was a queer activist thing or if bad feminist heterosexuals could also attend. I asked her and Vivian assured me that the workshop had nothing to do with sexual preference, in fact the whole point was to abolish your identity. The thought was comforting. To be nothing, nobody. I watched Vivian tousle her short, asymmetrical front part. It made me think of Antifa and then, for some reason, I was telling her.

"You know," I said. "This weird thing happened last year where a guy wouldn't leave my apartment." My chest tightened. "We went to a bar and he tried to explain Marxism and then he came home with me and wouldn't get off my couch."

"Was he drunk?" Vivian seemed suspicious; of me or the Marxist, I couldn't tell.

"No," I said. "He just didn't see why I deserved to be in my apartment any more than he did."

"How did you get him out?"

I wasn't sure about that part. If my head on his thigh had repulsed him or if it was some sort of revolt against my privilege? Had I made myself too human or else dehumanized myself by showing off my good luck? All I knew was that it had been my choice. I'd chosen not to shame him, to keep his ego intact. And by choosing to submit, I'd kept myself separate and safe.

"It's okay," I assured her. "I'm not a survivor."

Vivian dismissed my joke with a penetrating stare. "I think you should come to Greece."

I laughed it off. But five days later I was on a plane.

Part Two

Lesvos

I only really read about the meditation center on the train to JFK. From the internet I learned that the center's guru had been a controversial Indian philosopher whose followers had tried to create a utopia in the English countryside in the early 1990s. The disciples had quickly found themselves in an ugly dispute with the local unemployed who believed their disappearing factory jobs were due not to the early effects of globalization but to the presence of these neo-hippie immigrants from the encroaching continent. MI5 had gotten involved, and even the queen had issued a harsh statement against what she'd called "an immoral cult." The conflict had climaxed in car chases and killer bees and the guru finally fleeing back to India, where his followers believed he'd been poisoned, and the English said he'd overdosed on happy gas. As much as I wanted to destroy my sense of self, I was excited to enter a world built on the teachings of a truly spectacular pariah.

Our plane was late so we missed the connection from Athens to Mytilene. The airline put us on a bus with rainbow-colored LED lights and a disco ball and dropped us at a hotel one hour from the airport. We spent five hours checking in, eating cold pasta at the buffet, and lying wide awake in our rooms before the bus returned for us at dawn. Then we took a propeller plane that rattled through Aegean gusts with all the agency of a kite. When we finally arrived in Mytilene, it was midway through the first day of the ego death workshop.

The airport was one long, shiny room with a currency exchange booth and a Coke machine. Lesvos, it seemed, was not a major tourist destination. The airport brochure said that the sea around the island was cold and a darker blue than the more popular islands and that the accommodation and dining were "traditional." I hid my disappointment; we were here to die.

Outside the airport the sky was a blasted white. The small city was gray and haggard and lacked the superficial charm of a destination. People squinted and turned away as though annoyed to be visible, to be made self-conscious by the presence of outsiders. We hailed a cab and asked the driver to take us to the meditation center on the other side of the island. He took his hands off the wheel and studied us in the rearview mirror.

"You know what this island is famous for?"

I tried to think back to the airport brochure. "Freshwater sardines?"

"Sappho." The driver grinned. "You should be going to the beach."

I understood that he was talking about lesbianism and smiled at Vivian, who had also understood. "Thanks," she said. "But we're here to kill our egos."

The driver had no follow-up questions; in fact he didn't speak to us for the rest of the drive. As we traversed the island, the landscape shifted quickly from drab highways to emerald pine forests to bald, rocky mountains. The stone was a pale green that made the hillsides look lunar. Just before we reached the last set of hills, the highway took us through the little beach town. There was a slim boardwalk lined with mostly empty cafés and stray cats slinking around the table legs. The sand was gray and the sea was flat and dark with a huge black rock in the middle. It thrust up out of the blue like a giant loaf of rye. The only men I could see all seemed to be jumping off the top of it.

The beach town didn't feel like the kind of place you would travel far to see. Maybe if you lived on the west coast of Turkey or just above, somewhere in the Balkans. Even then, you'd have to have bad taste or not very much money. It was vastly different from the resort beaches of my childhood vacations. I could recall the joy of arriving somewhere hot and tropical in pleasant wooziness and all the doting smiles of service workers in their crisp, clean uniforms. These resorts were womb-like—everywhere a warm pool to sink into, a soft massage or pampering treatment to receive, somewhere to lie in baking sunshine or float in cool, fragrant darkness. It was pre-life or post-life but never *actual* life and I had loved that feeling of seamless and unerring care.

When I told her this, Vivian said my childhood sounded exploitative. That all tourism was. I supposed she was right, or rather I didn't have it in me to be contrarian. I was fighting that urge, and what I now suspected was the engine of my personality. Although my contrarianism was why, in my adult life, I'd always rejected travel and so, actually, avoided exploiting people. It was embarrassing to gather with strangers somewhere known for its tendency to inspire awe. I preferred to be surprised by nature and art; to let them sneak up and astonish me, alone.

Vivian had moved on and was now observing the passing lesbians. There were a few walking in the street and sitting on idling mopeds. They were older, in cargo pants, and all had short hair, weathered Scandinavian faces, and the uncanny look of genetic relatedness. The driver explained it was still low season and that the summer only kicked off the following week. Vivian sighed; we had other plans. After the workshop, we were headed to the detention center on the other side of the island. It was the largest one in Europe and had been plagued by overcrowding, riots, fires, and deaths. Our purpose there was altruism. Pure and simple. I was even enjoying the blasphemy of this; still feeling a little angry with Ayn.

Winding up the hill toward the center, I noticed two young people walking by the side of the road. One was a petite, heart-faced girl with loops of red beads hanging at her chest like many smiling mouths. She was draped over a long, lithe boy with white blond dreads wearing a ratty T-shirt. Both of them were barefoot and smiling with an inflamed, demented-looking happiness. The boy stuck out a hand and the driver made a tiny dodge with the wheel.

"Can we pick them up?"

I was surprised to see Vivian looking eagerly out the back window. Was she already trying to help the island's destitute? Maybe it was part of our journey; if they robbed us, we'd just be one step closer to enlightenment. As the driver huffed and slowed the cab, I couldn't help thinking that in one way Ayn was right about altruism; that it seemed to court the death drive. The car idled in the dust, but the couple didn't increase their pace. As we waited for them I watched Vivian's face begin to strain with anxious regret. Her foot tapped rapidly against the front seat. I knew what she was thinking; we were missing Day One.

As they came around the side of the cab, I caught a glimpse of the boy's T-shirt riding just above the small fuzz of his pubic bone. Then the door opened and they slid in with a heady waft of salt water and body odor. The girl gave us a big, effervescent "Hi!" and the boy murmured something and then looked out the window. As we drove on, a warm, humming excitement filled the car. Vivian gushed about the beauty of the volcanic hillsides and the girl gushed back. Carefully, I watched the boy's face. It was angelic, though he had an angry patch of acne at his chin and a catlike coolness in his eyes. Beautiful but probably sixteen.

The girl began to tell us how wonderful the center was—calling it a "commune" and punctuating her speech with breathy sighs of pleasure. She sounded Slavic and I guessed that both of them were. A couple, I assumed. They were too physical for siblings. After a few minutes we turned off the main road, scrabbling up onto a dirt trail. It was rocky and kicked up a red fog of dust. Now we beetled along through a dense olive grove, until the trail narrowed between two flanks of bamboo. At the end was a long line of mopeds parked outside a low stone wall. I saw a sign with a mandala painted on it. A gray-bearded Indian man smiled out of the center. The guru.

We pulled in at the wall. I tried to lift my bag from the trunk but the boy snatched the handle from my fingers and yanked the suitcase down onto the road. He did the same for Vivian and then went silently to the gate, saying nothing when we thanked him.

Once the couple were gone, Vivian immediately resumed her panic about how much of the death workshop we were missing. I paid the driver and we wheeled our suitcases through the dust and up to a small stone house with a hand-painted reception sign on its door. Vivian gave an urgent knock. I could hear a fan rattling inside and then a chair squeaked and now came a light, lazy footfall. Vivian bugged her eyes at me. I wasn't sure if she was thinking *Greece* or *meditators* but I could see the frustration in her face; the languorous pace here was going to be a problem. Finally the door opened.

"Welcome, beloveds."

A tall, handsome Greek man with light almond eyes and fine, doe-like features stood in the dark entrance. Vivian apologized and immediately launched into the story of our airline misadventure. The man stood back, waiting for us to enter. Vivian remained at the threshold. I could see she was resisting him. She didn't want to surrender to their time zone, their *sense* of time.

"Please," he said at last, gesturing to the two red floor cushions positioned in front of a low wooden desk. Vivian relented, hurrying inside and sitting up very straight as if her diligence might hasten the proceedings. The man drifted in behind his desk. He knelt slowly and then held out two worn pamphlets. In here were photos of more beautiful, radiant people dancing under orange lights or legs crossed in lotus position or at an outdoor buffet, serving themselves big glistening leaves of lettuce.

"You can jump straight into the workshop," he said. "Or you can take things a little bit slower and first get used to the place."

I detected a hint of wariness in his tone. He seemed unsure of us and I wondered if it was just Vivian's pushiness or something deeper and more fundamental that he sensed in our natures. I wanted to reassure him; his warm, happy presence was making me want to abandon my nature, and everything about myself.

Vivian was less enchanted. Despite all her recent growth, she was still highly sensitive to not getting the exact thing she'd ordered online.

"We came here to do the death workshop."

"Jhyes," he said, a twinkling sympathy in his eyes. It was

clear that already Vivian and I were failing. Too goal-oriented; too intent on succeeding; unable to hold a paradox in our tiny minds. And yet, even in this exchange, the manager appeared to be aimless. He didn't need to teach or help us. Such needs were beneath him. He rose with gentle indifference and led us back out the door.

We left the suitcases on the porch and walked down a dirt path to another large stone hut with a pile of shoes at the door. An attractive dark-skinned man was hurriedly removing his sneakers at the entrance. He wore a white turban and robes and had the round, lively features of what I assumed was a Moroccan or Tunisian face. I felt my body instantly soften and sway in his direction.

"And here is our other American," said the manager.

My heart sank. The turbaned man put out an awkward hand and introduced himself in a whiney New Jersey accent. He was an Armenian American psychoanalyst from Newark who seemed equally unenthusiastic to discover his compatriots. We hurried through some geographical banalities and then the manager instructed Vivian and me to remove our sneakers. When we were shoeless he put a long, graceful finger to his lips.

"Silence, beloveds." The manager turned and glided serenely away.

I opened the door and we stepped into the cool, dark room. It took a moment for my eyes to adjust to what was happening. The ocean of white eddies was actually a large group of linen-clad bodies whirling all over the room. One boy in the center wore a skirt that was spinning like an umbrella around his slim hips, and each of the whirlers looked like a glowing jellyfish floating in a dark sea. It was so beautiful, I felt weak. Which made me wonder how the heat and the spinning might interact with my severely sleep-deprived brain. But even this was exciting. Fainting, falling, knocking myself unconscious—all of these sounded like useful tactics for ego death.

I started to step around in a tight circle, the left foot leading the right in small pivoting movements. The instruction was to breathe away your thoughts, spread your arms wide, and spin. I became instantly nauseous but worried that stopping would be more dangerous than continuing. I stumbled into someone's arm but they seemed to bounce right off me, giggling and spinning away. I giggled too. My body felt light; my mind was an airy scrawl. When the music slowed, everyone was instructed to wrap their arms around their shoulders and bow to themselves, then sink down to their knees. A tinny recording came over the speakers and a sleepy Indian voice began to tell a joke.

It was about a nagging wife, the delivery flagrantly deadpan. I felt myself chuckling before the punch line, which, when it came, sent a shot of laughter up my spine, pure as light and somehow detached from its content. The whole group was laughing and a strange atmospheric heaviness filled the room, which made remaining upright hard. I found myself lying on my back, legs wheeling up like a cockroach.

I had never believed in a Jewish God or secular Pilates or anything that any large group of people were doing. But I surrendered to this laughter and somehow managed not to think anything funny or smart or contrary.

After the morning session Vivian and I got a short tour. The dining area was a vast, open space with a thatched roof supported by three wooden pillars. Below this a small, vegetarian buffet swarmed with bees and wasps. A lot of things at the commune, I learned, swarmed with bees and wasps. The toilets were another thing. We were taken there next. The bathroom block was also a wall-less thatched structure with toilet cubicles at one end and shower stalls at the other. These were partially closed off by low wooden doors or shower curtains. Even at two o'clock in the afternoon the bathroom was busy with showering and urinating and the swift ploppings of shit. Vivian exhaled loudly at the sight of each naked ball sack that emerged moist and swinging from a stall. The men here were very slow to wrap around their towels.

Next we dragged our bags to the small wooden hut we would be sharing. The manager led us down a dirt path, past other huts and tents, through the speckled shade of olive trees. Here, he asked for thirty euros and, once again, I handed over my credit card for both of us.

"Jhyes," he said, taking the card. "Come get this later. And if you want to stay longer, just let me know." He smiled beatifically. "Welcome, beloveds."

Inside the hut there were two single beds separated by a space of one foot. Opposite the beds was a small dresser with two drawers, a mirror, and a fan that blew hot air around the room. The windows were gray with mosquito netting but otherwise paneless. We lay on our beds and Vivian told me she was concerned.

"A lot of boundary issues here," she said, frowning at the low ceiling.

"Yes," I agreed. "I'm a bit nervous about pooping."

"It's like they don't believe in doors."

We lay there for a few more moments and then Vivian told me she had noticed a woman with a bowl cut in hiking boots, pouring drinks at the little outdoor bar. She was definitely queer. I hadn't seen the bartender but I had noticed a young, handsome Italian in our workshop group. He had a dark mop of sun-streaked hair and piercing eyes of a psychotic turquoise.

Still smarting from Big Boy, I feared and dreaded the Italian, which only made me madly excited for the afternoon session.

Back in the group room, I sat just behind the Italian while our group facilitator talked about the word "forgiveness." He was stocky with a prow of silver hair and wet brown eyes that sat eggy in his sockets. *Synchoresi*, he told us, was the Greek word for forgiveness and could be translated as "the space you make to include your opponent." Inside the idea of *synchoresi*, he explained, was a kind of death. To include something always required a small surrendering of the ego. An inclusion was always a type of self-cancellation. Then he started quoting someone called "the Master." The guru, I presumed. The Master had practiced Sufi whirling, said the facilitator, because it was about inviting things into your orbit—including your enemies, who were the keepers of your shame and thus the key to your whole personality. To me, it sounded a little bit like Nietzsche. To endure injury without suffering. To be merciful.

"The Master," he said, "believed that ego death comes only when you can enjoy the farts of your adversary."

The group chuckled, and I smiled, remembering the communal toilet block, as another piece of my enlightenment slid gently into place. Then the facilitator's eyes got shinier. The personality, he said, was nothing but an elaborate shame deflection mechanism. And once you invited people in, there was no room for shame and the personality lost its purpose. His eyelids fell closed. The only thing left to listen to then, he said, was the loving silence of the heart. I glanced at Vivian and noticed that she was glaring at him. When the session ended she seized my arm at the door.

"*Master?*" Vivian was outraged.

"Yeah, it's a bit dated."

"I think it might be a bit worse than that."

Vivian marched us straight to the Wi-Fi room. It was a tiny airless space with a wonky bookshelf full of the Master's books, a broken office chair, and a barbaric old PC. Luckily, you could also get patchy internet service on the patio outside.

Vivian, it appeared, had not done her research. We sat on deck chairs under the vined canopy, swarming with bees and wasps, and she began to google. Vivian knew about the original utopia but not the conflict with the local workers, whom she immediately identified with. She scanned the Wikipedia page with rising fury.

"The cult bused in Pakistani migrants to increase their council votes."

This struck me as a sound strategy but I kept it to myself.

"And after they voted," she continued, "the migrants were all sent straight back to Liverpool." Vivian read rapaciously on, then frowned. "Although it does look like the Pakistanis had some trouble fitting in."

"Trouble?"

"They were strict Muslims. And it was an evil sex cult."

"It doesn't feel like an evil sex cult."

But Vivian's eyes were bulging again at the screen. "They were bio-fucking-terrorists."

I scanned along anxiously beside her. I knew that the cult's leaders had released a vicious strain of European bee into the hostile neighboring farmland. A ninety-six-year-old woman had been stung in her snow pea patch and died of anaphylactic shock. But I'd missed the second incident where the whole commune had thrown a wild all-night dance party outside the town mayor's house, causing the stress-induced death of two beloved guinea pigs. Vivian was appalled by their tactics and I conceded that there had certainly been some bad elements. In particular, the Master's own daughter. A fierce and electric woman who went around puncturing people's car tires and calling their babies ugly. She had also been the loudest advocate of her father's voluntary sterilization program. On the airport train, I'd scoured this section hungrily, my chest swelling with vindication as I'd read that the Master saw overpopulation and the toxicity of family dynamics as the twin evils in modern life. But more importantly the woman was, like her father, dead. Or at least defanged in a Danish nursing home. Crucially, the Master's ideas were good, and the man himself was gone. He couldn't rob or brainwash or molest us.

"But, Viv," I said. "Isn't it kind of like hearing the accusations and still watching *Hannah and Her Sisters*?"

"I wouldn't participate in a workshop based on the philosophy of Woody Allen."

"No, but you know what I mean."

Vivian looked conflicted. She leaned right back in her chair and stared off toward the distant hills.

"The workshop's only three days," I said hopefully.

I could see that she had spotted two young women in booby peasant tops bent over a bush and plucking off the fat figs. Vivian twisted in her seat, moaning.

"Three days," she said. "And there's no way I'm calling him 'Master.'"

The evening meeting was held in a huge circular courtyard of pale pink mosaic that spiraled out around a deep shaggy tree. Behind this a green field peeled back toward the lunar hills, the crests of which glowed orange in the sinking sun. The sky was luminous like submerged coral and already stars were glittering above. Goat bells tinkled in the distance. A few grinning mongrels strutted around on short legs, humbly seeking pats. It was beautiful in an unobtrusive way and I felt moved to genuine awe.

The atmosphere that night was ceremonial. People wore loose-fitting white clothing and swayed to slow, synth-y rock music. I stood among them and let my limbs slacken, then start to flail about. It was embarrassing to move like this—cultishly—but my resistance was weak and I found myself gradually submitting. I was here to let myself go. I began to smile, my mouth stretching so wide that laughter bubbled out in little spittly side-bursts.

When the music stopped, everyone sat abruptly down. They closed their eyes as gentle sitar music began playing through the speakers. I sat but kept my eyes open, taking in the scene. A small dog appeared beside me and presented his filthy belly. I stroked him as I glanced around at the dozens of peaceful faces. I wanted that peace; to sit in a dusk-lit grove tickled by bees and wasps and now mosquitos too, without flinching in body or mind. I closed my eyes and tried to feel my breath. It slowly synchronized with the steady rise and fall of the dog's chest and for a moment we seemed to be conjoined, a vast breathing emptiness. My mind slid out from under me and there was a second of deep felty black, before my thoughts came rushing back in.

Soon after, a gong sounded and everyone lay prostrate on the floor. I wiggled myself down and lay there, feeling the cool tiles beneath my belly. Now a crackling din came through the speakers. It was an old recording: a thick, expectant quiet broken only by the odd car honk or grumbling cow. Cows in traffic, I decided, must be the sound of being in India. The ambient noise of this Indian street went on for a long time and I began to wonder and then to worry about its significance. Or rather, I worried that its meditative effects weren't working on me. When I could no longer bear my failure, I peeked an eye open.

Everyone was sitting up again, cross-legged and gazing intently at a huge flat-screen that had appeared under the tree. Filling almost the entire frame was the bluish face of a sad-eyed man with a wizard beard and a bright white beret. It was the man from the mandala; the guru, the Master. The street rumbled on behind him, and then he blinked with slow, bovine indifference as his jaw wheeled open.

"The family is wrong," he said in a soft, sibilant monotone. "And must be destroyed."

A bright streak of elation ripped through me. It was his words but also, somehow, the slow-landing impact of his intonation. It felt like truth. Powerful, ancient, counterintuitive truth. The mystical twang of paradox. The kind of wisdom my ever-deflective heart could absorb.

The Master continued. The family, he told us, had come into existence with private property. It made women the property of men and children the property of parents. The family drew a boundary around the child so that they were told what to think, how to be, and the love of their feudal parents was rationed to them. As I listened, my body seemed to float in the warm air, my cells vibrating with the dusk's gentle buzz. Our parents, the Master cautioned us, simply had to be ignored. They had tried to make us into moral beings and thus missed all that we actually were. They dismissed our energy, our essence, and our life force. They made us feel wrong and unnatural; made us perform. Yes, I thought, practically levitating; our parents made us all into narcissists.

A furrow came into the Master's brow as he raised a large,

flat hand straight up like a traffic paddle. Morality, he said, had been weaponized against us. Through television and the media and the whole chastising superego of Culture. Whereas morality was actually deeply personal—the domain of the individual—where each decision could be made only from the silent intuition of the heart.

Silence and intuition were foreign to me, but I was eager to learn. And the idea of a "sacred life force" I recognized from Nietzsche and, in an unsettling way, from Ayn. But maybe living for one's own sake could just mean nurturing this essential life energy, absent of the egotistical self? I would ask the facilitator first thing tomorrow.

The discourse concluded with another joke. This time it was about Haimy, who couldn't get it up for his long-suffering wife, Leah. The joke played on some stereotype of the sexually neurotic Jewish male, but that didn't stop me from laughing. I recognized the minor transgression and laughter came rushing up. The high, giddy laughter of getting away with something, of getting off. We were all transcending morality, together. It wasn't an orgy, but it was in the ballpark.

After the discourse, I drifted blissfully to the dining hut. There was a buffet table in the center of the space with four large bowls full of tomatoes, peppers, cucumbers, and onions, a smaller bowl of feta, some lemon quarters, and a collection of chopping blocks. Here, Greek salad became a meditation. People sliced and chopped and sprinkled crumbly cheese into their bowls and then glided away in contented silence. Nobody sanitized their hands.

Vivian and I sat at a table marked "In Silence" and watched a shirtless boy with a top knot eating his Greek salad with chopsticks. His eyes were closed and he moved with Noh-like slowness.

It took him three minutes to raise a cucumber slice to his lips and bite down but when he did the experience appeared to be transcendent.

There were several of these wiry, monk-like boys who floated around shirtless and opiate-eyed. Though their asceticism seemed to contradict what I had read on the Wikipedia page. The Master said there was a balance to be found between the spiritual and material worlds. He'd kept three hundred and fifty Harley-Davidsons in a garage on the original compound, taking a different one out each afternoon to roar around, terrorizing the English countryside. On the way to enlightenment the Master encouraged people to make lots of love and a decent amount of money. He condemned abstinence of all kinds as a cheat that curbed the mind's greed; a greed, he said, that caused useful suffering and taught profound awareness. There was also a footnote on the Wiki, explaining the motorbike collection as merely one of the Master's "sublime cosmic jokes." These sexless monk boys appeared to be in the wrong commune.

In the middle of the evening meal, a cowbell was rung and a spindly Englishman with a ruddy, sated face stood and announced that there was a lecture tonight on the male orgasm. Vivian pretended to gag but then shrugged and kept eating—relaxed and newly tolerant. The Englishman said that the lecture would be held after dinner in the geodesic dome on the hill and that both men and women were welcome.

We washed our dishes at the outdoor sink with its wild, sputtering hose and brown dish soap, and then walked over to the outdoor lounge. This was a low, canopied area with daybeds and rattan chairs scattered across the dirt floor. Colored bulbs lit it into a dark, fairy-tale forest. Here we were almost immediately accosted by the American, who started complaining to Vivian that they were the only two queer people at the commune. As Vivian began pointing out all the latent lesbians and their unsuspecting boyfriends, I made a hasty retreat to the geodesic dome. It was up the hill behind the bar—a glowing red testicle in the black sky.

Already it was full, and men and women of all ages sat spilling out the opening and all the way down the stone steps. I perched on a rock at the bottom of the stairs and peered in at the spindly tantra master who sat on a raised platform in the center of the dome. Throned up beside him was a voluptuous Italian woman cross-legged on a red satin pillow. The two of them sat there, eyes closed and swaying to imaginary music. We all watched in silent anticipation until the tantra master finally paused and opened his eyes. His high, nasal voice rang through the dome.

"Tantra is all about the polarity," he said. "The woman has to be receptive to the man's needs. Just as he has to be a sensitive instrument to hers."

"And, ladiez-uh." His tantra queen had a sensuous, heaving lilt. "Our needs iz as deep and mysterious-uh as the ocean." She closed her eyes again and felt, presumably, the oceanic depth of her needs.

Then they gave a demonstration, the queen straddling her master and the two of them breathing loudly as they began to rock back and forth. Were they naked I supposed that what they were doing up there might possibly be considered sex. But I was disappointed. I realized that I wanted to be shocked; scandalized into some kind of radical transformation. Flung so far from my comfort zone that I lost myself, lost touch with reality (the one I hated); was re-formed by the will of others. Which sounded a lot like sex in my twenties. And then I wondered—had I come to the geodesic dome secretly hoping to be ravaged?

The tantra master slid out from under his queen's wide hips.

"Now," he said, smiling at us. "I want everyone to close their eyes and place two fingers on their perineum."

I closed my eyes and nestled my fingers discreetly between the folds of my shorts, praying I was not the only one doing it. The tantra master directed everyone to breathe in through their genitals, pressing their fingers into the fleshy bridge between crotch and anus as they exhaled.

"And now," he said softly, "I want the men to bring the other hand over the shaft of their penis. And to squeeze."

It occurred to me that every man in the dome, probably forty of them, now had a raging erection. My body tensed up and my movements became infinitesimal.

"There iz no goal here," said the tantra queen. "Nobody iz trying to ejaculate-uh."

I pressed harder and started to enjoy the spreading warmth. It was a whole different class of sensation from the imperative "to come." After a few moments I peeked an eye open but nobody was looking. They all had the same inward expression of private focus. I wasn't afraid of these people. They were not here to coerce me into sex. They were barely even taking my money. In this day and age, the most tantric experience one could hope for was probably just a bit of group masturbation.

Eventually, the men were told to release their penises and everyone was asked to remove their fingers from their perineums. I experienced no tantric orgasm, but glancing around the dome I felt the soft sheath of affinity slide on like a robe. I had managed to share something intimate with a whole large group.

When I got back to the hut, Vivian wasn't there. And her bed was also empty when I woke the next morning with the blazing

sun and shrieking birdcall. I found my friend at breakfast, wash-
ing her bowl in the sink. As we walked together to the toilets,
Vivian regaled me with the previous night's sexual conquests. In
one evening she had managed to get naked with both the bartender and a Belarussian ex-model on the run from her oligarch
boyfriend, and now had a serious crush on the beautiful Asian
boy in the white whirling skirt who she believed was demisex-
ual but misidentifying as a demigod. One of the sexless monk
boys. They had meditated together that morning on the swing
seat above the river bed and as the boy jangled his bracelets over
her belly Vivian had almost come.

"Oh, and how was the male orgasm?" she asked me.

"Very inclusive."

"Glad to hear it."

We pulled our towels off their hooks and marched happily
toward the showers.

Returning from the bathroom, I came upon the outdoor
art station. Under the shade of a gnarly olive tree, several large
sheets of tarpaulin were spread out, covered in brightly colored
canvases. The art station appeared to be a place where adults
painted flowers with other people's children while their parents
were off living their own lives. During his evening discourse, the
Master had said that children should be raised not in modern
nuclear families but by nonjudgmental, unconditionally loving
communities of spiritually enlightened people. The only problem,
he'd joked, was that these people didn't yet exist and so really
most children shouldn't be raised at all.

I stood there watching the art station for a while. No one in-
dulged the children or even spoke to them in an altered tone of
voice. I observed a stiff German woman with a wispy mullet tell
a tiny noodly-haired child that his painting was "interesting."

There was no talk of the child's talent; he wasn't "amazing" or "special." My father had probably over-praised me and my mother had obviously made me hungry for validation. Whereas the commune children seemed neither coddled nor judged. They were gently, adjacently loved and appeared to embody what the Master believed about emotional self-sufficiency. They had a natural confidence that appeared to need nothing. They were pure propulsive energy, and responsible for their own inner lives, already, at ages six and eight and eleven.

I noticed now that the German mullet was eyeing a large blonde woman in an optimistic floral onesie talking to one of the monk boys. I had noted this woman at the tantra workshop—in particular her luscious mouth and dark, penetrating eyes. As she'd come back down the stairs with a cute Greek boy, I'd thought she sounded Bulgarian. She was confident and attractive and the kind of person who usually made me want to go and hide.

But the German mullet seemed to loathe her. She made a face of wincing distaste as she watched the Bulgarian chatting away obliviously. I quickly learned why. The German leaned down and whispered something to the noodlehead, who then ran happily toward the Bulgarian, shouting "Mama!" The Bulgarian sat up glaring at the German and even the monk boy looked annoyed as he extended his thin arms, shielding himself from the oncoming child. It was sad but true: most children really shouldn't be raised at all.

That afternoon the death group was told to assemble again in the parking lot. We were driving to the beach for a full-moon fire ceremony. Vivian hopped in a car with the whirling boy and

I found myself hovering around the Italian like a sad, witless insect. After several awkward minutes I was finally invited to join his convoy and we headed off down the dirt road.

The car belonged to another Italian, skinny and coarse-faced, who wore Thai fisherman pants and no shirt. I had noticed him doing yoga under various trees around the commune, always beside some nervously laughing woman. I sat in the back of his tiny, filthy sedan and listened to the fast, luscious mouthfuls of Italian. Neither man paid any attention to me and I took pleasure in surrendering my need to be known. Watching the landscape, I felt myself merging with the green fields smudging by outside the window.

We bypassed the town, turning off down the long, cratered road that ran toward the cliffs. The skinny Italian parked his car at the foot of the dunes and the three of us walked over the sand to where a sparse row of straw huts sat overlooking the water. I knew that this end of the main beach was nudist and immediately began to fret. I could see Vivian sitting outside a hut with a group of young people I was beginning to think of as "the popular group." There were two couples—the men broad and ponytailed and the women petite and curvy—and the little Slavic girl from the day before. The men had a laconic slipperiness about them and the women seemed performatively orgasmic. When she waved I pretended not to see Vivian and remained with the unfriendly Italians.

The two men laid their towels out in the sun and stripped down to their underwear. They were both wearing Hugo Boss briefs. No heterosexual American man I knew would have worn these unironically. But the Italians seemed comfortable, proud even, of the machismo bestowed by this iconic underwear. It was all so simple here, so primal and innocent. And the Hugo Boss underwear activated something inside me—a broad softening of my pelvic region. I felt like flopping down and lying belly-up on the sand.

And then the underwear were coming off. Bunching down their hairy thighs and exposing their limp, bouncy penises. This wasn't so bad. It certainly wasn't intimidating. I crawled into the little straw hut to strip off. Somehow this seemed more dignified, more seductive, than doing it in front of them. From the cover of the hut's thinly layered palm fronds, I now observed my two companions. They were lying eyes closed on their backs; their flaccid shafts curled inward like shy slugs. It really was the safest, most nonthreatening sex cult I could have imagined. And without an enigmatic leader, things were unlikely to descend into the usual paranoid mass suicide and murder. The cult seemed to thrive because it was *not* an idealistically deranged utopia. It was, rather, a capitalist enterprise run on accommodation fees. People had not given up their homes, jobs, or life savings. The Beloveds were economically independent, disinvested, and free to come and go. Something about this pleased me. The system wasn't Randian but it also wasn't the opposite. All my hard research and recently held convictions felt slightly less stupid and not like a total waste of time.

I slid my top off and eased down my shorts but before I crawled back out of the hut, I considered the arrangement of my labia. If I lay down, up-beach of the Italians, they would see quite literally into my vagina. Perhaps it was self-conscious, but I wanted to leave just a little bit of room for mystery. I decided to lie stomach-down, facing the water. Almost as soon as I did this, a beautiful Dutch girl walked over and put her arms around the handsome Italian's shoulders. I was suddenly ashamed of my nakedness and sat up, reaching for my towel. The skinny one seemed to notice my discomfort. He patted my arm and told me we were going for a swim. I appreciated this and hurried off behind him.

In the water we chatted.

"What your zodiac sign iz-uh?"

"Pisces," I said. "Although I heard they recently moved the cusp?"

He shook his head and grabbed my hand. It wasn't quite affection he was giving me but rather a deeper form of assessment. He studied the lines of my palm with tense concentration and then, having divined nothing, he let the hand abruptly go.

"Enneagram number?"

"Enneagram?"

"Myers–Briggz-uh?" He was getting frustrated.

"I think I'm the 'natural leader' one?"

"No," he snapped. "Maybe you iz 'feeling introvert.'"

"Okay," I agreed, though it wasn't a question.

"Do you know where iz the planets at the moment of your birth?"

"I'm really sorry but I don't."

He sighed and looked out to sea. There was something slightly fascistic about the skinny Italian's interest in personality typing systems. Especially when we weren't supposed to have personalities here.

"Your friend who iz in the basketball shorts?"

"Vivian?"

He chuckled. "She have made a bondage with the man."

Now I was confused: Had he misread Vivian's queer signifiers? She wasn't into bondage and she definitely wasn't into men.

"I don't think she even knows any men."

"She hates the man and so she has become one."

I tried to believe this was just a Mediterranean thing, and

became gently instructive. "You know, in America, all people wear basketball shorts . . ."

He laughed, slapping a hand hard across the water's surface. "Impossible to surrender to the Master in a-pants like thiz-uh!"

It seemed to me now that the Hugo Boss underwear meant women like Vivian harm. I looked back at the shore and saw the white and terra-cotta houses jumbled all along the green escarpment. The brown cliffs were misty to either side, the darker green mountains loomed over the town. The freedom of my nakedness felt suddenly impersonal and I tucked myself into a bobbing ball, trying to reclaim whatever it was I'd just lost. Whatever my passivity had taken from me. After a few moments I sensed the Italian approaching.

"Now I will float you," he announced.

I was suddenly supine, ears submerged, mouth sucking in air like a whale spout. The Italian cradled my back, gliding me through the water. It took me most of the three minutes to relax and by then he was tilting me back up again.

"Now it iz my turn."

He withdrew his arms and lay back. His torso bobbed up into a plank and with it, his fully erect penis. I quickly submerged my hands and began to float him through the water. But an alarm was sounding in my body. Much to my surprise, the erect penis was freaking me out. I floated him with my arms fully extended, keeping his torso literally at arm's length. Turning him slowly through the water, I asked myself why the erect penis felt so menacing. It was only an admission, an invitation; less a demand than a request. But I found myself resenting his audacity and even taking on his (imagined) shame. As if *I* were the one to be imminently rejected. Or maybe it was the feeling that with his blatant request all the nonsexual parts of me had been somehow rejected. But was that actually true? Did his lust have to delegitimize my whole being? And why was his sexual desire less legitimate than my need to be engaged in meaningful conversation? Did I feel powerless simply because I was new here and he was not? Where was my ego now?

But my questions seemed out of place. They were feminist questions and I was here for something much bigger than that. I unfocused my eyes and let the sudden boner just be there. Like a tree or a rock. It was only a dare. The boner's seduction technique was to shock and disturb, but it was as harmful as a light slap or a nudge in the back. A penetration technique for someone frightened of actual intercourse. It wasn't the intuitive dance of tantra; it was more like comedian pervert behavior. And of course I could relate to someone just trying to get a rise.

After a few minutes, I removed my hands from the Italian's back and began frogging around him in widening circles. My teeth were rattling and he heard this and seemed to understand.

"Now you iz cold."

Watching the sun blink on the horizon like a huge copper coin, I tucked myself back into the ball.

On the beach again, the facilitator instructed us to go find an object representing an aspect of the self we wished to see engulfed by flames. I found a hard, stinky knuckle of sea sponge, which I decided was the joking, contrarian part of my brain. Returning with my sponge, I saw that a huge fire now blazed at the foot of the dunes and the whole naked group had formed a circle around it. I joined them, and then the facilitator walked into the center of the circle, and told us we were all failures. *Meditators*, he clarified. Because meditation was all about failure. If you tried to meditate, you failed; if you tried to stop trying, the moment you noticed that you had succeeded—that you had surrendered yourself to *something*—you were instantly failing again. Meditation was the process of accepting failure, over and over, in each new moment. There were only brief glimpses of something else (emptiness? aliveness? connectedness?) but when you tried to name that thing, you just failed once more.

And now, one by one, all thirty members of the ego death group walked up to the fire and threw their symbolic object into its roaring mouth with ritualistic flourish. When it was my turn, I shuffled up to the fire and knelt down. I stared at the sea sponge, trying to will a revelation. None came. And then, with the focus of a marksman, I tossed the sponge into the fattest flame and watched, intently, as the fire ate it up. Still nothing. No transformation. In fact, I just seemed to get closer to myself, jumping down my own throat like someone who'd just coughed in a theater. I was failing. My face burned; my brain was a choking lung. I gave up, and then my thoughts were moving like blind fingers through fur. The thoughts were just outlines, form without content. Amazed, I watched them for a moment, then decided I must be doing it, meditating. And the feeling went away.

The next morning I was late to breakfast, where only the bees and wasps were in full attendance. They blackened the honey jar and rolled in gauzy waves through the open containers of marmalade and raspberry jam. They lay in wait on sliced watermelon, camouflaged as seeds, and had even developed a taste for hard-boiled eggs, which they dive-bombed in a frenzy of psychic attrition.

I took my naked yogurt to the end of a long, largely empty table. Just a few chatty older women at one end and the young

Slavic boy in the middle, his blond mop with its prongy dreads monstering down his face.

"You are scared of the bee?"

I looked up. He was talking to me.

"Yes," I said, observing his bowl. It was tiered with condiments that rose over his muesli like a mad frilly hat. I felt ashamed; it seemed you were supposed to be so meditative that the insects treated you like just another inanimate object. The boy frowned and slid toward me down the bench, snatching up my bowl. Then he slunk back to the buffet. His face maintained its angelic repose as he lumped honey, then tahini, and finally two big spoonfuls of raspberry jam onto my yogurt. Without even looking, he pinched up a slice of watermelon and combed it in like a tiara, ordaining my breakfast a festive dessert. He returned and plopped the bowl down in front of me.

"Technical support."

But before I could say anything he was loping off to the kitchen. I called out a breathless *thank you*, which, once again, the boy ignored. I wondered if his rude benevolence was a Slavic thing or a teenage thing and, most importantly, how old he actually was.

Eating my breakfast, I watched the commune children. They seemed to run around all day, seducing adults into games with their confident eye contact, and tripping over without crying. The Bulgarian's child was there, darting between the legs of the sexiest men on the commune, as if specially trained. He dashed from man to man and then back toward his mother, who was always belly-laughing with someone young and attractive while carrying a basket of raw potatoes. It might have been her big Bulgarian flat-footedness, but the woman seemed solid in her body and at home in every space she occupied. It was also, somehow, the fact of her child—flitting around with animal grace and his own natural entitlement—that gave the Bulgarian that extra degree of earthly affiliation. She seemed to have it all; a child *and* her freedom; young, handsome paramours *and* the absence of an ego. The Bulgarian and her child made me feel silly sitting there, eating my indulgent breakfast. My appetite felt shameful. As if I had already had enough, had my fill, and someone else—younger? more productive?—deserved it more than I did. Was I here to kill that sense of shame? Or to kill the self who felt it? I figured I was about to find out. This morning was the final death journey.

After breakfast I went straight to the courtyard outside the stone hut, where I was cornered at the shoe pile by the American.

"Vivian said you were writing a book about Ayn Rand."

But he was smiling. I guffawed through the question: "You *like* Ayn Rand?"

"Oh, I loved her in high school. She helped me through my cystic acne and probably, if I'm honest, through my parents' whole divorce."

It was a shock to hear her name here. Yet it didn't feel misplaced.

"I think she got the stuff about self-esteem right," he continued. "She just failed to remove the 'self.'"

I nodded, unsure. I didn't want to be thinking about Ayn Rand. Especially not at this critical moment. It had disturbed me that, with her invocation, I'd felt my heart lift, nudged by the tough stem of pride. Thankfully, the gong rang and the American took my hand and led me into the hut. Inside, everyone already sat facing a partner. Ayn hovered in my thoughts, edging the question toward me. *Could* I still be writing a book about Ayn Rand? Did I even still want to be a writer? Being one seemed counterintuitive to the eradication of the ego. If the personality was a defensive response to shame, then writing had to be a full artillery assault.

The American and I walked to a pair of yoga cushions at the far end of the room and sat facing each other. The curtains were drawn and the room became cool and dark and smoky with incense. In my periphery I could just make out Vivian entering and scuttling over to the whirling boy, who welcomed her into the deep folds of his skirt. The facilitator was walking around the group, stopping to murmur aphoristic encouragements and ask profoundly rhetorical questions. When he got to me, his sad eyes pinched with scrutiny.

"Something has already killed you."

For a moment I thought he meant I had won. That my ego was already dead. And then I realized he was asking me a question.

"Yes," I said. "It was *The New York Times*."

He nodded. "You were sacrificed. For the betterment of society."

I held my face very tight, trying not to dissolve into tears before I had received his wisdom.

"Sending the individual into exile to cleanse the sins of the group." He looked sagely into the distance. "Is a very ancient practice."

By now I knew the drill. "That the Greeks invented?"

"The Greeks *updated* it. Instead of sacrificing the goat, they drove the man out with stones."

"Lucky for the goats."

The facilitator ignored this. "The Greek word is *pharmakon* and it means 'sacrifice' and also 'cure.'" His wet eyes pooled toward me. "Because the poison and the medicine are one."

"Like Big Pharma?"

He raised a flat, obstructing palm. "No politics please."

"Sorry, I was joking."

"Yes," he said pointedly. "Time to get rid of that too."

His chastisement felt good, or at least, it made me want to die. The facilitator took a deep breath and exhaled it slowly right into my face. The warm air parched my eyeballs and I blinked back at him, grateful but afraid. He moved on and then, through the speakers, sitar music began its twangy serpentine ascent. A few moments later the facilitator was back at the front of the room, ringing the Tibetan gong. Then he gave us our instructions.

Staring into our partner's left eye, we had to apologize to someone in our lives whom we had hurt. And then another person. And then the person we felt least like apologizing to; someone who still made us feel wronged and hurt and angry. And then we had to apologize to that person, over and over again.

The room devolved into screaming quickly followed by howling. For the first few moments I could think only of my reviewers, which now seemed petty. And then I thought of my mother. I knew my crime. Painting her walls with poop the week her baby died. I had no memory of the painting, no recollection of pooping into the bucket or swishing my mother's hair brush through the sludgy paste. The only part of it I could recall was Jackie's reaction. And it was small. A silent pain rising in her face like water behind a door.

"Sorry," I said to the American. But the word was like tissue in my mouth. Like hollow sound, like the human microphone. The more I said it the less meaning it had, like I was speaking gibberish. And then something strange happened. The singular left-side focus along with the dim light, sage smoke, and collective will to die started playing tricks on my vision. The American's face flashed black and white like a photo negative and he began to peel back in layers, sliding through the different stages of a human life. First his features had the soft roundness of a child, then a sharper boy, an angular young man, and soon he was gaunt and finally the skin wizened and cracked and the bones began protruding whitely through his cheeks. In his old man's face I was surprised to see Antifa's. Old Antifa. And in Old Antifa's glazy eyes an ancient hurt glistened; in his quivering mouth a deep anguish gaped. My heart rushed toward Old Antifa and I felt the silky, sickening breach of our beings.

"I'm sorry," I whimpered.

Because somewhere on the space-time continuum Antifa was already dead. I saw the death in him, how it drained the color from his face and made him seem delicate and vulnerable. Removed and preserved. My eyes burned with tears. To see your enemies as *aufheben* must've been some sort of spiritual practice. Encouraged, I tried to picture Jackie dead but her face wouldn't materialize inside my partner's, and then trying to kill her made me feel bad. In the middle of this confusion, the gong rang again and the facilitator told us to lie down and cover our eyes with a meditation mask. I felt disoriented but the facilitator had already begun to lead the group through a guided visualization. This flustered me; I was bad at making my mind conform to someone else's vision. He asked us to picture ourselves on a mountain, and I forced myself up onto a lunar hillside, staring out over the dark blue suit of the Aegean. Then he told us to place a hand on our hearts and feel the emptiness. To hear the deep silence and let the total nothingness fill us. It was this acceptance of ourselves, he said, of our essence, and of reality itself, that was true happiness. A bliss that was the actual texture of existence. It was an abundance, he said, that flowed from our hearts and out into the world. I remembered the overflowing joy of Ayn's metal enthusiast, Hank Rearden, and then I tried to feel what the facilitator was describing as a bliss so powerful it split the skin, shooting out in flashes and flooding the whole universe with light.

But I couldn't quite see it. Or rather what I saw was a goat. In my mind's eye it stood beside me, nibbling at my shoelaces. The goat looked bored, which made me giggle. And now I felt bad, like I was undermining the exercise. But this only seemed to make the goat more willful. I tried to stay with the group as they shot through the sky like comets of white light, and into the outer strata of the atmosphere. I drifted along behind; flying over the Earth, the goat flying beside me, nibbling at purple tufts of stardust. I decided that the creature had to represent my contrarianism and felt that I was momentarily succeeding, a feeling of competence at killing my ego that then immediately served to strengthen it. Faintly in the distance, I could hear the group being guided back to Earth, floating down over gray Europe and the Greek Islands, sailing lower toward Lesvos and the commune until they were all sliding one by one down the chimney and into the dark stone room. They had all merged with their enemies, dropped their shame, and died, I presumed, and were now back to live lives of blissful, egoless freedom.

Whereas I felt unchanged. I hadn't even dropped my shame; that sadistic welder of my personality and art. And with the goat I had somehow made a joke of the whole exercise—worse, a kind of *pun*. I floated down the chimney, making my ignoble reentry with the stubborn ungulate drifting along behind, dropping shit pellets on all the silky eye masks.

At lunch, everyone looked enlightened. They sat in silent, happy groups, relishing their hummus and pita and the air in their lungs. Even Vivian looked content. She sat on a bench at the far end of the dining hut, cross-legged and facing the Belarussian ex-model. They were eating Greek salad very slowly while gazing intently into each other's eyes. I hated hummus. It made me think of camel shit mixed with sand, of desert fertilizer—an observation I couldn't even make in this sanctimonious company, where satire was considered evidence of a robust ego. Alienated, I went to lie down in the hut.

Having failed to die, I was now left with the worst possible outcome. My self was wounded but it wasn't dead. I could feel it dragging along behind me like a limb I'd tried to sever. It was angry. Bitter and vengeful. And all the lentils and chickpeas they fed us were giving me gas. I lay in the tiny sweating hut with its sauna walls and its porky pink curtains, hating the smell of my own farts. At least I wasn't a narcissist. But whatever this was felt terrible.

There was only one thing that ever helped me. One thing that had always been there, tingling at the base of my brain, pinning the moments, prodding and flipping them. Only writing promised me happiness, or at the very least progress. But I knew that it required an ego. Especially my kind of writing. The kind of jokes that I was craving; all the spiky little adjectives marinating in my saliva. Already I could feel the details of the Bulgarian's camel toe crowning in a laugh at the back of my larynx. And what about the rest of them? Evidently, if humanity killed their egos, people would move like sloths, lacking the motivation to call insect exterminators or erect functional doors. Nobody would bother to make art, or not good art. Maybe they'd make the kind of art I'd seen at the children's art station. Big happy sunflowers and people holding hands. Maybe bad people made good art and good people made art more suitable for children. And maybe I wasn't actually here to merge with the group. Maybe some people simply had to be separate. How else would we know which parts were funny?

I took my laptop and walked up to reception, where I had noticed several bicycles thrust up against the side wall. None were locked and I figured it was an honor system like the laundry room floor onto which people threw their white linen garments and then, with astounding optimism, retrieved them from the clothesline six hours later. I took a red bicycle and pushed it out the gate. Looking back at the compound I felt sharp and sealed against the world, like the cone of a pencil.

The beach town was now packed with women. They walked the streets in pairs and small groups, drinking beers and pinching each other's bottoms. I rode to a café at the end of the board-walk where there were a few empty tables. On the window I saw a poster for something called the Women's Festival. It was vague on details but appeared to have attracted hundreds of middle-aged and older Northern European lesbians. They had occupied much of the beach below: spread out on towels, warming their tan, leathery limbs.

I took a table near the taps and gazed out at the huge, loaf-like rock. Big Cock Rock, I thought, as I watched a man go hurtling off the top of it. Why did men need to do this? My father was always jumping off cliffs into bodies of ice-cold water. As a child he'd dragged me along with him, bullying me to the top of precarious boulders that sheered off into deep turgid pools. Having already lost a boy, my father was somewhat nonbinary about placing me in confrontation with my own mortality. There was often a rope swing and a set of shivering teenage boys egging one another toward the edge. I felt for them, seeing the mix of fear and defiance on their faces; the shame of cowardice and the loneliness of knowing that no one was going to protect you. Maybe because a dead boy was just a soldier; whereas a dead girl was now named and invoked as tragedy, inciting mass movements. I could feel all my wrong opinions bubbling back up, and enjoyed the little bump of self.

The Beloveds, I knew, believed in the very passive notion of karma. Passive and thus controversial to those in the business of world-impacting. At dinner the night before, I had heard an energetic Australian man say climate activists were interfering with the natural course of karmic destruction. I liked the contrarianism of this, the nihilism of it. The fact that we were all, ultimately, going to be canceled. There was ego death in this idea but there was also just the potential for a whole lot more fun.

Behind me, I heard a loud slurping sound, and then a glass clanked down on the table. I turned around and saw the Slavic boy, sitting alone in his filthy white T-shirt and shredded track pants. His hair sat up in dready yellow spooks. If I hadn't known where he lived, I would have assumed he was homeless.

"This lesbians have the aura of ancient beings." He nodded down at the packed beach. "Like they is from the nother planet."

This was better, at least, than the skinny Italian's homophobia. And it was true that the lesbians possessed a sort of geological dignity lying there in their silent pairs, enjoying the gentle broil of the sun. But now I was worried about Scientology.

"Do you think aliens should be allowed to wear basketball shorts?"

The boy squinted at me. His small eyes slit as his mouth bunched right up into his nose. And then, just as suddenly, the tight screw of his face unsprung.

"Baby, this is very hectic joke!"

"Thank you." I was blushing. Flattered to have animated this surly teenager. Bewildered by the "baby."

"This Beloveds is clueless," he said, rolling his eyes, then bouncing his hands emphatically off the table. "They think only the Master can make jokes because they haven't read his books. They is big basics who think it spiritual to be wearing dick out of pants."

The description made me laugh. So we *were* allowed to make jokes; the Master decreed it.

"They is not like the original revolutionaries." His eyes got a sly twinkle. "This is why I am liking Americans. It is a very horny people."

"Uh, I think that's just the internet."

"Come on, baby!" He stared at me, incredulous. "Look at all the movie stars!"

"You mean the porn stars?"

"I am talking about *Tom Cruise*!" He threw his hands up in mock exasperation. "Matt Damon! Brad Pitt! Leo!" His face was pink with feeling. "They have huge life force! Huge spiritual potential!

"You think Leonardo DiCaprio has huge spiritual potential?"

"Oh, it is hard-core. You can see in his eyes."

"Isn't that just his ego?"

"Behind big ego is always big spiritual potential."

"But he dates teenagers?"

He shook his head sadly. "Leo have been wasting his life force like a basic pussybitch."

He was flirting with me and I felt dazed. Luckily the waitress was suddenly upon us, sliding a sticky menu under my nose. She looked tired and harried, and feeling guilty I ordered a beer.

"What about you?" I asked him.

"He just have water." The young woman swiped up his menu and marched off.

The boy took a big horny sip of his complimentary water and plonked the glass down, sloshing an ice cube over the side. "I am having no choice to be here," he said bluntly. "They is having a war in my country and my mother is crazy big drunk."

My body hunched toward him, but the boy remained stoic, informing me that this was the only commune where he could follow the teachings of his master, that he was lucky it was only a three-day train ride from his city, followed by a fourteen-hour boat. I felt bad that I'd taken a plane, that there was no war in my country, or not a bloody one, and that despite her quirks my mother was a stable person. Even so, I knew the boy didn't actually care about that, didn't see himself as a victim. It was cringe, he continued, that the Beloveds were horny but not for all of life, that they were unambitious but about replacing the internet router. And yet, he had found a way to exist here; meditating or else watching funny internet videos which, were he still alive, the Master would have loved.

I had to refrain from gazing at him with eyes of adoration. I felt awe at this boy, who had found spirituality even in YouTube videos. I had so many questions but once he had finished his story he stood. I thanked him for sharing and he leaned in over his chair, smiling, and then he kept smiling in a way that I knew meant sex.

"How old are you?" I said.

He blew a raspberry and started to walk off in his silent, dismissive way. And then he turned back.

"Eighteen."

Now he did a mad little jig with his eyebrows, which, in the eccentric alphabet of his repertoire, almost certainly meant he was lying.

I drank my beer as the sun set and then rode back to the commune. I took the main road out to the small gas station and turned off onto the dirt path. Here, the darkness swam in fast. To either side I could make out the low walls of large compounds, blank as passing freight cars. There were great blue swathes of creeping foliage, the odd window jeweling through like a citrine pendant. Their private warmth was somehow mine; a secret light had gone on inside me.

Halfway up the final incline I needed, suddenly and powerfully, to shit. I slammed the bike against the front wall and hurried down to the toilet block. The stalls were thankfully empty and I threw myself into one, latching its tiny door. The small shiv of wood hid my body from eyebrows to knees, so for privacy I dropped my head into my hands. Certain I was alone, I emptied myself, rapturously, into the toilet bowl. Then I heard the patter of bare feet.

"Baby? It is you?"

I froze and waited there, in hell.

"Seriously, baby! I am sure you are just running in here."

Under the door, I watched his big filthy feet slap away into the opposite stall. The shower whooshed on, and with it came a torrent of atonal babbling. I had heard similar sounds each morning coming from inside the stone hut and assumed this was another kind of meditation, which meant I might have time to escape the toilets without dying from shame. For the purposes of expedience I decided to utilize the fearsome bidet hose. I hadn't braved it before, having no sense of how to aim the hose and dreading the force of its spray. In my haste, I yanked the head off its hook and foisted it up between my legs. Then I pressed the lever down and felt a mighty blow to the face. I dropped the hose and it spun out, writhing between the wall and my thigh like a trapped snake. It shot mad arcs of gray water all over the stall, drenching my face and T-shirt. Finally I got hold of its neck and flicked the lever back, killing the jet. I was cold and wet, and tinglingly numb with what felt close to something like total egoic disintegration. I wiped and flushed and hurried out of the stall. But I was too late.

The boy was leaning against the sink mirror, naked and wet and grinning at me. I smiled back, dissociating. His body was a lean wash of golden tan; hairless except for the reddish fuzz of pubic hair. It was a body between forms—sliding toward adult musculature while maintaining the softer ebbs of boyhood. His penis was flaccid but man-sized.

"I am not having the towel."

He stared at me, poker-faced, as if daring me to find his naked body sexual. My heart pounded in my ears, making me dumb and focused like an animal.

"Take mine." I pulled my towel from the rack and held it out to him, averting my gaze.

He shook his head. "I am always like to be drying natural."

I nodded, keeping my head up and my eyes off his penis. Meanwhile he happily took in my soaking wet T-shirt.

"It was hectic job in there?"

I blushed and brought the towel up to dry my face, then rubbed my neck roughly, bringing a little sensation back to my body.

"Hummus is the garden fertilizer of the Middle East."

He grinned at me, understanding, at least, that I was attempting a joke. There was no trace of disgust in that smile; he was totally comfortable with the knowledge that I possessed a digestive system. I had never experienced this kind of mercifulness in an American man. Or actually.

"My old roommate used to leave his turds in the toilet."

The boy slapped his chest in amazement and water sprayed off his small pectorals and into my eyes.

"Your roommate is a Sufi!"

"Ah, no . . . I think he was Iranian American."

"He was a Sufi whirler! He has been trying to include you into his orbit!"

"Mmm, don't think so. Raffi was gay."

He clapped his hands in delight. "They are having so many gay in America! Such a big gay horny country! Such a huge spiritual potential!"

I was astonished. "You think Americans have huge spiritual potential?"

"Oh, it is hard-core." He was suddenly moving toward the exit. "Americans has gone crazy for the freedom."

I watched his long, lean body stride out into the moonlight, the bare buttocks slick and blue like some wonderful piece of machinery. I liked how strange he made me feel. Spiritual because I was American. Sexy despite having diarrhea. And like it might be possible to get enlightened and still keep your sense of humor.

Vivian didn't come home that night either. In the morning I dressed and took myself off to the early meditation. My commitment had waned but I found that this made it easier to relax. I didn't care if I failed, and inside the dark oyster of failing sat the shining pearl of success. Allegedly. Entering the silent void,

I couldn't help thinking of Baby: his cherubic face, luminous inside a mandala of fire. It wasn't total emptiness but it still felt like spiritual progress; of all the Beloveds, Baby was the closest to enlightened. And at least I wasn't seeing a goat.

At breakfast I made a majestic dash from muesli box to yogurt vat to honey jug, which I scooped up in a graceful arc, looping its amber tongue back into my bowl. My fingers danced over the apple slices, wasps spinning away in violent arabesques. Eating my hard-won breakfast I felt happy and just the tiniest bit entitled to my place here on Earth. Walking back along the path, Baby came up behind me.

"You know this movie: *Wolf of Wall Street*?"

I spun around, nodding cautiously.

"It is seriously magnificent movie." He sighed up at the sky. "There is very much life I am finding in it."

"You like bankers?"

"Bankers has enormous potential."

"They do?"

"And I love this guy: Yo-nah Hill."

"He's excellent."

He wagged a finger and told me that Jonah Hill had huge potential but not like Leo. Leo, he said, was hectic. He was the banker with the most spiritual potential because he was the one who had a nervous breakdown.

"Nervous breakdowns make you more spiritual?"

Baby nodded, his dreads bouncing out with spaceship gravity.

"Closer to enlightenment."

We wandered down to the empty bar area and then over the little bridge. There was a wooden plank bed strung up over the dry creek, but a couple had occupied it; the waifish man vigorously massaging the large woman's shoulders. Baby pointed out his tent farther down the ravine. He had erected it on the silty floor of the creek bed.

"I am sleeping with the spiders," he said, grinning diabolically.

I worried that this was where we were headed. The tent was small and sunken and all of his clothes seemed to be spilling out the open folds and into the dirt. I observed the grim tableaux of pant legs kicked out over slimy rocks and shirtsleeves punching across the mud. Baby's home had the grisly aesthetic of a special-victims crime scene. A filthy teddy bear sat up on a large rock, appearing to lay claim to all the carnage.

"I am showing you," he said proudly. "But not today."

I felt quietly elated as we bypassed the tent. Baby led me up the hill toward the geodesic dome. In the daylight I now saw that it was built from tent poles and strips of orange fabric. It looked less like a glowing testicle and more like a gigantic basketball. Inside, the sun bent through the gaps in white-hot shafts. Baby flicked out a couple of yoga mats and then lay down on his stomach. I minced over and lay beside him, propping my chin girlishly on my hands. We were playing, I understood. Whether it would ever amount to actual physical contact, I had no idea. Though I knew I should be careful. He was very young.

After a few silent moments, I sensed he was staring at my profile and so I turned coquettishly to face him. Now his eyes dipped lower, to my lips.

"Nice mustache."

But before I could plunge through the gelid waters of shame, his face was blurring fast toward me. Baby's lips pushed wet against my mouth, opening into a forceful kiss. I could feel a light, grazing stubble on his chin and some crusty acne scabs, but when my hand found the bulk of his shoulder I relaxed in the knowledge that he was considerably bigger than me. He rolled on top of me and his genitals pressed thick and ropey against my groin. I fastened my legs around his hips and we began to slowly grind. I felt like a teenager—locked with some sweet-smelling boy in a fumbling ecstasy of frottage. Whatever his age, I told myself, the rules in Greece had to be looser. And then, rushing toward climax Baby suddenly stopped, raised his hand, and squinted at me hawkishly.

"Tom Cruise high five," he said, smiling with all his teeth.

I froze and waited for Tom Cruise to go away.

"Don't leave me hanging, baby."

My hand slid up and limply met his palm. I felt helpless and confused and somehow humiliated. And then as he resumed his grinding, I felt the flinty beginnings of an orgasm. Baby whipped himself back up into a humping frenzy and then, again, he froze. High-fived me. And the cycle repeated. Each time he got too excited, Baby paused in the spiritual essence of Tom Cruise. I came three times. It was some combination of the psychotic look in his eyes and the feeling that he wasn't actually looking at me at all. After the fourth Tom Cruise, Baby let himself flop off sideways onto his back.

"I am preserving my chi," he explained. "Coming is for basics."

Afterward, Baby had to send an email. To his mother, who was desperately worried about him. He had escaped conscription and a war zone and yet, according to her, he'd still done the wrong thing. I didn't want to psychoanalyze, as Baby (or at least the Master) didn't believe in it, but the woman sounded borderline. She thought he'd be safer back home with her in the one-bedroom apartment they shared with a floorful of Georgian truck drivers. Baby wiggled his arm out from under me and jumped up. I wished him luck with his email, careful not to sound too invested in his life.

Walking back down the hill and into the commune, I felt a sharp new aliveness. The sort of feeling I had anticipated having after the death journey; how it felt jumping off large rocks into freezing cold water. It was a deep sense of integration; as though my cells had rearranged themselves and somehow stumbled upon some meaning. Like my life was, in and of itself, significant. Worth living. Tears sprang to my eyes, and I felt gratitude. I even felt gratitude for the cynicism I felt feeling gratitude. Whatever I was, in that moment, it was okay.

And then I saw the Bulgarian's noodlehead. He was at the art station, painting a picture of a woman with full bosom, smiling serenely. At first I thought it was his mother, but then I saw the book lying open beside him. The noodlehead was painting the Mona Lisa. I approached him gingerly; I was bad with children and wanted no trouble with him or his formidable parent. When I reached the tarpaulin, I paused and made a noise with my feet so as not to startle him. The kid turned around and looked at me, warily. I understood. I had nothing to offer his mother.

"Do you like Leonardo da Vinci?"

The noodlehead shrugged and returned to his painting. "No, but other people does."

For a moment I felt a strange compulsion to test my parenting style on this conveniently communal child. "You know, it doesn't matter what other people like."

The boy shook his noodles dismissively. "Matter if selling on Facebook Marketplace."

So this was her scheme. The child painted Mona Lisas for the ironic internet while she slept her way around the commune. I was appalled and impressed and wondered how much money he got for them. But I didn't ask. I could sense the kid was uncomfortable and wanted me to leave. So I continued on up the path to the outdoor bar, where I lay in a hammock for what must've been the duration of an email written to a borderline mother. Baby found me there afterward and suggested we ride bikes to the beach.

We took two from the front wall and rode down to the nudist end. Reaching the sand, Baby flung off his shorts and started marching toward the straw huts. His body had a muscular ranginess that made me think of a big cartoon cat up on its hind legs. I shimmied off my sundress and skipped along behind. Inside the hut, he took my phone and typed something into a Google search. The title blinked up over his shoulder: "Best of Tom Cruise Running Montage." I squeezed in beside him and together we enjoyed the eighteen-minute video.

There was Tom Cruise running across the tops of buildings; Tom scrambling over landing planes; Tom's legs pedaling through the air as buildings exploded behind him; Tom fleeing from alien spacecraft and lurching tsunamis and great black plumes of tumbling smoke. I watched with smiling delight and then I watched Baby watching—intently, almost prayerfully— as his hero ran and ran and ran. When it was finished he tossed the phone onto the sand and rolled on top of me.

"Baby is big Hollywood writer," he cooed.

I wriggled under him, trying to turn my embarrassment into more of a sexy, slithery dance. I was not a big Hollywood writer and I wanted him to like me for my soul (despite the fact that they were all famously equal) and how it expressed itself in my unique physical form. That he'd appreciated my mustache had felt like a promising start. Baby pinned me under his hips and planted a kiss on my left breast.

"Brad," he announced. And then my right. "Pitt."

I smiled up at him, mystified.

"I think they are looking something like the face of Brad Pitt."

I wondered if he meant that my nipples resembled the wizened pink pucker of Brad's aging lips or something even more insulting. But there wasn't time to get upset.

"Now we are making love."

It wasn't phrased like a question, though Baby had learned English from the Master's books and videos where everything he said was a statement of fact. I was not about to correct his grammar. I kissed him and he nudged his pelvis at my crotch, then slowly pushed himself inside me. But as soon as he was in Baby went completely still. He squeezed his eyes shut and ground his jaw.

"No, no, no," he whispered.

It was mortifying. Was he trying to retract his consent? While he was still inside me? I searched his face but already the tension was fading and a smile had curled into his lips. Baby cupped a hand to his mouth and gave himself the soft roar of a cheering crowd.

"I have preserved my chi," he announced, and began to push himself deeper inside me.

Baby moved extraordinarily slow. His momentum was barely perceptible but he built gradually to a trembling, eye-fluttering climax that he then, once again, suddenly terminated. Squeezing and clenching and seemingly trying to disappear until the threat abated and he relaxed. His palm sailed up and he squinted down with the wolfish smolder of Tom Cruise.

"High five, baby."

And now came a huge yawning heat. For a moment I considered preserving my own chi, but then I thought, *No—chi is different for women.* Especially older women who might not get another chance to waste their chi on a beach in paradise with a beautiful young boy. I looked into his piercing eyes and let the enemy in.

This time, as I came, I felt a tickle in my ribs and then a fast, rising laughter. It surprised me, rushing up on the hot current of orgasm. My eyes burned and tears came bursting out in big, luscious splashes. I was crying but even the sound of it, the rolling *huh-huh-huh* of my sobs, threw me back into rapturous laughter. My mind turned like a wheel, my thoughts like water slipping through its spokes; a downgoingness that resisted everything but the sensation of the fall. The Tom Cruise dropped from Baby's face as he watched me, enthralled.

"Baby," he congratulated me. "You are having the nervous breakdown."

I wondered later if the sadism of having to high-five Tom Cruise had temporarily annihilated my ego. Leaving the straw hut it certainly felt annihilated. As I walked out onto the beach the world was once again sharper and brighter and coursing with new significance. The dark sea lapped against the stones with rumbling, elemental mystery; the evening sky was a tease of euphemistic purples. Walking along the shore, my atoms buzzed at the perfect pitch; I was pure gliding energy, matter without form. I didn't need anything. Not food nor sleep nor conversation. Death didn't scare me; becoming nothing but dirt or sand or seaweed. And if I stayed like this for days or weeks? I didn't care. If it killed me, that was perfect too. I wondered if all the Beloveds felt like this. It seemed unlikely that they, too, had discovered such a specific form of tantra.

We found our bikes and rode to a tiki bar on the boardwalk. Baby ordered a banana split and we sat on the deck in blissful silence. My joy skirted over surfaces, landing on the gold froth of the tide or the deep blue of the sand or a seagull gently planing. Every few minutes I would burst into a big, loony smile. Baby sipped his complimentary water, grinning like the doctor of a convalescing patient.

The thought of altruism seemed absurd now. The boundless ecstasy I felt was the only thing that people needed, and sharing it the only way to truly help them. Though even the concept of help felt anathema to such a vast and all-encompassing joy. A drag on the totality, a small, human interference. I also noticed another, less enlightened feeling. Baby was treating me *a lot* like his girlfriend. I could feel the little puff of ego but I didn't want to make it die. It seemed possible for both things to exist: spiritual enlightenment and emotional attachment to a cute boy. The Master had managed to be both sage and lover. Why couldn't I? I was like Baby, like the original revolutionaries—horny for all of life.

As our young waitress set down Baby's banana split, I could sense her discomfort. I knew she was trying to figure out whether the age difference between Baby and me was diabolical or just eccentric. What this oddball, Slavic Adonis was doing with a boring, middle-aged American woman. Watching him spoon the whipped cream onto his tongue, I began to feel proprietary. Not just because I knew I would be paying for his food, but because the joy of watching him eat it felt earned.

And so I was happy now to think of Ayn. Her belief that intellectual courage could be sexually attractive. That a desire for the highest caliber of woman—a free thinker who wasted no time trying to be hot—was a response to one's own values as expressed in the Other, and a sign of mutual exaltation. Unlike

Ayn, I had even been brave enough to have a nervous breakdown. Once Baby was finished I paid our bill and left the waitress a big, smug tip.

When we returned to the commune, Baby went straight to the
Wi-Fi room and I headed to the hut for my reading material.
The week before, unsure that I would succeed in killing my ego
and thus never write again, I had packed my one unread Ayn
Rand biography. I had never successfully abandoned a project;
the waste of time and energy felt nearly intolerable. I realized it
wasn't like a miscarriage, but it was like losing some sort of little
life. I knew the biography mostly explored the affair Ayn had
had in late middle age with a man twenty-five years her junior. I
hadn't opened the book yet, but now I was curious.

I took it out to the lounge area and lay down on a divan
below the buzzing canopy. The bees and wasps swam between
the green and the whole sky fizzed with photosynthetic activity
while that wild objectless joy kept rising through my cells. For
the first time in my life I felt no fear of tiny stinging insects.
And in this ecstatic, loving spirit, I began to read.

The philosophical connection between Ayn and her cute
young acolyte had gradually become sexual, and after many intense late-night colloquies, Ayn and Nathaniel had agreed to
tell their spouses, rationalizing the affair as an act of selfishness
in tune with Randian philosophy. Ayn's husband, Frank, and
Nathaniel's wife, Barbara (also a Randian and the author of this
biography), were both told that the open marriage was an ethical opportunity for all of them. No one mentioned the word
"ego" but the implication was that love could breach marital
bounds without hurting the self-esteem of the individual. There

was no limited supply of love; loving Nathaniel wouldn't make Ayn a less doting wife to Frank. It was also a wonderful test of self-resilience and emotional independence. Furthermore, jealousy was anti-rational and barbarous insofar as it threatened the highest human value: individual freedom.

Reading this in an ecstasy of postcoital bliss, it felt profound. Like Ayn was speaking to me from the grave. As if, despite her atheism, she lived on in the ether, inspiring tech savants and finance bros and even little old traitorous me. Her message was newly clear: there was enough love to go around. You really could love two men and all billionaires and maybe even a bee. A whole swarm of them. Ayn believed that *love*—of the self and those who loved themselves—was our greatest asset and anyone who tried to regulate or restrain it was constraining the very lifeblood of our humanity.

Across the bar I saw the young Slavic girl rise from her hammock. She was wearing a blue bodysuit much like the one I had taken to the laundry two days earlier and never recovered. The suit was a striking departure from the whites and creams of the group aesthetic, and although it was painful to observe the bodysuit's fickle elasticity—its dark skin stretched in rapturous bloom across the girl's full bosom—the garment obviously belonged to me. But I was determined to maintain my good mood. The laundry was a communal affair. The only separation that existed there was whites from colors. It was probably an honest mistake. As the girl approached, I smiled and waved.

"The suit looks amazing on you," I told her.

"Thank you so much!"

She did a little twirl and then continued walking slowly toward the bar. My joy dipped. I had just merged with the whole cosmos but sharing Lycra was obscene. The Master didn't believe in parents owning children but he definitely believed in people owning *stuff.*

"I actually lost one just like it in the laundry."

"Yes!" She paused, beaming at me. "We all lose things in the laundry!"

Her statement was less an admission of guilt than a bad aphorism. I was getting impatient.

"You mean we lose them," I said. "And then we find them again?"

"Or the thing was never ours."

I blinked at her. Shaken to my core. Then I searched her face for a twist of irony, a twinkle of humor. Finding no trace of either, I became frantic.

"So you're saying that it's *your* bodysuit?"

"I'm saying the world of objects is mysterious."

"You don't think it's a crazy coincidence?"

The girl threw her hands up and laughed. "Let yourself be surprised!"

"Surprised by what?"

"How things always seem to be all about us."

I watched the shapely ass glide away, held in the humble grasp of my own aged nylon. I felt sick and wanted nothing more to do with the bodysuit—seeing how beautifully it accentuated her figure. But I was baffled by our interaction. It seemed pointed, and Baby-related, though I'd already confirmed that he thought of the girl as an older Slavic sister. Meeting in the showers on his first day, she'd taught him how to shave and later how to use a knife and fork and now he had all her streaming passwords. He claimed they'd never slept together. *I am not like American man,* he'd told me. *Sleeping with the horny stepsister.* Whatever it was I didn't trust her, and later that night I told Baby.

"In Polish," he said, "there is thirty different word for 'thief.'"

It was a relief to be back in his arms, in my hut, away from the prying eyes of the Beloveds. I told him that the girl had made it sound like we were just sharing and Baby said that no, you couldn't share clothes, but also, you couldn't get attached to objects. I thought of the Master's three hundred and fifty Harley-Davidsons, but before I could say anything Baby had knelt and pulled his pants down.

"I am putting my penis in your mouth."

It wasn't a question but I took the feminist trouble to ask myself and discover that I did, in fact, want to have his penis inside my mouth. And he knew I did. We were in tune, his sensitive instrument predicting my oceanic needs. Kneeling on the bed I leaned toward his naked crotch and Baby placed his flaccid member onto my waiting tongue like a fillet on a grill. He remained stubbornly soft for the first minute of my exertions. I worked hard, the penis bobbing in my mouth like a blind sea vegetable. When he did eventually start to stiffen, Baby extended his arm for a Tom Cruise high five.

"Jehweemohgwhaya," I responded.

"What, baby?"

I withdrew my mouth and blinked up at him.

"Jerry Maguire," I requested.

Now a trembling intensity came into his face. He kicked a leg out and then wheeled his arms around, drawing the hands up into two tortured claws as he breathed through clenched bottom teeth.

"Help *me* help *you*," he pleaded.

I redoubled my efforts. As I lurched back and forth, Baby threw punches in the air.

"Help *me* help *you*!"

He wheeled his arms around again and let his other leg flick out, making familiar exasperations from the famous locker room scene. My mouth sounds got wetter and slappier and then cruelly flatulent, but this only increased the sublime sense of degradation. I tried to tighten my grip and then to loosen the suction's seal but nothing would stop the constant stream of gastric audio. I gagged and hot tears came stinging into my eyes. Now Baby's body began to shudder. It heaved with the onrush of a monstrous orgasm.

"Uh-oh."

The friction of our flesh made one final squeak before cold shame shot like torchlight through my body. My mind went black and starry as my mouth filled with liquid heat. Receiving him, I felt somehow that I *was* him. All my mental chaos condensed, conducted pin-like by the steel instrument of his being. And for one deep, vertical moment his power over me was mine.

"My chi," Baby said sadly, extracting himself from my mouth.

But he came over every night. Baby walked his sandy feet across my floor, left the mosquito door open, broke the lamp. He lay in bed eating from a box of Cheerios and watching YouTube compilations. There was mid-career Tom Cruise and late-career Nicolas Cage. There was everything that John Travolta had ever done. It had something to do with nostalgia, I thought. And possibly dads. He hadn't told me about his own father but I assumed he was dead or not in the picture. When we talked it was about the Master or my life in Los Angeles or New York. He loved to hear about the other boys, the older men, the goat yoga. He delighted in all the new American religions—the juice god, the sugar demon, the gender holy wars. We had much to teach each other.

Vivian had also decided to stay at the commune a little longer. The whirling demigod had turned out to be a Chinese Brit who'd left his job at an Oxford think tank to study Sufism with various gurus around the world. Vivian preferred the exotic Belarussian with her llama face and the monkish bowl cut she'd just received to mark her queer transition and hide her from all the jet-setting jealous lovers. Vivian still intended to take her own newfound enlightenment across the island to the detention center. But carrying on a queer romance among Syrian and Afghani asylum seekers would be tricky, and so she was delaying her expedition. In the meantime, our living arrangement—that I would remain in the hut and Vivian would sleep in the Belarussian's tent at the other end of the commune—fell naturally into place.

Each morning Baby and I went to the early meditation. Then it was breakfast and a morning discourse or yoga class taught by a long-limbed Norwegian person. Baby usually disappeared after that and I rode my bike down to the beach, where I wrote mean descriptions of commune members or else read my Ayn Rand biography. I wasn't sure how to bring the two worlds together. Ayn Rand would never have visited a place like this, or only if she'd been promised an island full of adoring young men. Though, reading on, I learned that Ayn's taste for young flesh had begun to sour when her affair with Nathaniel took a nasty turn. After several blissful years, Nathaniel Branden had stopped wanting to sleep with Ayn. He'd called it everything from gas to stress to hero worship. What it was really about was age, aka his fear of dying. Nathaniel had stopped feeling attracted to Ayn but couldn't tell her and risk losing his mentor and business partner. He couldn't risk undermining their whole philosophy and calling the bedrock of Objectivism into question. And, of course, the waning of their sex life had made Ayn paranoid and depressed.

She'd stopped writing and spent hours each day on the phone to Nathaniel, trying to talk through his "emotional blocks." But they went in circles; Objectivism was useless on a subject lying to protect his interlocutor's feelings. Ten years on, Nathaniel had become just another middle-aged man, terrified of losing his boner. And Ayn Rand, though she would have railed at the verb, had been badly gaslit. Her ideal man was less than ideal.

All of this gave me great confidence in Baby. Not just because he was young but because I knew he'd never age. You couldn't, claimed the Master, when you didn't fear death. Baby was fearless and even welcomed death-fear as an opportunity to kill off more of his ego. My pruny elder nipples, I conceded, were just more shining stones on his path to enlightenment.

—

Baby didn't believe the rumors about the Master. In fact, he had little interest in history and distrusted anyone who tried to wield their knowledge of the past. In this way, he was quite Randian. Believing in the pure, unmediated will of the present moment, Baby took this disinterest in historical circumstance impressively far. He claimed to have never heard of 9/11. He thought Osama bin Laden was a former American president and got #MeToo confused with Y2K, which he then mistook for a type of K-pop. He listened wide-eyed to my stories but sometimes I wondered how much he could truly care about contemporary urban life in America. He had never read a novel and was saving all of Western philosophy for after he had attained enlightenment; there was no point knowing things, he said, until you had the spiritual depth to understand them.

Baby's favorite was the laughter meditation. It was infrequently practiced at the commune, which he claimed was more

evidence of the group's pathetic reformism. The laughter meditation was the most radical and transcendent of all of the Master's techniques. People had gone mad. They had fallen into
rapturous fits and had to be hosed down. A few had continued
laughing long after the gong; hours, days—unable to stop themselves. Existence itself had become terminally funny. In other
words, the laughter meditation really worked.

At the end of that week the dinner bell rang and a stern,
skeletal Austrian woman announced that there would be a
laughter meditation that evening in the grove. Baby was ecstatic.
He high-fived me over the table and then hurried off to clean his
dinner plate. I felt exposed by the high five. It was part of our
private sexual language and the sacred key to my pleasure and
here he was flouting it in the crowded dining hut. But I made
myself let it go. I wasn't going to miss tonight's meditation.

When I arrived, a large group was already assembled under
the oak tree. I walked straight to Baby and sat down. A few
people gave me knowing smiles. Mostly the older Scandinavian
women; the blue beads of their eyes shining back from some
gauzy sexual other side. Young men had loved them too, I imagined. Baby said it was because we had less ego than younger
women, yet also, somehow, had more of ourselves. What exactly
was that "self" we had more of that did not involve our egos? I
had no idea. But by now I understood that the ego came and
went and was something you killed gradually over time. And
also, whenever things confused me, I called it paradox and an
opportunity to die.

We waited on the cool tiles for several minutes before the Master's voice came slithering through the speakers. "There is almost
no difference," he susurrated, "between the child and the sage."

Baby's body tightened beside me. The Master was talking

about him, or someone like him, and Baby knew this too. He was special, and nothing like the American boys I had met, saturated with information but scared to test their knowledge on the teeth of the world. There was something both innocent and wise about Baby. Something I wanted to protect. A familiar quality of youth. An irreverence removed from meanness or hatred; a genuine sense of playfulness. Baby wanted the dour veils to lift, to bring life to what was dead.

The Master had continued, imploring us to reclaim our childlike innocence. Meditation, he said, was the obvious way to do this. By silencing the thinking brain, you were restored to your natural state of childlike wonder. His dopey eyes got a devilish glint. But the other thing that did it, he said, was laughter.

The screen went black and the stern Austrian appeared in front of it. I had often seen her humming beside a tree or else shushing the chatty Italians. Now she stepped up onto the low parapet surrounding the oak and raised the meditation cymbal. Her eyes fell closed and she paused in a long spell of waiting that began to feel punitive. Only once the whispering had completely ceased did she release a deep, humorless sigh, and strike the gong.

The familiar sound was twangier and somehow comic, and I watched the Austrian's face break into a smile and then, amazingly, she was laughing. It was infectious and immediately low chuckles began rumbling through the group. People around me started rocking back and forth, hooting at one another. I saw Baby make eye contact with the big, buff Cretan who wore a toga and was always braiding some woman's hair. They watched each other, laughing—Baby's voice husky and the Cretan's oddly high and squeaking. Their laughter lit the furnace of my own and with it rose a hungry inner eye, searching for material.

My gaze landed on the frizzy-haired Parisian woman I'd

seen scrubbing the bathroom floor in expensive-looking kaftans. She'd handed me a business card alleging she was both a PhD and a shaman. Locking eyes with her now, I began to find something very funny. Nothing specifically, and sort of everything. From the woman's large, placid eyelids to the mole on her chin, and the relentless fact of her laughter—her whole face burning and gleaming at me. I was doing it, I congratulated myself. Losing my mind. And as I thought this, the laughter naturally receded. But I knew I'd come close.

Delirious, the shaman and I drifted apart and I found myself crawling between other crawling bodies or bodies that were rocking or rolling on their backs, all eager to meet my gaze and catch new strains of the contagion. At the foot of the oak tree, I stopped and stared up at the leaves, my whole nervous system moving in harmony with breezy nature. I could feel the giggles waiting, a cresting wave at the prow of my chest. And then a shadow moved across my body and I saw the American stagger past, his shoulders spasming in laughter. Baby was pursuing him; his arms bent dorsally at either side of his chest, hands flapping, in what appeared to be a crude pantomime of homosexuality. I glanced around to see if anyone else was objecting, but the only witness was the Oxford Sufi watching with his usual calm detachment. Baby slunk toward the American in a demonic catwalk, and now the Sufi giggled. Baby spun around. Seeing the Sufi, he raised his fingers to his eyes and then drew them outward into two dark slits.

"*Ching chong cha!*" he chanted. "*Ching chong chu cha ching chong cha!*"

Baby had stepped off a ledge, and the three of us went with him. Surrendered. Or submitted. Surrendered, I decided, laughing harder. It was wondrous. My laughter rolled into tears, forgot its own subject, and spilled over into mindless rapture.

We laughed and laughed, held together, suspended in audacity's high bouncing net. This was where I wanted to be. Forever. In the bliss of a collective nervous breakdown.

And then the Sufi looked at me and threw an arm out across his own chest, extended from the shoulder to the flexed beak of his fingers. Recognizing the gesture, shock slapped me right out of my body. He was doing the Heil. I laughed, but it felt forced and this killed my joy. I was suddenly dry, untickled, untouched. Slowly, I drew back from the others, from our warm, amniotic unity. It was hypocritical and terribly off-brand, but I was offended.

My dad didn't pick up. He was probably fitting someone's night retainer to send the twins to their Marxist summer camp. I sat in the hut and thought about his obsession with making me a brave little boy. There was one summer in junior high I'd gone swimming with him. Off the coast of Cape Cod. Insanity, but I was depressed. I had joked (painfully for him) that I was doing it because I no longer cared if I lived or died. And it had worked; the swim was like a sustained, mild panic attack, but leaving the water I'd felt happy to be alive. Now I was remembering a moment during the swim when I'd sensed the hulk of his body at my side, and how it had felt, sort of, like protection. It hadn't removed the threat of sharks but it had bestowed a strange haze of impunity; immune to death because I was loved.

Baby didn't come back for hours. I tried to read my Ayn Rand biography but this only made me more insecure. Nathaniel Branden, I learned, had been sleeping with another woman. A much younger, prettier woman who was also not his wife. Nathaniel had turned out to be, in Baby's words, a big basic. A pussybitch. A person of great spiritual potential, horny with life force, but unable to align his mental and physical values. In this sense Baby was more evolved, but I was worried I had disappointed him. I had failed to find *all* of existence funny. Exposed my susceptibility to history, to a wound from the collective past that he probably thought was just some level in a violent video game.

When he finally returned Baby was tired. His Nicolas Cage lacked verve and he quickly softened in my mouth.

"Is something wrong?"

He shook his head and mounted me. But his heart wasn't in it.

"Don't you find it exciting to come in the mouth of a woman with a postgraduate degree?"

He cringed, which felt unfair; American meritocracy was perfectly aligned with the Master's values. Some people were born unlucky and others were not. Leveling the playing field was against both human nature and the laws of the universe. I was sure the Master would've agreed that abolishing standardized testing was like trying to abolish karma itself.

"Seriously," said Baby. "All this *knowledge* is just feeding the self."

And this disturbed me. If my knowledge of the world meant nothing to him, what was my value? He looked at me and raised his palm. I brought mine up but Baby wasn't high-fiving me. He let the hand hover over his left eye, obstructing his view of my face.

"You should take a new name," he said.

"A name?"

"The original revolutionaries were all given Sanskrit names."

But a name was an identity and surely just bolstered one's sense of self? I grinned and got slithery under him. "I thought my name was *Baby*?"

But he didn't want to play. "The name is like a mantra. It is instruction for the soul."

"Well, do you want to give me one?"

"Only the Master can be giving it."

So that was that. We made love but it was mechanical and distant. And then, as I felt him stiffening toward orgasm, something in me began to rebel. I scooched up the mattress and slid across the pillow, then turned back to face him.

"Chase me!" I cried.

Baby froze. On my knees I made a little pivot, flashing my ass.

"What you are doing?" He looked annoyed.

"I just want you to . . . grab me!"

"But I was already inside you."

A cry caught in my throat. "I guess it just wasn't quite enough."

He sighed and collapsed onto the bed. I watched the thick slug of his erection dip ominously toward his thighs. My appetite at that moment felt insatiable. Nothing would satisfy my need for him. Nothing could bring me close enough to his flesh, his heart. Only if it was beating between my own ribs.

"*Vedanta*," he said gruffly.

I couldn't remember if this was an ancient text or a type of yoga. I risked a guess.

"I should read it?"

"It mean 'beyond knowledge.'"

He rolled over and started typing into my phone. When he turned back it was to show me a YouTube video; one of the Master's, called "Never Say I Love You." Dejected, I watched it over his shoulder.

Lovers, said the Master, had to see each other as strangers. When you decided you knew who someone was, however good or bad, you killed the possibility that they might ever become something else. The Master said there could be no expectations in love. Even the words "I love you" were an implicit demand—a claim made on the Beloved's emotional and physical freedom. Real love involved no ties, no boxes, no limitations. The only promise made to a lover, said the Master, should be the promise not to hurt them.

Baby was right. I shouldn't need anything from him. He did not belong to me. It was just the last part that bothered me—the promise not to hurt each other. How could you know what might hurt someone, or what exactly might hurt you? As if hurting and being hurt could ever be properly parsed into active and passive verbs. The promise felt unpromisable. An excuse to blame and be blamed. I wanted to own my hurt. How else could you endure suffering without injury?

"Copy that," I said and rolled the other way.

Within a minute, Baby was asleep. Lying beside him I was afraid to move. To make my breathing body felt. It was like we were in a primal struggle where my needs seemed to threaten his survival; as if only one of us could live. I worried he could hear my heartbeat and so I slipped out and into Vivian's bed. But I couldn't fall asleep there either and spent the next few hours scrolling through my phone.

In my YouTube sidebar I noticed new offerings. Mostly trauma therapy sessions from world-renowned facilitators. I watched Sia get diagnosed as "severely anxious attached" and Alanis Morissette blab for forty minutes about her "toxic triad of addictions." I wondered why the internet thought I needed trauma therapy. I had no trauma. I had not survived anything because nothing had ever threatened my existence. A mother not laughing at her daughter's jokes didn't count. Neither did Antifa. I had made my choice, and it was a choice. You couldn't be traumatized by someone seeing you as a set of bad beliefs and not a human being. Or you could, but what had happened in the Edelstein's pied-à-terre was not the same as the Holocaust.

In the morning it was raining. Loud and ecstatic like concert applause. I liked how it made the hut feel closer to our bodies. Made us feel closer to each other. Baby's sleeping mouth was ajar, the bottom lip slick and red and squished against the pillow. It made him look innocent and full of appetite in the way of actual babies; his need so selfish and pure it seemed to trump my own. His life felt both precious and fundamental; essential to the turning of the world. I watched him from the sad heap of my own body. My spirit felt zapped, my self like a silly dream I'd just woken from. Was this what motherhood would be like? Baby's dreads were shockingly still on the pillow and it disturbed me for a moment, the not-breathing boy. But that wasn't my trauma either. That belonged to my parents.

Baby finally stirred, and his eyes popped open.

"Rain." He looked at me accusingly. "Why you didn't wake me?"

Then he was up and bounding for the door.

I raced out after him through the muddy field and down to the creek bed, where a shallow torrent rushed through the slim cleft. Baby's tent had been washed away. There were a few clothing items slapped wetly against low branches or bunched in the ropey cradles of tree roots. The teddy bear was gone. Baby sat on a rock and cried into his hands. I considered my options. I could've told him that loss was an opportunity for death, that material possessions were a trap, that everything would be okay because I loved him.

"I'll buy you new stuff," is what I settled on.

"No, baby." But his tone was unconvincing.

I sat beside him and began to sweep the greasy prongs

behind his small, filthy ears; my whole body gathered over him like shelter.

"Seriously," I said, kissing his forehead. "We can put it all on my credit card."

We walked together to breakfast as Baby itemized his lost possessions. I typed them into my phone. He would definitely need new sneakers. A baseball cap. A backpack. Hearing how little he had, I felt wildly benevolent. I wanted to buy him an iPhone, an iPad, an N64. But Baby didn't want these things. He didn't even want the sneakers. He had learned to go barefoot at the commune and his feet were now calloused and tough.

"The less I have the less I am needing."

I felt like a deranged insurance agent, begging him to take my money.

"But the world is so crazy right now. What if you find yourself in a situation where you really need to wear a shirt and tie?"

Baby waved me off but I saw the change in his face. A small, private concentration. He was picturing something. The crumbs of a future I had sprinkled in his mind.

At breakfast it was announced that a sensual massage workshop would take place that morning. Baby had work to do in the Wi-Fi room but told me he might come later. He didn't like to be pinned down. In fact, trying to make plans usually just caused him to shudder and walk off in the opposite direction. But that was okay. Each time he did this I felt the cold air of solitude rush up all around me, as though I had been dropped from a great height. And it was fortifying. I felt strong in this enforced solitude, shored up against the world. Like he was giving me my medicine.

I hadn't laid eyes on Vivian in days and so was surprised to see her at the massage. She sat stiffly beside the Belarussian and when I waved neither one of them appeared to notice. They seemed morose, in a fight. I took a seat, feeling slightly uncomfortable to be there alone. The only other single person in attendance was the bald Israeli man who rarely spoke and always seemed to be hammering a nail into a wall.

The group was first asked to split into two lines. One for men and one for women. When everyone was assembled, the facilitator—blond and rakish with manic blue eyes and an ambiguously Northern European accent—turned to the women. He told us to breathe in the man's loving energy through our vaginas and return that love by breathing out through our breasts. I could feel Vivian's eyes burning into me, but chose to ignore her. I didn't want to be cynical. Maybe it was petty and apolitical but I really wanted to get good at sex. To be more receptive to the man's needs; less selfish, less the flawed female protagonist. The facilitator addressed the men next. They had to absorb the women's heart energy, inhaling it through their chests, and expelling their own love back through the eye of their penises.

"Can there be a gender nonbinary line?"

Vivian, I now saw, had hung back in the far corner of the room, while the Belarussian was happily breathing male love energy in through her vagina.

The facilitator regarded Vivian warily. "Whichever one you feel, masculine or feminine, you can join this line."

"I feel both," said Vivian. "And neither."

I noticed I was holding my breath. A conversation about gender-as-construction seemed unlikely to play out well here.

"What is your resistance?" the facilitator challenged Vivian. "What are you afraid to lose?"

Vivian puffed up. "What are *you* afraid to lose?"

His boner, obviously. But the facilitator didn't answer her. He just watched as Vivian marched across the room, took the Belarussian's hand, and walked her into the men's line.

"Is this an LBGT thing?" the facilitator asked, annoyed.

"A *what*?"

The facilitator's gaze flicked to the Belarussian and then to me, as if he feared some sort of violent queer uprising. His voice became gentler.

"Trust me, beloved. When you are too opposed to something you just become its slave."

"Trust *you*?" Vivian scoffed. "A sixtysomething white male massage therapist who calls it LBGT?"

"He's right, beloved." This was the shaman PhD. "You can't hate men, you can only hate the past."

"What the fuck does that even mean?" Vivian was yelling. "History is real, people! So is science!"

"When it suits you."

"Excuse me?"

The skinny Italian had stepped sideways out of the male line and was facing Vivian with his feet in a wide martial stance. Through the threadbare fisherman pants I could just make out the stubby contours of his penis. The one that feared actual intercourse.

"You LGBT don't believe so much-uh in the biology, do you."

Vivian went red. My face blazed too; I felt complicit. I knew he'd been harboring an ancient Neapolitan hatred toward her and I'd done nothing to fix it.

"Congratulations, little man!" Vivian shrieked. "You have a penis!"

And she was off, flying toward the door as the room erupted

into relieved laughter. I felt queasy. Vivian had, until recently, believed transgenderism was all Hillary Clinton's idea. But I knew she'd changed her mind about that and I also knew how she felt right now—like she was being laughed out of the room.

"In America," I yelled at the Italian, "only gay men wear Hugo Boss underwear."

And now a small mutiny proceeded. Me at the head, the Belarussian behind, and then, surprisingly, the skeletal Austrian brought up the rear. If Vivian really wanted to achieve nonduality she'd have to drop the acronyms altogether, but at that moment I was on her side.

Out in the courtyard our little group disbanded. Vivian and the Belarussian were suddenly, wordlessly, storming up the path, and the Austrian closed her eyes and turned to commune with a tree. I felt a little sheepish—realizing I'd made a gay joke to defend the lesbians, though nobody appeared to have noticed. I figured I'd just go read my book at the outdoor bar until Baby was free. But entering the grove I saw the Polish thief. She started walking straight toward me; her face a flat, Slavic wall of concern.

"You must be careful with him," she said obscurely.

"Careful?"

The thief nodded. "His mother is narcissist."

I felt my shoulders hackle up like a threatened animal. What was she saying—that his narcissistic mother had ruined him? A man was not his past, and what was a mother to a man, but the past? And what about his absent dad, who—if you thought about it—was just a narcissistic father? I looked at her and shrugged.

"Why are you telling me this?"

"Please don't buy him an iPad."

The thief was vivid now. Something dangerous moved inside her, ruthless and precise as a shark. There was a moment, just a breath, where I could have stepped into her orbit, met her inside that deep, jealous pain. I sensed myself waiting at the edge of it. For a soft inner nudge or sudden upswell of sentiment—all my joyful abundance overflowing onto her. But it wasn't there.

"Why not?" I snapped. "So he learns to steal?"

Marching off down the path, my body was stiff and burning, a branch in the flames. There was ecstasy in this, in walking away. It wasn't an orgasm but it was still a little bit like coming.

After lunch a sing-along materialized outside the kitchen, around the German CEO with his twelve-string guitar. Baby had told me that the man came here each quarter—parking his Tesla at Athens Airport, and growing his beard and the boundaries of his marriage in an unironic costume of white satin robes. The sing-along was comprised mostly of Germans who ardently wished to sing the Beatles because they knew all the words. They gathered in around the dormant hearth, beginning, rather dogmatically, with "Let It Be."

Baby and I stood on the outskirts of the little group. I hummed along softly but Baby didn't sing. He muttered a stealthy commentary—a mini discourse on language, according to the Master. The Slavic languages, he claimed, best expressed emotion and so were ideal for poetry and novels; Sanskrit's grammar was perfect for philosophy, but English was dominated by "I" phrases, making it the lingua franca of pop music.

"And solipsism." I added. "And iPhones."

Singing softly, I kept hearing my own "I" bob up on the calm sea of sound. It seemed significant but I wasn't sure how. I could share; I just didn't want to share the same thoughts as others. The quality of my thoughts still mattered to me, even if Baby was losing interest. I wondered if the Master also thought novelists should be paid as much as janitors. If art was just another healthy, human activity, like sex or making a salad. If smiling sunflowers and stick figures were the price you paid for spiritual peace. To me, ego death and literature still seemed incompatible. But many things about the commune remained elusive. You were meant to kill the ego but a dead ego could own a Tesla and cheat on its wife. You could steal people's clothes but buying someone a new baseball cap was possessive. They called themselves a commune and yet nobody ever seemed to do any chores. The chorus swelled around me. *Whisper words of wisdom, let it be.*

That afternoon Baby and I rode our bikes down to the village. He sang all the way to town, some sad Russian song that I could tell made him feel separate from me and more like himself. I tried not to take it personally. As we turned onto the main road I called out and offered to buy him a banana split. Baby looped back around, weaving the bike like sexy twisty hips, eyes hot with confidence. It was a barefaced seduction—there was no showiness or play, nowhere for the air to hiss out. He wasn't kidding. Today, Baby seemed to know the bargaining power of his youthful beauty.

When we got to the tiki bar he walked to the edge of the boardwalk and jumped down onto the sand. Then he started stripping off his clothes, flinging them out like orbiting planets. I admired his nonattachment to objects but couldn't help regretting all the nice new things I'd just ordered him online. Baby kept his underwear on and then, beckoning me, ran straight into the sea. I tied up my bike and hurried down the steps after him.

My body quickly adjusted to the cold, and the physical exertion felt good. Baby had bad style but his long limbs compensated for this. He was fast and stayed ahead of me, never looking back to check that I was still there. I tried not to take this personally either. He was a child. And a sage. He was killing my ego and edging me closer to enlightenment.

About halfway to the rock my arms began to tire. They felt heavy, the skin loose. I had a mental flash—Ayn's fleshy upper arms sagging beneath her cape. I imagined my arms were hers, weighted by the sodden garment. Had Ayn done much swimming? Had she ever even gone to the beach? I knew she'd avoided the west side of LA, where the Frankfurt School exiles had lived. But she'd spent summers in the Crimea at her family's seaside home, and it didn't seem beyond her capacity to enjoy the pleasures of the ocean. As a young woman she'd loved musicals; her biographer had gone into great, patronizing detail about her lowbrow fondness for their corny ostentation and the simple joy they inspired. An ordinary joy, she said, that Ayn had sought her whole life. Though nowhere had I read of any vacations taken after childhood. Her life had been dedicated solely to work; to building a philosophy, a movement, and to imagining a man who might offer her the kind of life where that ordinary joy was possible.

And then, thrashing along behind Baby, I had another thought. A thought like a vise on the world, squeezing everything into tight, palpitating focus. My period was late. Really late. Later than the usual lateness. I felt glee. It wasn't about babies. It was the thrill of the momentous, of The Real. A disaster to refocus and rearrange my life. Pregnancy. My body swooned into the big strong arms of this idea. Was a child what I'd actually needed? Secretly even wanted? And could Baby somehow be a part of it? A child-sage raising a child? As I swam, a series of images scrolled through my mind. Baby holding a swaddled infant. The two of us being married at sunset in the grove. The German mullet squinting at a crude drawing of a tree.

When he reached the island, Baby scrambled up onto the weedy rock shelf and then disappeared behind a boulder. I found it hard to get my footing and haul myself out. Baby wasn't there to help me and I felt his absence, newly, in the depths of my womb. But I soothed myself, deciding that his help would've made me feel old and decrepit. I didn't want to be like his needy, narcissistic mother. And I wasn't. I had all the life force that she lacked, because I *didn't* need him.

Baby was waiting for me just around the first big rock. There was a small triangle of flat ground hemmed in by three large boulders. Seeing him, standing before the rock face, I knew instantly what he wanted. And I was right. He took my hips and pushed me up against the steep incline. The rock was cold and bits of it dug into my back. But I wanted him; I wanted our closeness. As we kissed, Baby pulled my underwear aside. He edged himself in and it was painful—a coarse burn I remembered from being a much younger woman, and especially a girl. But male impatience could be a turn-on and so I waited for my body to respond. Baby pushed in deeper and the burn branched wider. But I wanted it. I looked for Baby's hands and saw that one was fastened to my hip and the other mashed hard against the rock. I knew it already: he wasn't going to high-five me. There was no Tom Cruise in his face, not even any eye contact. I was too dry and now my cervix was on fire. If I was going to get wet, I knew I needed him to care more. And not about my life.

"Strangle me," I said.

He ignored this, or maybe he didn't hear it. I took the hand off my hip and placed it on my neck.

"No." He yanked the hand back. "This is porn. Please, baby—you are cringe."

I pushed myself out from under him and started climbing away up the rock. I was hurt, though already I could tell it was misplaced. Baby came climbing after me, laughing and muttering something about my big gay country with all the horny stepsisters who wanted to be strangled by their horny stepbrothers. It was true: porn was full of women being strangled. And whose fault was that?

Ayn had strangled all her leading ladies. They'd loved it, begged for it. Sexual strangulation was one of the individual's great freedoms. You had to reclaim this right from all the boring feminists who said it was just misogyny. But now I wondered, was it really free will when being choked was the only way you could come? Was that really a choice you had made, for yourself?

I had reached the top of the rock. Today there were no boys or men. I walked to the edge and could hear Baby still scrambling up, somewhere behind me. It wasn't his fault but he still felt *symbolically* responsible. For the way being objectified felt like rejection, and how its opposite did too. I didn't wait for him. I just stepped off into the cold rush of air.

We didn't talk again until we were sitting outside at the tiki bar. Baby ordered his banana split, then told me he was going for a walk. There was a new petulance in him but also a more palpable connection between us. Like an invisible wire or electromagnetic leash that made him feel somehow present in his absence. Our chemistry was waning and yet it seemed I had made him nonconsensually attached. Was it me? Was it just the banana splits? I could feel that his attachment to me meant I had more power in our situation. Though not because I was older or richer or from a country without thirty different words for "thief." Was it related to his mother? Was it because I was less needy or could at least hide my feelings behind humor? I sensed I was hiding them from myself. But self-deception couldn't be a power or, for that matter, even much of a choice.

I felt a presence in the doorway and looked up just as the beaded curtain scattered around Vivian's dark form. She planted herself on Baby's stool and informed me that she was leaving tonight. We hadn't discussed it yet but now felt like the right moment to ask Vivian if she thought she'd killed her ego. She looked affronted and then said no, but this was only because the Beloveds were a bunch of neo-hippie luddites who thought a woman's highest aspiration was belly dance. I wasn't sure what she was referring to. There were a couple of cute Turkish girls who wore midriffs, but Vivian was definitely being unfair to all the emergent bisexuals.

"And anyway," she continued. "I think I'll lose more of my ego helping people in need."

This annoyed me. The old altruism trick. That life's larger meaning only derived from confrontation with the suffering of others. I shrugged and told her I was staying here.

"To fuck that boy?"

"He's legal." My cheeks burned. "And he's actually very wise."

"If this was America there'd be a power imbalance."

At that moment I felt so yawningly far from my friend, from everything she stood for; things I could imagine only from the most gruesome memes on the internet. Were Vivian and her furries trying to ban personhood now? Would they come for first names next? Favorite colors? And then there was the slim but angsty possibility that I was pregnant with Baby's child. I was so angry all I could do was glare at Vivian and tell her to get a fucking life.

"Was that Humbert Humbert's defense?" she said.

"You'd probably like to ban *Lolita*, wouldn't you?"

Vivian leaned back on her stool, observing me. "You didn't kill your ego either. As usual you've just been sitting there, making fun of everyone."

At that moment the owner appeared with Baby's banana split and placed it down in front of me with a proud little flourish. The large phallic banana was positioned just above two scoops of ice cream, a curly whip of cream framed the testicles like pubes. Vivian and I remained stoic as the small, sturdy woman moved expertly around us, laying out the silverware. We couldn't laugh at her, and this mutual understanding helped us. I didn't make a joke and, realizing this, something in Vivian relaxed. The owner settled the plate into its rightful geometry between the tiny spoons and miniature fork, and with a short regal bow she left us.

Vivian looked at me. "I don't think you're a bad person."

The tears came before I could blink them away. I turned my head and pretended to look at the ocean but I was sure Vivian could see the steam rising off my eyeballs and misting into the air.

"And you're very nice to boys," she said sternly. "Too nice."

I nodded but I couldn't speak. She was right about the boys and although I had my reasons, they felt impossible to articulate, even in my mind. Vivian reached out a tentative hand and squeezed my shoulder. It was stiff and unpracticed but the gesture made me melt. She squeezed me harder and then stood.

"Well," she said. "If you change your mind . . . the door's open."

"Unless it's on fire."

Vivian giggled all the way out of the café.

I waited at the tiki bar for Baby. For a while I watched a sun-burned European family wading in at the shore. The parents stooped identically; her bikini line was too high, hinting at a long-faded raunch confirmed by her husband's sorrowful expression. The children were wheezy and overweight and committed to tormenting each other. The younger brother had small, conical titties and kept splashing his sister, whose wide flabby breasts bounced inside a wireless tube top each time she dunked him violently under the water. I watched as the four of them started swimming together toward the rock. The boy paddled beside his mother's sensual breaststroke; the girl kept up a prissy splash beside her father's plodding hulk. This was it. Their vacation. The peak of their year. What struck me most was the formation they made. Four depressed bodies moving through space, oppressed by their mutual proximity, yet lacking the will for separation.

Watching the sad European family, I wondered—could I actually stay here? With my new spiritual family, bound by nothing but philosophy? A family that shared meals and meditation but no labor and very little conversation; one that encouraged self-responsibility and personal freedom above all. Where people could come and go and nobody was ever hurt by it. I saw no life for myself in the US. Or only if I could take a piece of this place back with me.

When the sun dropped behind the cliffside I ordered the check. The owner stared sadly at the browning banana submerged in its creamy pool, but she was gracious and said nothing. Cycling along the boardwalk I kept an eye out for Baby, peering down side streets and onto the main road. It was only once I hit the highway that I really began to worry.

As I veered off onto the dirt trail, tiny insects swirled into my mouth and died acridly against my tongue. Could something have happened to Baby? Should I return to the beach? Alert the police? It seemed prudent to check first at the commune. And feeling that this was the right choice, I knew I'd been wrong about the stronger connection between us; the electromagnetic leash and my power to keep him close. That the more likely scenario wasn't drowning or death, but some very ordinary sexual betrayal.

I found him lying in the creek bed, curled up with something small and brown and furry. For a moment I thought he'd retrieved his drowned teddy bear but then I saw its breathing chest. Baby was snuggled up with the commune dog. The same blissful mutt I'd meditated with on my very first day. I trod carefully down the rocky incline and into the damp soil.

"Baby?" I said softly.

The dog wheezed up at me, smiling with the humble genius of its species. Baby didn't acknowledge me at all.

"Do you want me to go away?"

He shook his head, then buried his face in the animal's fur.

"My mother have made for me some hard-core trauma."

He might've been crying so I didn't mention the fact that Baby didn't actually believe in trauma. That being in the present moment made the past moot. Instead, I leaned in closer and in my gentlest, most non-prying voice, I asked him what she'd done.

Slowly, he released the dog and sat up. He stared straight ahead and in a quiet, angry voice he told me how she'd thrown shoes at his head and burned his dinners and finally just stopped leaving the apartment. At fourteen, he'd had to take work in nursing homes to pay their rent. I felt a little jolt of gratitude for Jackie and then I told Baby how sorry I was.

"Because of her," he said. "I can't be close to people."

I stroked his shoulder. "That makes perfect sense."

"When they touch me I am wanting to throw up."

I withdrew my hand and pinned both arms to my sides. "If you need to cuddle the dog instead of me, I totally understand that."

"What I need," Baby said sadly, "is to be healing this trauma."

I was confused. Wasn't all the Sufi-whirling and laughing at other people's trauma supposed to solve that? When the ego finally died, surely so did all of its problems?

"Won't the meditation heal you?"

Baby pulled the dog into his lap. He rubbed its scabby belly and shook his head. Now I remembered the YouTube videos on my phone. All those erratic, middle-aged pop stars dissecting their dysfunctional romantic relationships. How they'd chosen narcissists and other shades of the Emotionally Unavailable to play out their childhood traumas, until a suicide attempt or re-hab stint finally broke the toxic cycle.

"So you want to go do a trauma workshop with Alanis Morrisette?"

But my joke belly-flopped in the deep sincerity of his plea. I knew what he was asking.

"People have always been telling me to try the acting."

The Master said one should never hope. Hoping was for idiots. Even the Greek root, *idiotes*, meant "one who has a private goal, a hope against the whole." Hoping thrust you into an imaginary future, far from the perfection of the present, the truth of the moment, the sublimity of the real. One had to live utterly without hope and one shouldn't even hope to achieve hopelessness. And yet here we were, back in the hut hunched over my laptop, planning Baby's new life in Los Angeles.

I didn't mention the possible pregnancy. Even if it was true, anything could still happen. I didn't want our plans marred by what might've felt like an overwhelming obligation. He had mother issues; we had to go very slow. I kept things light and optimistic.

"We'll find you an agent and, worst case, you'll get something temporary like an internship."

"What is internship?"

"It's sort of like an assistant."

"No, baby. I am not wiping people's asshole now. My soul have become too free."

In that case, I would email Terra and ask about paid work as an extra. Or an unfeatured actor. Or whatever you had to call them now. Maybe Baby could even model. We skipped over the issue of visas and moved straight to the fun stuff. I told him about acting studios and show reels and headshots. And then I told him none of that might even be necessary. If he made micro-content. And got himself an agent.

"Yes," said Baby. "I am needing an agent with the life force of Jerry Maguire."

And now I looked into the eyes of my beloved and said the seven sweetest words in the English language. "I can introduce you to my manager."

Baby reached over and squeezed my right nipple. "Brad." And the left. "Pitt."

Then he sat up very straight, eyes rounding as he huffed on some mystical inner vision.

"This is my American dream," he said. "To be taking the magical mushroom with Bradley Pitt."

But that night Baby didn't come to see me. At nine o'clock I went to join the late-night meditation to calm my nerves. In the stone room I found ten people gathered in a circle, staring at a single candle burning on the floor. I slipped in beside them and stared down at the shimmering flame. But I couldn't focus. My mind was splintery and my back was sharp with eyes, like a huge torch sweeping the room for Baby. After a few minutes I gave up and slunk back outside. Hurrying along the path, my body rang with fear. That he was out here somewhere, shining his attention on someone, some woman, several women. The moon seemed to hound me all the way down the trail. It had his pale, luminous beauty, and a colder, more impersonal scope. But I wasn't supposed to be jealous. I was spiritual. I was a sharer now.

Back in the hut I opened my laptop and found the thief's Instagram. There were lots of bikini shots and smiling selfies. The thief didn't use filters or makeup, and her perfect, unimprovable beauty caused me actual physical pain—an ache in my heart and a clamping of my nether regions. I sat in bed and doused myself with images, like a Tibetan martyr in screen swiping self-immolation. I scrolled right back through the photos and, as if by conjuration, in the corner foreground of a selfie, I saw a long, smooth male hand. Baby's. The photo was a week old. No one else appeared to be there; just the thief and the hand resting on a blanket on the sand in the pearly blue dusk. I scrolled on for more evidence of Baby. Now every shadow was his body standing just out of frame; every picturesque selfie bore the artistry of his photographer's eye. I spent forty minutes analyzing two photos of the popular group, whose time stamps seemed to contradict the thief's photo location for most of an afternoon three days ago when Baby had also been missing. I created whole itineraries for Baby and the thief, sought evidence, found only the barest scraps. At the end of my hour-long investigation I had nothing conclusive, aside from a shimmering ocular migraine.

I left the hut again, searching for headache pills and Baby and the inner strength to accept his absence. The Master said romantic love was the most common way of accessing the divine; that relationships were the gateway drug to God but ultimately impeded one's spiritual actualization. The final step was to let go of other people, to need nothing aside from the (egoless) self. If romantic love really was just an exercise in ego, it was probably time to let Baby go. But what if his child was growing inside me? And what else, besides a few plotless pages, did I have? I'd never sell another book. No one wanted to read *Eat Pray Love* narrated by Humbert Humbert. I felt like Barbara the jilted wife and biographer. Barbara, the one who could only go and write it all down.

Reaching the bar area, I was surprised to find it empty. I walked beneath the low canopy down the tiled path to the grove. The lights were out. It wasn't even eleven p.m.

"Good evening, beloved." The Oxford Sufi was sitting crosslegged in the tree swing.

I nodded curtly. I had always been suspicious of men with posh accents and bare feet. "Where is everyone?" I asked him.

"Everyone," he said. "Or just your beloved?"

He was insufferable but I needed information. "Correct," I said.

The Sufi looked very pleased with himself, great diviner of truths that he was. He put his hands out and beckoned me into a hug. I didn't want to hug him but mostly I didn't want to make a scene. I moved toward him and when I was close enough to the swing, he pulled me up and into his arms. I rested my face away from his, against his shoulder. My body relented, capitulating to yet another coercive hug. Eventually he pulled back and we sat there facing each other. He beamed at me.

"I've also had sexual experiences with older women," he said. "And they were wonderfully healing."

I couldn't tell if he was gloating, sympathetic, or horny; a problem I often had with these sustained periods of eye contact.

"Healing?" I heard the irritation in my voice. "But what can you heal without a past?"

I admit I was confused. Baby had told me to ignore the past and now he wanted trauma therapy at a bougie rehab center in Big Sur. Couldn't the past just be meditated away? Wasn't that the whole point? That you canceled the past, not the individual? I looked at the Oxford Sufi's billowing white sash and saw the logo: YSL. I knew this guy and that he, too, understood me perfectly well.

"I don't need healing," I said pointedly. "Because nothing bad has ever happened to me."

The Sufi watched me intently. "There's historical trauma."

"I'm not fucking him because of Hitler."

He smiled and his gaze pressed on me with its shining little significance. It was the look of someone who was about to teach me a spiritual lesson.

"What scares you most about death?" he said.

But I wasn't scared of death. I wasn't using Baby to avoid questions of mortality. I was deeply aware of my own aging body. In fact, sex with Baby was all about death. Each time, I seemed to fall through a well of shame into blissful emptiness. I disappeared into his will, his pleasure. It wasn't news to me that I was playing the masochist. Baby didn't make me feel better about myself; he made me want to die.

"Oh shit." I jumped down from the swing and started walking quickly up the path.

"*Beloved*," the Sufi cooed. "Everyone is in the dome."

I ran up the hill. Orange light spilled across the stone steps and, with it, mediocre house music. The Beloveds were having a dance party. As I came up the stairs I could see them all, bopping and swaying to the music. People danced in couples and small, erratic circles. The thief was there, and so were all the other cute young girls. But Baby wasn't here either. And I couldn't picture him on a dance floor full of uncool Europeans having a fantastically good time. And of course not. He was a child. A boy. He should've been playing video games or fingering some village girl on the back of her moped. Watching from the dome's opening, I was suddenly sad realizing that he'd never join me here. Dancing would have felt so good. And then I was sadder; wondering if I'd mistaken a life of refusal—to conform, to fit in, to disappear—for that feeling of aliveness. If my father and all the boys jumping off rocks had mistaken it too. The intensity of challenge for the gentle joy of being alive.

I left the dome and walked down the hill to my bike. I started cycling into town, though I wasn't sure why. It wasn't to catch Baby doing something nefarious. It was just to get away. From the Oxford Sufi and all of the Beloveds. But after a few minutes my legs began to ache. My belly cramped and my head pounded. Coming up the last scrappy incline, I felt my strength ebb away. I stopped and the bike rolled out from under me. It curled in on itself, then collapsed; the front wheel bent out like a snapped bone. I sat down in the dust, blue and crawling from the light of the moon. The fields were blue too, everything squirming right at the surface.

And then it hit me. Sticky in the seat of my underwear. It was late, later than late, but my period was here. Nothing, in reality, tethered me to Baby. There was actually no reason to stay, to give my life up for some boy. A selfish stranger. It wasn't about him anyway, I thought or, rather, let myself think, with shame. The masochism was about my baby brother. Him instead of me. That life instead of this one. I stared into the blue field and felt my whole body squirming along with it. I hadn't made choices with younger men; my choices had made me. I was not in control. I had chosen, against my will, the trauma narrative.

I rose at dawn. The hills were black against the pale sky and a thin red line ran along the horizon like a power cord. It was time to go home. I wheeled my suitcase up the path between the huts. They looked stunned and steamy in the early light, as if flagrantly hiding their occupants. At reception, I nosed my bike back up against the wall and left my suitcase on the porch. As I came up the stairs, I heard the chair squeak and then the three slow steps to the door.

His face was different this morning. The polished stone of his cheeks had a hard, sealed quality. He looked over my shoulder and pointed to the bicycle.

"You have been using this?"

I pointed stupidly after him. "The bicycle? Yes, I was borrowing it."

"Borrowing?"

"I assumed everything here was shared?"

His eyes glittered with cynicism. "It is shared with those who are contributing. The bicycle is mutual for people who understand reciprocity."

I wanted to laugh; I was being accused of bicycle theft.

"But this place is run on entrance fees," I said, bewildered. "And you still have my credit card."

"People here are working." His voice remained forceful. "They are helping in the garden, in the fields, the kitchen. They are cleaning toilets. You haven't noticed this?"

I tried to picture the kitchen hands but all I could see were the vague shapes of women and children, their faces blurred by steam. Perhaps this was part of the problem. The Beloveds had a shadowy presence, always flitting around, never stopping to explain or include me.

"Why didn't anybody tell me about the chores?"

"You didn't think to ask?" He was angry. "Why this CEO is emptying the garbage bins? Why this doctor is scrubbing the bathroom floor?"

And now I remembered. Or rather the unremarkable sights I'd been witnessing for weeks were suddenly recalled to me. The curvy Italian acupuncturist carrying a fresh bowl of lemon wedges from the kitchen. The buff Cretan deftly administering to the women's hair. The Israeli with his little hammer. It had all seemed so natural, like fruit slipping from a tree.

"I didn't realize."

My throat was closing in around an ache. I was bad and everyone had seen it. They had all been watching me not contribute, unwittingly, for weeks. I cowered from the big wagging finger of the group. It was desperate and pathetic but I asked him anyway.

"And what about Mischa?"

"What about him?"

"He isn't very 'reciprocal.'"

"Mischa is working every day in the Wi-Fi room. As technical support."

Mortified, I looked down at the desk. On the cover of a pamphlet I now saw that all of the young, beautiful bodies wore aprons and cleaning gloves; some held brooms and sponges and even pruning shears. How had I missed this? My own words came rushing back to me: I only knew what I knew, only saw what I could see. But I didn't feel merciful. I hung my head, and the manager seemed to take pity on me.

"Would you like to have the afternoon shift in the laundry room?"

"No thank you," I said.

And then I paid my outstanding bill and left.

Heading up to the road, I passed the Bulgarian's hut and was struck by a powerful bolt of intuition. Baby was inside. I tore across the grass to the hut's front window. The curtains were drawn but there was a small space between the flaps. On my toes, pressed right up against the boarding, I looked through the gap. The hut was just like mine. Two beds placed a few feet apart. In one, the Bulgarian stretched out in an oversized T-shirt. And in the other, besieged by an army of grimy soft toys, was a sleeping Baby and the noodlehead curled against his back. I hopped down and stepped away from the hut.

The scene was so strange that for a moment I couldn't make sense of it. Were they sleeping together or was the Bulgarian just babysitting? Babysitting felt equally bad. That both of us were just better versions of his mother; projections of his trauma and phantasms of his past. And now I felt furious. That he had hurt me like this. Made me share with this woman who was no better or worse than I was; more horribly, she was the same. I waited outside the hut for a few moments, considering my options. I could've just left. Done the dignified thing; the enlightened thing. But I wanted him to know what I thought of him. What I thought remained the most valuable thing about me. I knocked angrily on the glass. The Bulgarian stirred and opened her eyes. Seeing me, she frowned and then tapped Baby. I knocked louder and he sat straight up.

"Baby!" He smiled and spread his arms wide. "Good morning!"

I went for the door handle and then I was suddenly inside, huge and throbbing at the foot of the bed.

"Why do you think Tom Cruise is always running?"

Baby squinted at me. But I didn't care if I was being cringe.

"He isn't your hero," I cried. "He's just your trauma."

Baby burst out laughing. He clapped his hands, rocking sideways on the mattress and waking the younger boy. I looked at the Bulgarian, who was slouched up in her bed, squinting at me with profound irritation.

"I am right here!" Baby cried. "You are the one who is running!"

And I was out the door, walking swiftly through the grass. Cold and hard, a glittering rock shooting through the dark.

Epilogue

Athens

I n the cab back to Mytilene I texted an old friend from college. Jaclyn had fled New York in 2008 (thinking the next four years would be "boring") and arrived in Greece just in time for the debt crisis. She'd been living in an abandoned laundromat in Athens ever since, while writing short, confusing fiction about her encounters with young male refugees and letting her teeth go brown with nicotine and wine. Jaclyn, I knew, wasn't going to judge me.

The laundromat was in an ugly, shuttered neighborhood that was brainy with graffiti. I left my suitcase with a group of young Arab men smoking out front. Jaclyn had arranged this. She was already at work when I arrived and so the men had been paid to watch my bag while I explored Athens. At eight o'clock that evening Jaclyn would meet me in the arts district for a drink.

I walked right across the city. I had barely slept and exhaustion made my thoughts vague and my sadness Technicolor and dreamy. When I wasn't thinking of Baby, I found myself thinking of Ayn Rand. Barbara's description of Ayn's final breakdown. How she'd screamed and collapsed into a chair, then started hitting Nathaniel, helplessly, like a child. And what she'd said to Barbara later, sobbing on her sofa. *The best mind I knew . . . the man closest to me in every way, rejected me as a person. There is nothing for me to look forward to, nothing to hope for in reality. My life is over . . . he took away this earth.* Until the day Ayn died, the specter of this mediocre Canadian psychotherapist had loomed large. She'd removed his name from all their publications and gone about destroying his reputation. She'd also never written another book. I suppose with Nathaniel's betrayal Ayn's project had ended. The Ideal Man was a fallacy; she should have kept Nathaniel as a fiction. Sadder still, Ayn had lacked the inner strength to transcend him.

All over the arts district I saw anarchist symbols and slogans. Scribbled on elegant old facades and imposing sandstone walls were aggressive imperatives to *Fight the Power*, *Stand in Solidarity*, and *Fuck the Fascists*. There was an equally ubiquitous tag by a group called the *Yo! Gang*, which made the whole thing feel deeply European and uncool. By a fountain in a leafy square, I saw a group of young, scruffy men dressed in black. They were smoking cigarettes and glaring at two police officers standing across the road. I wondered if Athens attracted rebellious types like Jaclyn. People who got passionate about veganism but forgot to text their dads on Father's Day. Which of the Penguin philosophers had said it? Revolution was both radical change and also a complete circle.

I got to the Acropolis at dusk. The stone floors were slippery from overuse and people kept sliding around on them—men jerking forward as they offered factoids from ancient history, and women clutching at their boyfriends in gross displays of physiological need. The Parthenon was netted in scaffolding and on each step people clustered out of breath, phones dutifully raised. I felt no awe or sense of mystery. I wasn't inspired to coo at the cradle of Western culture. I had never really believed in much of anything. Except, maybe, books. Books, which were not a boyfriend or a baby, not people at all. Books, which could stomach paradox, and knew that both things—good and bad—could be true. Baby was wrong about books. You didn't have to be enlightened to understand them. Great art was a gateway to the sublime. Why had I been listening to the righteous ramblings of a child? But I knew the answer: low self-esteem.

I sat on a bench in the busy courtyard. When I closed my eyes, thoughts of Baby rushed back in. His rosebud lips, his smiling eyes, the fuzz patch at his lower back, that laugh. His absence felt like my absence. My insides had a cold, scraped-out quality. A trembling ether, a void. But that emptiness was me too. That breath. That breathing body. Emptiness was not death, I reminded myself, but aliveness. I thought of something the Master had said about letting go, then realized that actually the Master hadn't said it—Ayn Rand had.

One had to choose people, she'd written, along with every aspect of one's life, moment to moment, unburdened by the past. Freedom emerged in the aliveness one felt at severing a tie or breaking a bond—be that with an idea, a culture, a guru, or any other human being.

Doing this—letting each thought of Baby dissolve with a gentle exhalation—I found some relief. And each refusal to think, to dwell in lack or shame, felt like a small act of self-love. Was it a bounty overflowing? Not yet. But the day was still young.

When the sun finally dipped behind the mountains I got up and saw that I had a missed call from Vivian. I almost allowed myself to wonder if something bad had happened at the detention center, but then I stopped that too, and just enjoyed the sunset. Walking back down the long incline, I realized I was hungry. I found a restaurant back in the artists' quarter. It had a leafy courtyard and white tablecloths and leathery old people in soft silks and linens. I ordered saganaki with honey, grilled prawns, and a glass of white wine. With nothing and no one to think about, I found my attention focused on the experience of eating. This produced the strange double sensation of doer and observer, as if I were *with* myself, like a mother watching her child. A generous, careful attention. For the first time in years, I ate until I was full.

On my way to the bar, I stopped in the square where the anarchists were still standing in quiet menace. It was too early to meet Jaclyn and so I found a bench by the fountain. I sat down and closed my eyes. We'd been told that meditation was all about acceptance—accepting your thoughts for what they were. But maybe meditation was all about denial. Denying the validity of thoughts, of feelings, discomforts, the hauntings of certain people. Maybe it was the ultimate contrarianism—a denial of perceived reality. A gentler way to release attachments and feel the life waiting underneath. I meditated for a few minutes and then, from the silence, emerged a good sentence. Clean and punchy and unapologetically itself. I took out my phone and typed it up. Then I sat there for half an hour, writing notes. Ideas I was having for the book. When exhaustion set back in I stopped writing and started practicing a new signature. Tracing my finger over the screen with the phone's paintbrush function. What to remove and what to preserve. In the end I kept only

"Vedanta." Was there ego in choosing a new name? Yes. Was there ego in worrying if there was ego? Yes. So then, like the Buddhists said, *whatever*.

Looking up from my work, I noticed one of Jaclyn's neighbors standing with the other boys across the square. He was the sweet-faced one with light stubble and a beguiling widow's peak. I caught his eye and waved and he walked over.

"You are enjoying Athens?" he asked me.

I nodded. He was cuter up close.

"You have been to the Acropolis?"

"Yes." I gestured to the square. "But I find this more interesting."

"Antifa," he said proudly. "They have world headquarters here."

I regarded him warily. He was wearing black, though this seemed incidental. His socks were blue with small white clouds. Still, I had to ask.

"Are you an antifascist?"

He shrugged and squinted across the square. "I have to be careful or they'll send me back home."

Home, I imagined, being somewhere like Syria or Afghanistan. And then I went red, remembering Vivian's missed call. I nodded at the boy. Pretending to comprehend something of his plight. I was Jaclyn's friend, after all. He must've thought I was half curious, half going to use him for a short story. And maybe he was right. But it wouldn't be that kind of story. Where the writer relayed the trauma of a destitute subject, making them the helpless victim of circumstance.

"But actually," he said. "I don't so much like groups."

"Me neither," I said.

There was a short, warm silence, and then his eyes lit up.

"I'll show you something."

We moved through the shadows toward the fountain and emerged under an orange streetlamp. The water had been switched off and so the pool below was still. Where it wasn't clouded with algae the surface reflected back the rusty evening light. It smelled like the commune toilet block. I waited and watched, beginning to wonder if he was mad or just romantic or maybe going to steal my handbag. And then a small black beak breached the water. Next came the slow yellow eyes, straining folds of neck and the little bobbing head, watching us. Another head popped up, and then another. Three more were gliding in like submarine periscopes from the other side of the pool. Soon there were ten.

"They've come to listen to a discourse," I said.

"A discourse?"

"Yes." I was smiling despite myself; a broad, giddy grin. "They want to hear from their master."

The turtles made a semicircle in front of us—heads poised, listening. I was about to tell the boy to address his audience, but seeing the phone in my hand—still lit from the fresh rush of ideas—I thought, *No; I don't write that kind of story.* I paused.

And recentered myself.

Acknowledgments

Thank you to my fabulous agent, Susan Golomb, and to the whole wonderful team at Catapult. In particular my brilliant editor, Kendall Storey; who else would go back and forth eight times over a camel shit joke? Thank you to early and encouraging readers Emma Cline and Sara Freeman. And thanks to my family: Jutka, John, Paul, Jen, and Nagyi, for loving me, supporting me, and putting up with me. That said, a huge and heartfelt thank you to the person who spent hundreds of hours writing a novel: me.

© James Bennett

Lexi Freiman is an Australian writer and editor who graduated from Columbia University's MFA program in 2012. She has been a recipient of the Center for Fiction / Susan Kamil Emerging Writer Fellowship and an Aspen Words scholarship. Her first novel, *Inappropriation*, was long-listed for the Center for Fiction First Novel Prize and the Miles Franklin Award. She also writes for television.